On a Northern Shore

JANIS MACKAY

Luath Press Limited

EDINBURGH

www.luath.co.uk

First published 2025

ISBN: 978-1-804252-26-0

Printed and bound by
Clays Ltd., Bungay

Typeset in 10.5 point Sabon by
Main Point Books, Edinburgh

This novel is dedicated to Mark, with love.

'Without the story in which everyone living, unborn and dead participates we are no more than bits of paper blown on the cold wind.' George Mackay Brown, *Winter Tales*

WOOING THE SEA-SPIRIT was an old custom Rob's dad had practised. Waking groggy and it still dark, the last thing Rob wanted was to get up and make some weird offering to the sea, but here he was, pushing the rough woollen blanket off him. He didn't hold with the old superstitions, but it was hard to ignore them. He checked the clock. Six am. Six hours into the new year. At least the fireworks had stopped. The seabirds hated them.

He could almost hear the voice of his dad, encouraging him on. *A fisherman needs to first-foot the sea. Up yea get laddie and sprinkle a wee dram in till ee water. Don't forget the selkie, noo. That way your nets will be filled, your creels too. And she'll calm rough seas.*

'Oh aye? And who is it drinks the whisky?' Rob had said, back 'to live quiet' in Ronester, and ashamed his dad believed in foolish notions. Plus, Rob had enough going on in his head without adding sea-spirits and selkies to tip him over the edge.

'She does,' his dad had said. 'She likes a nip, same as we do. It's called a libation.'

'You've got to be joking.'

'I wouldn't joke about the selkie spirit, son. It's not so much the dram. It's more, she wants taken into account. And she loves music.'

He might throw her a dram, but he wasn't about to serenade some nymph in the sea! Rob brought down his half empty whisky bottle and poured a measure into a jar. He paused after a dribble, then thought of his dad, could almost feel him nudge his elbow. *Ach, go on, son. At least a double. We're asking the sea to fill our cup, so we have to fill hers now.* Rob topped the jar up, imagining his dad watching and nodding. Then he pulled on his jacket and went out into the night.

All seemed quiet in Ronester. Doubtless the revellers would be well stoned and drunk by now, slouched around Mrs Gow's living room up near the hall, and Jake Henderson would be there, playing the rock star and giving it slide guitar. But down here, in his cottage by the shore, the only music, bar the constant keening of wind, was the low moaning of a few seals and the sigh of waves rolling over the skerries. The moon lurched between clouds like she was drunk. And here was sullen Rob the fisherman, off tae first-foot the sea!

Still thick with drink from the night before he wanted to tip the generous nip back himself, but there was his dad again, on about the sea-spirit. So Rob, knowing the beach rather than seeing it, made his way over the stones and down to the water's edge. He unscrewed the lid of the jar, breathed in the good peaty smell, then, wind in the right direction, flung the whisky to the sea, muttering, 'Happy New Year'. Then louder, why not. He had to make sure any sea-spirit heard, and maybe this was for his dad too. 'Happy New Year,' he called, but his voice was a muffled thing under the crashing of waves and the wind moaning like a banshee.

Job done, he stuffed the jar into his bulky pocket and was about to make his way back when his foot brushed something, not hard like a rock. He thought it was a seal. It didn't move when he rocked it gently with the toe of his boot. A dead one, he guessed. Peering closer he could see only the pelt remained, slumped on the stony beach. He heard a cry from the sea and swung round. A half-moon appeared, just enough to outline a shape in the water. Fogged with drink and unsettled with notions of sea-spirits, Rob thought he saw someone in the sea. He rubbed his eyes. Slapped his face. Peered again. Something was in the water. It looked like a naked woman. Or some creature with arms. Splashing. With hair, massy, and skin, white as moonshine. And she was laughing and throwing water into the air. Then she plunged under and was gone.

Imagining he'd raised the selkie this New Year's night, Rob backed away from the water's edge, heart racing, desperate to see the magical creature again, but half terrified. Some deep longing in him was ready to run after her, scoop her into his arms, but his racing heart kept him backing away. Plus, he didn't trust his senses. The cry could have been the wind, and the hair likely was spume in glinted moonlight, for any naked selkie woman he'd conjured had gone.

He slithered over seaweed, muttering how selkies don't exist. Neither do sea-spirits. He fell over the slippery pebbles, cursed, then hurriedly staggered to his feet. Ghosts don't exist. Neither do men with halos of flame.

Though he knew that wasn't true.

From halfway up the beach, he looked back to the black, whisky-sprinkled sea, where there was no high-pitched cry of laughter. No selkie luring him into the waves. 'You're imagining it, Robbie,' he said, out loud, laughing himself now. Laughing down the other thing that threatened to roar out of him.

From the dark sea a wild laugh echoed back. He bolted up to the cottage.

Rob was no stranger to imagining things.

He finished what was left of the whisky as dawn tinged the east on the first day of the new year.

2

WIND-BLOWN; LAND of edges, ledges and big skies.

Where great curtains of rain sweep the North Sea, and winds roam untrammelled, whipping up white horses, crashing spume over jutting skerries then fleeing inland to batter the flat, treeless county.

Where the gull's cry and the peewit's piercing song echoes on.

Caithness.

Her sparse-strung necklace of villages hugs the cliffs: Berriedale, Dunbeath, Latheron, Latheron Wheel, Lybster, Thrumster, Wick, Staxigoe, Reiss, Keiss, Freswick.

And, end o' ee road; Ronester.

Ronester's one pub is called The World's End. The one hotel is shut. A handful of farms sprawl into the interior. Near the village hall there's a huddle of cottages, and a few council houses up by The World's End. A church with a small but consistent congregation and a shop with the same. Near the church is the village hall. And down in the harbour three fishing boats rise and fall with the tide. South of the harbour lies a stony beach and by the shore two white-washed cottages, set well apart from each other, brave salt spray and high tides.

Ronester. Where the seals howling on a moonless night can tear your heart.

Rob lives in one of those cottages near the shore. His is the only boat that works the sea. The *Stella*. It's his now, his dad in the windy churchyard. If it's true the dead forget then he's at rest, worry for his only son over. Except this far north, they say the dead are with us.

Rob was born here. Bred here. Knows the tides and shifting winds. The seabirds that nest on the Ronester cliff ledges.

Afternoon of the first of January and Rob, breaking custom, took his boat out.

Winds skimmed the flat lands like shearwaters to where jutting cliffs plunged to the sea. Fulmars, puffins and black-backed gulls returned year after year to these craggy ledges. From his fishing boat, out in the bay, Rob lay on the deck, blowing up smoke rings and picturing what might fly into his circle of smoke. An avocet. A lost albatross.

A selkie?

He reached for his binoculars and followed the flight of two fulmars. What a sense of freedom, the way they rode the thermals with stiff wing beats. It fascinated him the way they came inland every January, from far out at sea to check and prepare their nesting ledges. He watched the fulmar circle four times then try and land on a crag ledge at the far end of the beach. Each time the bird hovered, came close, hovered, then swung away. Probably the aerodynamics and positioning needed to be just right. 'You can do it!' Rob muttered as the bird slowed near the ledge for its fifth try. 'Well done!' Rob cried, seeing the seabird finally land.

His dad, that shy, quiet man, had liked fulmars. Little sayings, too. His parents had had that in common. If at first you don't succeed... was one, especially when Rob came back from Aberdeen. Home to lend me a hand on the boat was how his dad tactfully put it, but for months Rob hardly got out of bed.

Try and try again, son, was another. Ours is a clan that don't give up!

'Aye, but every clan's got its black sheep,' Rob had said, mumbling.

A son of mine deserves the best. Dad again. Ha! That was a joke of a saying. There's a good woman out there, son, and don't settle for anything less!

Rob uncorked his hip flask and drank to good women and persevering ancestors. While the boat bobbed and gulls circled overhead he pulled his notebook from his shirt pocket. With a stub of pencil he added a bit about fulmars hovering and judging their landings. They don't give up, he wrote, under the page on fulmars.

They find mates, he wrote, but wondered if they all did? Were there single fulmars, who didn't make the grade? Didn't succeed in wooing? Were there females out there, who never laid an egg? Were there snubbed tube-nosed males who were not good enough?

His dad, despite all his little sayings, hadn't succeeded in keeping a good woman either.

Like father, like son.

Rob had the sea to himself. That's what it felt like. The two other fishing boats in the harbour never left it. Rob cut the outboard motor. The radio was still on, Karine Polwart calling a heron home. He let the boat coast to her song then turned the radio off when the news came on. He'd start hauling creels soon. After this smoke. And this quiet. A few wheeling gulls. This doing nothing except bird watching and gazing out to the horizon. Empty apart from the oil platform, that blight on the seascape.

'Here's tae possibilities,' he said, raising his flask to a passing gull. He took a swig, smacking his lips at the rush firing up his insides. He thought of his dad, but wasn't about to share this dram with the salty sea.

Rob extinguished the glowing end of his cigarette between his thumb and forefinger before stuffing the dout into his pocket. He pulled the lever and the motor puttered into life.

Surly, the villagers called him. Rob went away then came back. Saw things it doesn't do for a man to see. Now wants to live quiet, the tongues wag. Born in an ill wind, that one. Such a shame, though, about dour Rob at the shore. Mad keen on seabirds. Daft if you ask me.

He never did.

He lay wrapped in the cradle of his boat with the picture-filled clouds above; a dancing girl, a seal, then an elfin face. Gulls swooped low in a tang of salt and brine. Rob trained his binoculars on the soft white underside of a banking fulmar, watching the stiff, straight wings ride the updraught.

Lying on the deck of the *Stella*, it occurred to him the mad escapade to first-foot the sea had been a dream. To the north curtains of rain fell. By the time the rain reached Ronester, Rob, with a bit of luck, would be inside, fire on, a beer to toast the year.

With a groan Rob sat up and eyed the land. Seaview cottage still felt like his dad's place. He still expected to moor his boat, go into the kitchen and find him there, asking about the catch and the swell, back from the dead and ready to make him a brew.

He pulled the throttle into a low growl. The old boat still felt like his dad's. It moved off and at the bow his frayed Saltire flapped. The wind tugged at Rob's hair, whipping it back like a ragged flag from an annexed, broken country. His pet gull trailed, hoping for fish, but Rob's catch had been poor. These few hours out on the *Stella* weren't about fishing for bait. He wasn't sure what this trip was about. Some kind of prayer for a man who does not pray.

Rob worked the tiller, bringing his boat through the swell and on a course, bow-nose to the harbour. Like a lot of fishermen, Rob had salt blue eyes and brine thick hair. The lines around his piercing eyes were crinkled with years slitted against spiralling cigarette smoke, stung by wind and salt spray. With the way binoculars made you screw up your face. Maybe, too, with loneliness. Handsome, some of the locals called him, or used to. Rough, with that scar down his cheek. Haunted, others said, shaking their heads. He could do with a good bath and a set of new clothes, they said of poor Rob Sinclair. And a wife.

Betsy, his neighbour from the cottage along the shore, and tired of their tongues, said we're all different and thank God for that, and there's someone for everyone. When she had gone, the gossips raised their eyebrows, muttering how Sinclair Senior had had zero social skills and that fairly rubbed off on the son, and the lack of a mother did him no favours either. As for Betsy Manson, had she any idea how many single men were rotting away in hovels, dust an inch thick on their mantlepieces. And she was hardly one to talk, a spinster.

With the boat on course, Rob looked to his own stony beach. It was seldom anyone save him set foot there. Seals sometimes. It flashed back to him, the way visions do; a cast seal skin draped over stones, a naked woman dancing in the sea and him standing at the water's edge wanting her. Wanting her so bad it hurt. He battened down that longing and pulled his thoughts back to seabirds. You knew where you were with seabirds. Oyster catchers, seldom alone, the heron, seldom in company. Gulls, ducks, snipe, divers, waders. Avocet, the beauty, seldom seen.

With his binoculars he followed a fulmar banking over the roof of his cottage. By its skill in flight, he tried to work out how old it was. Hard to credit, but some were as old as he was. Near on forty.

But this was a young one, struggling to land on a cliff ledge. Rob followed the bird as it swooped back over the beach, where there was something else, some creature. The thing was moving, crawling over the stones. But then the creature rose up. Rob adjusted the lens, and now saw it was a woman, who seemed to be wearing a brown fur coat. Rob stared, transfixed. His pet gull cried as if snubbed. The woman stood, letting the coat drop behind her where it landed like a slumped bear. Or the cast coat of a selkie. Rob's heart raced. Under the coat she was wearing a long, green dress. The woman pulled that off, then, naked, waded into the sea.

The boat was close to the harbour now and the woman up to her knees in water. Then it was her waist submerged, then just her head visible, her hair floating behind her. If Rob wasn't mistaken, she was looking at him, or at least in the direction of his boat. What was she doing in the freezing water and it only the first of January? Maybe this was some kind of New Year dooking ritual? Or did she need help? It was too far to shout. Rob cut the engine then trained his binoculars on her again, adjusting the lenses to make out the expression on her face, like relief it seemed, or mad joy. Or regret. Then she was gone. Rob rammed the throttle and revved the *Stella* into the small harbour like he was the coast guard, responding to an SOS.

He leapt from the boat, flung a rope round the bollard, then bolted along the road towards the bridge that spans the river. Crossing the bridge, he lost sight of the sea. On the track to his cottage, he ran faster. He felt a jab to his chest, but kept on, coughing, batting away the haunting images of men leaping from the burning rig into the water. Men he hadn't saved. And the one with the flaming halo.

He reached the cottage then ran up the slope to where he had a view to the shore. No-one was swimming in the sea apart from a few bobbing fulmars. The young one was still trying to land on a ledge. The fur coat was gone. On the beach, two oyster catchers preened their feathers; a sign of rain to come. Maybe she had been a figment. Or a seal. It wouldn't be the first time Rob had been seeing things. Twice now he'd dreamed this selkie woman. It's a thin time, he recalled his dad saying of these days over New Year. Plus Ronester, his dad often reminded him, a glint in his blue eyes that Rob could never quite fathom, is a thin place.

Rob clambered over the stones to the shore and studied the water, just to check. With piping cries the oyster catchers flew off.

Then, sure enough, the rain came.

The cottage felt emptier than ever.

3

JANUARY THE 3RD and still a few sore heads were going slowly about the village, into the local shop for the hair of the dog, a few cans of lager, vodka for a Bloody Mary, and then heading home to coal fires, their collars pulled tight around their necks, as if the prevailing north easterly might sever their fragile heads from their queasy bodies.

The bell on the shop door tinkled, letting the shopkeeper know another had joined the queue. He lifted his head, pausing in his wrapping of sausages, noting her who doesn't take a drop had entered. 'Happy New Year one and all,' Betsy Manson chirped, bustling into the shop and too bright for the others there. 'All the best for the new year. Or as much of it as we're spared to see.' She laughed. She was a great one for laughing.

'Happy New Year,' the others muttered back.

Undeterred Betsy breezed on. 'Oh, a guid New Year then, was it?'

Rob gave her a brief nod. 'Yea didn't come over after the bells,' she chided. 'Here was I waiting for a tall, dark, handsome stranger to cross my threshold.' Then she winked. She had said the same thing the three New Years since Rob's dad died. 'I had black bun laid out, Rob.' She rummaged in her shopping bag, because wasn't she the lucky woman bumping into him like that with the very black bun right there in her bag. 'The sherry's up at the house, still on the sideboard,' she whispered, as if sherry was serious contraband. Like the corpse of Rob's father, up in the windswept churchyard, Miss Manson's bottle of sweet Amontillado had to be three years old.

Her Amontillado didn't escape the ears of Mrs Crowther, who could hear a dog whine down in Wick, so the saying went. The old gossip leant in. 'Aye, Rob,' she butted in, 'why don't you try her sherry? A bit company would do you good. Here was us, having a fine wee ceilidh in the hall and no sign of you. Your father wasn't one for company, but even though, he would have given us a tune.' The others in the queue nodded, as if remembering quiet old Robert Sinclair and his accordion tunes. 'Aye, then you're out on your boat like it's not the New Year.' Mrs Crowther cackled then coughed and Rob shifted uncomfortably. He'd forgotten this was the shop's first day open after the New Year closing.

'Your mother, as I recall, wasn't one for the sherry, mind,' Mrs Crowther went on, still leaning in so he could smell the onions off her. 'Only woman I knew who took tea at New Year.' Mrs Crowther nodded at Miss Manson, 'besides your good self, of course.' Rob's mother had been gone twenty-eight years, so she had good recall.

Miss Manson pressed the wrapped bun into Rob's hand. Muttering thanks, he stuffed it into his pocket. The queue shuffled forwards. Mackie's store had to be one of the few left where the shopkeeper insisted on fetching your items for you, lined up and nearing their sell-by date, in his domain behind the counter. Stepping into Mackie's shop, like stepping into the village itself, was like stepping back in time. It was Mrs Black's turn to be served and she peered at a list as long as her arm. 'Oh, and a bit of your best butter,' she said, when he came back with the bacon. 'And were the grandsons blind drunk by the bells?'

What these boys got up to down in Invergordon, he said,

was none of his business, and did she want cheese while he was over that way? It was, he informed her, from France.

Jean Black said if there was no Scottish cheddar she wouldn't bother.

'We'll be here till next New Year at this rate,' Mrs Crowther nudged Rob who was staring at the floor. 'Eh?'

'Leave the poor laddie, Gladys,' said Miss Manson, protectively.

'Laddie? He's old enough to have grandbairns.' She leant in even closer. 'Don't like the local lassies, eh?'

'He's just got eyes for the gulls.' Mr Mackie winked at Mrs Black who was slowly unzipping her purse.

Rob considered leaving, but Mrs Black was finally paying, then it was Crowther's turn and she'd forget about him. Anyway, he couldn't leave. He needed tobacco, milk and sugar. He couldn't abide tea without sugar, and UHT milk turned his stomach.

'He's saving himself,' Miss Manson said, 'aren't you, Robbie?'

Rob stared at the well-worn linoleum floor. While the women gossiped and Mackie patiently served old Jean Black her week's messages, Rob wondered how long the linoleum had been there? Thirty years at least. Was it Mackie himself who laid it, or Mackie senior? Whoever it had been, it was high time for a new floor. New shop. New life. New everything.

He made his own resolutions. No more looking back. And, resolution number two, which might be easier to achieve, use filters in cigarettes.

A hush fell over the shop. Rob looked up, snapping out of his resolutions.

'It's true,' Mrs Crowther was saying. 'She was blown in with the bells.'

'Where?' asked Miss Manson. 'What new lass? I've not seen anybody.'

Jean Black stopped fiddling with her change. The whole shop hushed in the wake of Mrs Crowther's announcement. She was tapping a finger to her nose. 'I saw her wandering about down by the shore, yesterday, and the day before. Like this biting January wind was nothing to her. Surprised you didn't see her, Rob. She swished right past your cottage. Pretty blonde-looking thing. About twenty-seven or -eight, I'd say. Probably foreign.'

Mr Mackie coughed. 'What can I get for you, Gladys.'

Gladys Crowther fished her shopping list from her coat pocket. '*The Press and Journal.*'

'Today's are not in yet. I can give you one from last week.'

'That's us,' sang old Jean Black as she shuffled down the shop, 'old news.'

A blast of cold air entered as Jean left. Old Gladys Crowther leant over the counter. 'Did the new lass come in here?'

'Soon as I turned the closed sign to open this morning, she was here.'

Rob hated the way they acted like spies. Even so, he was all ears. The few others in the shop fell silent too, all waiting for news of a pretty looking stranger. 'She came in here, muttering how she was supposed to get a job in the hotel.'

'She'll have a long wait.'

'That's what I told her. Easter, my dear, I said.'

'I told you,' Gladys addressed her audience, 'didn't I? Foreign. They all come here wanting to work in our hotels.' Then back to Mackie, 'Polish, was she?'

'Well, Gladys, she wasn't telling. She was wanting a place to stay. That much I understood. Then she's asking was there a farm name of Heatherlee.'

A pin dropping on the worn linoleum would have been louder than the collective hush.

'Lachlan Gunn's place?' Gladys raised an eyebrow.

'The very same. She'd heard he had a caravan. Don't ask me how. Something shady about her, all dolled up in that coat. Said she couldn't wait for the hotel to open. She didn't have much money.' Mr Mackie shrugged. 'So, I told her how to get there. And don't go asking did she have a ring on her finger for she kept her left hand tight in her pocket. All she bought was a packet of crisps and a can of Coke and she paid with an English note.'

'That could mean anything,' piped up Donalda. 'I got one when I was over in Thurso just last month. The dead Queen on it.'

'Anyway,' Mackie carried on, pausing to brush imaginary dust from his overall, 'I thought a bit company might do them good.'

More silence while the folk in the shop seemed to consider the Gunns and their need for a bit company. Gladys sighed. 'Where's she from? Did you find out?'

'You know me, not backward at coming forward but she acted like she didn't understand. And she was looking a bit, what's the word…'

'Shifty?'

'No, not exactly, more like…' You could almost see the *Sunday Post* crossword rattling through his brain… three across, D. Eleven letters, a sorry sight… 'dishevelled.' He nodded, looking pleased with himself. 'Aye, that's it, dishevelled, like somebody dragged her through a bush backwards. Her hair was a mess. Blonde it was, and in need of a good wash if you ask me.'

Nobody is, Rob thought.

Which wasn't quite true.

Gladys wanted to know exactly what she had with her. 'A plastic bag, Gladys,' Mackie informed her. 'Mind you, she had a fancy fur coat on her back.'

Rob felt his heart thump.

'A battered wife, I bet.' Mrs Crowther said, knowingly. 'On the run. Romanian, do you think?'

The shopkeeper smoothed out an old newspaper. 'I couldn't say. And she wasn't either. Like I said, she mumbled. I could hardly hear her. Right then,' he turned towards the cigarettes, 'the usual, Gladys, is it? Not giving up this year then, eh?'

Twenty minutes later Rob made his way down the winding track to his cottage. He might not have wanted to take a sherry with old Miss Manson, but he had six cans of beer he'd happily take by himself. The bag was also weighed down with tins of tomato soup, chocolate biscuits and a bumper bag of white sugar. Filters were in there too. Not giving up smoking exactly, but something to stop the coughing.

Mr Mackie had said her accent was hard to place and Mrs Crowther had said she was probably Polish, or Russian, because of the fancy fur coat, and who wore them these days. 'Reminded me of Julie Christie in *Doctor Zhivago*,' the old gossip Crowther's parting shot, clutching her scarf under her chins and heading out into the teeth of the wind.

Rob didn't see the stranger, but he did see Archie, the boy who often hung about the harbour to help him tether his boat and lift the catch. Spotting Rob, Archie waved wildly. 'Hello Rob,' he yelled, in that loud way he had of speaking, doubtless on account of his grandmother's deafness. Rob cut down the hill and approached Archie, who was grinning from ear to ear.

'Happy New Year, Archie,' Rob said, glancing into his bag of shopping. Biscuits, or Betsy Manson's black bun? Archie would prefer the biscuits. But so would Rob.

'Happy New Year, Rob,' Archie shouted, beaming up at him.

Rob pulled out the packet of chocolate Hob-Nobs and offered them to the lad.

'For me?' He was banging his chest. 'For Archie?'

'Yeah, Archie. All for you.'

'You're a great man, Rob, a great man,' Archie said, staring at the biscuits like they were diamonds. 'The best.'

A lump rose in Rob's throat. He laughed, and patted Archie on the back. 'You're the best, Archie, not me,' Rob said.

Heading back over the bridge, Rob stared down into the frothing, peaty water. It was a habit. And many's the fine trout he had lifted from that spot. He spied something down there, snagged on a rock. He shimmied down the bank and fished out a black leather glove. It could go into the outhouse, along with the other random things he had pulled out the river or combed from the shore.

Pushing open his front door he recalled the word Gladys Crowther had used; Zhivago.

The old woman spent so much time in about everybody's business Rob marvelled she had time to watch films. He couldn't cry out in the night without the whole village knowing, by midday next day, that poor Rob Sinclair had had one hell of a nightmare. Again.

Rob forgot about nosy Gladys Crowther, and imagined instead what Julie Christie in the film *Dr Zhivago* might look like. From the glimpse of the woman he had spotted through his binoculars, she seemed tall, curvy, a mass of blonde hair. He couldn't clearly bring to mind her face, just a fleeting, almost wildly happy expression. He took his cup of tea upstairs – the only place with a view to the sea. Told himself he was checking the weather but found himself scanning the shore for a film star in a fur coat with blonde, messy hair.

Or a selkie.

There's more in the sea than you think, his dad used to say. Fanciful thinking, his mother called it. That's what happens when you're too long out on the water, you lose touch with reality, she said.

Rob's dad couldn't argue with her. She'd wanted a good house with no drafts. She'd wanted shopping centres and coffee shops. Places to go. Dinner parties. A normal life, she'd called it.

Aye, Robbie, his dad said, when he'd taken a dram and played laments on the accordion, I couldn't give her what she wanted.

Before long the ache was back. It wasn't yet midday, but Rob opened a beer. Because it would be cold out on the sea. And because it was still New Year. Remembering old Miss Manson's cake, he broke off an end. He raised his drink and black bun to the window, toasting the sea, the gulls and the mysterious stranger.

That night he couldn't sleep. Maybe it was the ginger in the black bun. Or the stranger appearing just as he was getting a handle on life. Or at any rate, used to keeping his head down. Used to expecting little. The tap in the bathroom dripped. As he lay there the drip got louder, like a clock ticking the minutes and years of his life away. He cursed the landlord who took his money and left the place to rot. Rob staggered through to the bathroom, fumbling in the dark. He stuffed a towel under the tap. As he fell back into bed, he vowed to make more of an effort. Throw out stuff he never used. Like the piano.

The drip was duller now but still splatting. To mask it he turned his radio on, the signal torn between Radio Na Gael, the World Service and Caithness FM. He tried tuning to one frequency.

Closing his eyes he let the hissing poetry of the sea unjangle him; *Viking... North Utsire... South Utsire... Forties... Cromarty.... two... falling...*

4

MAIRI STARED AT the wooden sign propped against a stone: Heatherlee farm. The place then. 'Don't let on who you are,' Izzy had said, over and over. And still did, as if death had merely disembodied her but preserved her voice. Mairi snatched in a deep breath, readjusting her image of Heatherlee, reminding herself it was January. Of course it would look bleak. Nonetheless her heart sank. She couldn't help seeing the litter under jagged bushes, a blue piece of plastic snagged in a clump of heather. A rusted tractor-part in a muddy field and one bent and stunted tree. It was all flat, rough fields and low, tumbled walls. Desolate somehow. Mairi set her plastic bag down on the flagstone by the farmhouse door. The wind stung her cheeks. She kidded herself it was that brought the tears.

Don't give them the satisfaction. Her mother had warned her. *I was hurled from the clan and that means you too.*

Mairi breathed to still the storm. She ran her fingers through her hair, wiped the tears with her sleeve. After two days huddled over her suitcase in the hotel delivery cupboard she felt, and was sure she looked, exhausted. She had left the suitcase there for now, packed with ridiculous clothes she would never need, most of them Izzy's. She tugged her lips into a smile, then knocked.

As if Mackie had picked up the phone as soon as she had left the shop, to let the Gunns know a bit company was on the way, the door was opened immediately. An old man peered out. Her first impression of him was a flush of red. About his ruddy face was a shock of wiry grey hair. Hair from his nostrils, hair from his ears. 'Yes?' he asked, his voice cold and his look suspicious.

'I… I was supposed to get a job in the hotel.' Her whole body trembled. This was her grandfather. Here were her people. Mairi tried to find herself in his weathered face. She blinked tears away.

'What?' he called, as if he was deaf, or didn't understand her accent.

For God's sake, don't tell them who you are. Izzy had drummed that into her. But Mairi didn't need to dance to her mother's tune now. Though here she was, doing just that. *Pretend you're foreign, you're an actress, aren't you?* 'In hotel,' she said, grasping for some vague foreign voice despite her good intentions. 'For job, you know, but…' She shrugged, looked helpless, 'no hotel. So… I need place to stay. Man in shop said… caravan?'

She despised herself with this phoney voice. She had meant to be herself, whoever that was, but here she was, bowing to the mad demands of a dead mother intent on revenge.

The old man eyed her up and down. In front of him stood a young woman in high-heeled boots, a long, green dress and, over it, a fur coat, though by his blank expression she could have been a cow at the mart. Mairi glimpsed a white-haired woman in the hallway. 'In the shop…' she went on, trying to see the woman over his shoulder, 'they said, that, um, caravan… um…'

'Aye,' the old man said, 'it's round by the byre.'

He said she could have the caravan for £50 a week and he'd include coal for that. He didn't care where she was from or what she'd done. None of his business, he said as he showed her the old caravan behind the cow shed. It was painted a dull green colour, with mould patches and dents, decades past its prime. 'It's rain proof,' he said, not sounding sure.

Mairi mounted the two stone steps and peered inside. 'Aye, well, a bitty damp,' he continued, when still she didn't say anything, 'but fine when you get a fire going.'

The state of the caravan was the last thing on her mind. This was Izzy's dad. Right in front of her. Her grandad! And the woman she had glimpsed was surely her grandmother. They had cut out their daughter, Izzy had told her, in that airless flat in Magnolia Road, so that means you're cut out too. Izzy had snipped the smoke-thick air to ram it home. Just do them jobs then get the hell out of there.

And go where, Mairi wondered?

'Twenty-five, and that's my lowest offer.' He shifted uncomfortably. 'Do you understand? Do you speak English?'

'I can work,' she blurted. 'I am strong.'

'Aye, well,' he muttered, 'are ee sure?'

'Sure. I came to work in hotel, but, like I said, got wrong information.' She laughed mirthlessly. 'Is closed. So, sure, I can do farm work. Why not? Got to do something.' Her accent was doing that shifting thing. It would start to imitate the old man soon if she wasn't careful.

'You don't want to be working in 'at hotel anyway,' he said, shaking his head. Then he gestured in the direction of the crumbling walls. 'The dykes need mending, as yea can see. I'll get to it by and by. I jist need stones lifted oot the far field, not what you might call woman's work, but,' he glanced at her hands, 'it's a terrible stony ground.'

Mairi looked at the bleak fields. 'I can lift stones.'

'Pile them by the walls. At'll mak my job easier. I'll gie you boots, a jacket, thick gloves.' His gaze wandered off towards the farmhouse. 'And... if you can gie a bitty help in ee hoose as well.'

'Yes. Thank you for kindness,' giving a vague Eastern European throaty edge to her voice, but wanting to hug him, though Izzy had had nothing but scorn for him. He was old and broken now, she could see that.

As if her remark had loosened speech in him, he blurted, 'Aye, these dykes are far from what they once were. A guid mony stones have fallen loose and we've lost a few beasts on account o' these damn shoddy walls.' Mairi waited for him to mention a lost daughter.

The two of them stood outside the caravan, not speaking. In the distance a few sheep bleated.

'And like I said, maybe a bitty help for the wife,' he picked up his speech, 'for cleaning, stuff like that. She's not... not herself... but...'

Mairi nodded, picturing a grandmother in an apron, with soft white hair. Cakes and buns. 'The walls need patching.' He cut in on her fairy tale. 'We're aye buffeted by wind.'

He said he would show her the facilities. As they neared the farmhouse Mairi caught a glimpse of the woman at the window. 'Ye'll no be needing they...' he was staring at her, seeming to grope for the words, 'swanky clothes. Not for roond here.'

Mairi remembered that. How Izzy had said the old man had no time for women dressing up fancy. How he liked his wife plain as a ploughed field in winter. He tamed her, Izzy had said, her voice thick with scorn, but he could never tame me.

'I can be...' she looked around at the broken dykes, the tufts of thick grass, 'farm girl.' Like it was a part in a play.

'Aye well, if you're sure.' He showed her the back door to the farmhouse, how there was a toilet with a sink by the kitchen, and a bathroom next to that. He told her about mealtimes; eight o'clock, midday and five o'clock. They'd give her food, he said, for the work. He nodded back in the direction of the old caravan. 'It just needs warmed up.'

'Is fine,' Mairi said, because in that moment it was. Forlorn-looking but a million miles from Magnolia Road. Or the other sad flats she had lived in with her mother. In Carlisle, Preston, Crawley. And other places she couldn't remember. Always moving. Restless. Like leaves in wind. As if Izzy had always been searching for Ronester. 'But I'll be damned if I go where I'm not wanted,' she'd said, her jaw set tight.

Mairi looked at him and smiled. 'Thank you. Thank you for your kindness.'

'I'll put coal by,' he said, 'for the stove. And my wife will do your meals. She's good at that anyway. Look at me.' He patted his stomach and laughed, then stopped. 'So, a fair deal, I think. Work for food and board.' He seemed to run out of steam, like a man, Mairi thought, out of the habit of company. She felt a pang for him, for that much they shared. He went into the farmhouse and shut the door.

Mairi hurried past the cow byre and made her way to the old caravan, pushing back the mottled glass door, smelling the damp inside and looking for something to barricade the door with. There had been no mention of a key. Inside she let the tears come. For better or worse, she was home. These were her people.

The old man had given her firelighters plus twigs for kindling. He'd also left a bag dangling from the door handle with bananas and scones in it. Mairi wolfed them down, then managed to coax the fire into life. She stared into the flames, felt the heat and the possibility things might get better.

As the caravan warmed up, she emptied the contents of her bag onto the floor; her red dress, her scrapbook of film stars' pictures, a leopard print toilet bag, underwear, toothbrush, face cream, a hairbrush, a photograph of Izzy wearing a pale blue jumper; the mother photo, Mairi called it.

By the mother photo was the stolen golden ring that had belonged to her grandfather's mother; Elizabeth Gunn. A wonder it wasn't a fat diamond for all the stories Mairi had heard about this ring, this symbol of belonging. How ancient it was. Scottish gold, and how it meant family, pride and clan. And how Izzy, banished from both, nicked it. Mairi slipped it onto her finger. In a more straightforward world, this would be hers.

Alongside the ring was the cardboard box filled with Izzy's ashes. In an effort to jazz it up Mairi had wrapped the box in a red silk scarf. Mairi propped a photo of Marilyn Monroe against the shelf, and put the mother photo under her pillow. All the other things she had dragged up from London, the costumes, clothes, shoes, boots, to start this new life, felt a burden. They were still in the suitcase in the hotel delivery cupboard. For all the parts she might play. All the people she might be.

For a long time she gazed into the flames, as if answers were there. Perhaps they were, for it came to her, simply, without any of the Izzy drama. She wanted her own life. A place to belong. And a people to belong to. Home, was that too much to hope for?

The fire crackled.

'Aye,' she could imagine Izzy saying, 'way too much.'

But Izzy was dead.

A swift push over the cliff in the night-time would get rid of Izzy's clothes, and the boas and fans, the gowns and cloaks – the parts she'd never play and, free from Izzy's deluded ambition, realised she'd never wanted to. She pictured the suitcase crash to the waves below, smashing open, costumes billowing and curtseying in the salty sea.

Inside the damp caravan she lay on the narrow bench-bed, her fur coat wrapped over her. She guessed it was mid-afternoon, although the light was already draining from the day. And the fire had gone out. Good thing she didn't feel the cold. She gazed out the window, watching silhouettes of the barn, the slope of field, a barbed-wire fence. Everything became swallowed up by a darkness that came so early. She looked around for a light switch and saw, in a panic, there was none.

The cupboard in the hotel had been dark, but she'd been too exhausted to care. The hours in that cupboard now seemed unreal, a dream.

But this caravan was real. Night fell fast. She snatched in breath. Slapped her arms and legs to feel she existed.

Candle. Where was it? And why had she let the fire go out? Where were the matches? Looking out of the window there was nothing. At all. Not even a streetlight. It was unending black universe out there, and she was an insignificant dot. Her chest tightened. The dark could swallow her up and she'd cease to exist.

Then what?

Breathe.

She patted the bench, as if her trembling fingers might land on a box of matches.

Breathe. It's only night.

Then it came to her out of the terrible blackness; a life line of language.

Kind darkness.

It would not harm her.

Near dawn the dreams came. A vision of her mother, skeleton thin, looming over her, telling her to get on with these three wee jobs. Because dead, Izzy was moaning, is not gone.

Mairi woke from the dream, her heart racing. She batted her eyes open and saw where she was. The early morning light in the old caravan was grey, more a half-light. The bad dream was replaced by the hum of waves in the distance. The slow hush and drag of water worked like a spell. Mairi had gone into the winter sea the night she arrived and it hadn't killed her. She'd go in again, wash Izzy off her. Wash off everything.

Reaching the stony beach, and relieved to find it deserted, she stumbled to the water's edge. The glinting water drew her like a magnet. Already there was a pink tinge on the eastern horizon. Hurriedly she stepped out of the ridiculous high heeled boots, dropped her fur coat behind her and waded in. She yelped with the rush of cold around her legs. A crying gull flew above her. The sea rose higher and enveloped her thighs. She dipped her hands in the cold water, threw up spray and laughed. She had survived the night. She had tracked down her grandparents. She had a place to stay. And a job! Hardly the fabled West End, but it was real, like being an actress never was. Suddenly she felt euphoric. A wave rolled towards her, wrapping her waist. Exhilaration rushed through her. She screamed, laughed, pushed forward, her whole body tingling like something long dormant was waking. She managed two, four strokes, gasping, still yelping. Her fingers were shooting pins and needles. But she didn't care. She rolled over, gazed up at the vastness of the sky and a wave broke over her head.

In moments she was back on the beach, wrapping the fur coat tight about her. In the distance a dog barked. She clambered into the boots and hobbled back up the steep hill path, her breath billowing into the early morning air.

Not seeing the fisherman at his window, following her with his binoculars.

Back in the caravan, Mairi towel-dried her hair. Her whole body was glowing. She pulled on her green dress, trying to calm her breathing. With trembling fingers, she smoothed down her hair and left the caravan. At the door of the caravan were a pair of green wellington boots. Gratefully, Mairi pulled off Izzy's old boots and slipped her feet into the roomy wellies. Feeling like a country girl in an old rural film, she clomped her way to the farmhouse.

From inside she could hear the tinny drone of a radio. That stopped her. Izzy had been a radio fan. As the world (as Izzy had called everything else, as though they were somehow excluded from it) rushed on streaming films, with apps for this and apps for that, Izzy had kept faithful to the radio. When the old Hollywood movies were not on, the radio was. It's company, she had said. Now here it was again, the familiar tinny drone.

Mairi tried the door handle. It gave, so she let herself in to a small porch. 'Hello,' she called. She took off the wellies and in bare feet padded towards the cosy kitchen, a contrast to the wild, vast, cold, invigorating sea. There, by the kitchen table, with her back to her, was her grandmother, bent over some task. Tears pricked Mairi's eyes. It seemed she had traversed continents to reach this small, warm place and this old, bent woman, who appeared to be sawing at a loaf of bread. Mairi stared at the loose knot of her grandmother's apron, saw how her shoulders hunched over, strands of white hair spilled free of their pins.

The old woman cut on, humming along to the radio. Hm, mm, mm…

Mairi watched as the woman set the knife down and rubbed the small of her back, the humming shifting into little pained sighs.

'Um… hello.'

With a gasp the old woman turned round, knocking the knife over. It clattered onto the floor. 'Oh,' she cried, 'now would you look at that?'

Mairi stepped forward and bent to pick up the knife. 'I... I am...' she stammered, setting the knife back on the table.

'The worker,' the old woman said, smiling, her gaze flitting from the knife to the young woman now standing in front of her. 'I know. And that...' she gestured to the knife, 'is a sign a stranger will visit.'

Mairi stared at her, trying to see Izzy, or herself, in this careworn mirror. Maybe there was a resemblance, some turn to the nose, some dreaminess about the eyes. A softness Izzy never had. And a roundness to her that Izzy used to have.

'I... I'm... helping... clear the fields,' Mairi managed to say. 'Um... he said... breakfast...'

The radio had turned to chat, a road traffic accident and warning of snow. The old woman reached over and turned it off. 'We don't want the bad news, do we? Now,' she looked at her and smiled, 'porridge was ages ago.'

Mairi glanced out of the window. Then at the clock on the wall. Nine o'clock, and still not fully daylight.

'Sorry.'

'I said not to wake you. A cup of tea?' Her voice was warm, slow, 'and a fruit scone, yes?'

'Oh, yes, please,' Mairi could hear how eager her own voice sounded, how hungry. She forgot her foreign accent, and who she was supposed to be.

Who was she anyway?

'We like company,' the woman said, setting a brown teapot on the table and nodding for Mairi to sit. 'We get very little o' it, mind.' Then she pushed a heaped plate of fruit scones towards Mairi who took one and bit into it, ravenous. 'I made them for you. I hope you like them.'

Mairi nodded, chewing and forcing back tears.

'Now, just you wait right there,' the woman said, and

hurried off, leaving Mairi alone in the kitchen. But she was back in half a minute, carrying a thick pair of socks. 'I knew they'd come in handy, for someone,' she said, handing the socks to Mairi.

'I don't feel cold,' Mairi said, but pulled on the hand-knitted socks all the same, glad for their softness.

For a long moment the old woman stared at her. 'What's your name, dearie?' she asked. 'You didn't say. Lachie didn't tell me. Someone come to help clear the fields o' stones was all he said.'

'Hotel is shut,' Mairi said, as if that explained everything. Though hardly her name.

'Good.'

Mairi took another bite, then gestured to her full mouth, playing for time. She wanted to hold this moment, this lamplit kitchen, these scones, her own grandmother. Hand-knitted socks. As she chewed, her mother's voice whined, or maybe it was wind down the chimney. *Don't give them the fucking satisfaction, they don't need to know about you.* Mairi flicked through film stars, wondering who to be. 'Julia,' she finally said.

'Like Julie Andrews?'

Mairi shook her head, her hair falling over her face. 'Like Julia Roberts.' She remembered the Eastern European role. 'Actually, is Yulia.'

'Well, I'm Mary,' the woman said hurriedly.

Mairi gasped. 'That's… a nice name.'

Mairi had asked for the names of her grandparents, but had never received an answer, short of sergeant major and doormat. Izzy, with never a good word to say about her mother, had named her daughter after her.

Mary.

Mairi.

It means the sea, Izzy had said, because you were made to the crashing of the waves.

Mairi pulled her thoughts away from Izzy. 'I've always been Mary Gunn,' the old woman was saying. 'He married inside the clan.' She lifted up her teacup. 'Cheers,' she said, beaming from ear to ear, 'and Happy New Year.'

'Happy New Year, Mary.'

'That's Lachie,' she said, nodding to the field beyond the window. 'Short for Lachlan. He's not a bad man.'

Mairi felt a jab to her chest. According to Izzy, there was none worse. Or maybe one.

'More tea.' Mairi watched her grandmother's hands, veined, with a slight shake, grip the handle of the teapot. 'Whenever you want a cup of tea, Yulia, come away in and we'll have one. Like I said, don't be a stranger.'

'I am, actually… actress,' Mairi blurted, 'but is hard job. Too much competition.'

Mary nodded as if she knew all about acting and a thousand people competing for one role. 'No competition for farm work,' Mary said. 'I was a typist once, with nice clothes. I loved the dancing, and singing.' The old woman sighed, as if that was an eternity ago.

Mairi liked the simple ease of her. And felt the hurting in her too. 'I love the wide-open space here, the wind,' Mairi said, gesturing to the window, 'and the sea.' Her accent wavered but her grandmother didn't seem to notice.

'The sea can fair enchant,' the old woman said, her gaze as if set on some distant memory. 'And the wind can do strange things.' Then her expression shifted, like weather. 'I like the old films myself,' she went on, the cup shaking in her hand.

'Are you alright, Mary?'

The woman blinked then smiled and nodded. 'Oh, yes. Fine.'

But she rose and made her way to an armchair by the electric fire. 'You have more tea,' she said, her voice suddenly weary, 'don't mind me. Just a wee nap.'

In moments Mary was asleep. Mairi wondered if she should leave. But it was warm in the kitchen, and there was something tender about this soft old woman just feet away, sleeping. Mairi ate another scone. She would break the news gently, tell them about Izzy and the ring. About London and the other places. How Izzy never forgot Ronester. She would tell them about the cancer. And how she, Mairi, Izzy's daughter, their granddaughter, had come north in search of home.

Drawn to the Welsh dresser in the corner, Mairi noted the willow-patterned plates, and three milk jugs in the same blue and white design. Above the plates stood a small trophy and by it a framed certificate for Lachlan Gunn and his prize tup. On the top shelf her gaze was drawn to a neat line of small, framed photographs. Close by, her grandmother, in the armchair, slept on.

Mairi took down one of the small photographs. If she wasn't mistaken, this young child with brown hair, a round face and wide-eyed gaze, smiling down the years at her, was her mother. The child, not more than three, sat on a stone, smiling, happy, the open blue sky behind her. Mairi picked up another. There were eight in all, arranged in a line. Here was Izzy at school, holding a huge leather school bag. And another of Izzy about nine, with pigtails and a hen under her arm, sticking her tongue out, but looking happy. Then Izzy about ten with a blunt fringe, bottle feeding a lamb. In these photos this little girl looked healthy and round. The next was Izzy scowling and wearing her school uniform. She didn't look so happy. Mairi brought the photo closer. 'Bethie on first day at Wick High School,' someone had written at the bottom of the photograph. There was just one more; Bethie blowing out thirteen birthday candles. Mairi held it up close. She could see her mother's black nail polish. Her chubby fingers. Her scowl.

Behind her a door creaked. Mairi swung round. Then he was right next to her, fast for an old man. 'What the hell?' he barked.

'Sorry. I... I was just... dusting...' She pushed the last photo back on the top shelf, where it fell over, clattering on the wood.

Mary sat up, flustered-looking.

'Don't upset yourself, now, Mary,' Lachie said.

'I'm sorry,' Mairi blurted then hurried from the farmhouse, scooping up her wellies and scrambling into them, then she was at the field to start the business of clearing the ground of stones, and to put the sorrow of the house behind her. Her honesty speech could wait.

They were fucking crazy, Izzy used to tell her when Mairi begged for stories about her grandparents. Wanted to cage me up. The sergeant major wrote a list as long as my arm about what I could and couldn't do. So I did what I wanted. I went wild.

Mairi pulled stones out of the earth and piled them by the wall. It felt good to be outdoors, to carry weights, to tire herself out. To be away from images of her mother, a child forever, on the top shelf.

5

ROB GOT AS far as measuring it, but saw the piano wouldn't fit in the back of his van. He considered burning it, but that felt like sacrilege. So, he left it. And all the other things, while he drank tea, drank beer, smoked, went out on his boat, drank tea, drank beer and slept. Woke sweating in the middle of the night, shouting and thrashing.

Though with the turning of the year, something new pushed through. Even the nightmares were not as persistent as they used to be. He credited the beautiful stranger with that. He watched for her and tried to scrub the nicotine stains off his fingers.

She had drifted into his dreams.

Dancing by the sea… laughing, twirling round and calling his name… beckoning for him to follow, then she runs, still laughing, into the sea… the water froths up and he is swimming, trying to catch her… trying to touch her… to reach her… He can't swim, and when he brushes her skin she turns into a seal then the sea is on fire.

Rob woke, sweating and the fire over the sea fled. Heart pounding, he tried to slow his breath, until the dream faded. He stared at the knotted wood pattern on the beam above him, lit by a low sun ray. He threw the rough blanket off him and sat on the edge of the bed, ran a hand through his hair. It was well past his shoulders. Sometimes he wore it in a ponytail, tying it back with twine, pulling down a lock of hair to cover his scar.

He wasn't proud of it. It wasn't won fighting off a lion. Or trying to put out a fire.

He slapped his bare thighs then got up, swaying slightly. He steadied himself on the wooden bed post, trying to remember whether he had drunk much the night before. He took up the old, knitted jumper his mother had made his father thirty years ago. Young for a gansey, she would say. But his father must have been surly and ungrateful because she took off not long after. He shook it out, watching dust lurch in the morning light. Pulling it on Rob sighed, from so far inside he couldn't imagine an end. He was thirty-six, or -seven. And felt ancient. He saw his life going on like this, day after day, for years. Three, he'd give himself. Five tops. Then he'd be up in that churchyard with his dad. They'd have all eternity to talk about the wind over the sea.

And maybe then he'd get round to telling him about the man with the halo of fire. The burning man he couldn't save. The man he couldn't stop seeing.

He looked out of the window where the sea stretched for miles.

The beautiful stranger was out there somewhere, swimming probably, or walking up by the cliff, or in bed with Jake Henderson for all he knew. Face it, he muttered, whoever she might be looking for it isn't you. The image that had haunted him for ten years was back with a vengeance – the burning man with the halo of orange flames, wanting to be seen. And Rob closing his eyes, not brave enough to watch a man leap to his death.

Rob, barefoot, walked out of Seaview cottage, not bothering to close the door.

The earlier sunlight had gone, swallowed into cloud, and the wind was up. He kept walking, the lone resigned figure in this wintry picture, over the beach, not even wincing at the stab of stones. He drifted over tangles of seaweed, like a sleepwalker, and thought he saw a selkie rise from the waves. He found himself searching the beach for a cast seal skin. When he looked up, a seal was gazing at him from the shallows, then dipped its dark head under the water.

Something in him wanted to follow the creature. Leave the drudgery behind. No more man on fire, no more lobsters, no more Jake, no more folks feeling sorry for him, no more tins of beer and the ache under his ribs, no more arrangements with Maggie.

He started from his dwam, hearing the sudden piping racket of a pair of oyster catchers. Rob lifted his head. A large black bird flew low over the water, trailed by a herring gull.

In his notebook he logged a herring gull, two oyster catchers and a cormorant.

Back in the cottage he considered making his bed, bringing some kind of order, but the thought of tea put paid to that. 'A cup o' tea,' he said, his voice as dry as a heron's. 'Aye,' he went on, 'with three sugars.' He filled the kettle and set it down with a clatter onto the gas ring. Lighting it, he wondered how much was left in the canister outside. As the blue flame puttered into feeble life, he rolled a cigarette and bent to light it. With the first drag of smoke he laughed at the idea of a selkie. 'Rob Sinclair,' he said to himself, 'you need to get out more. It's a bit company you're needing. You need to get the old man and his daft beliefs out of your head. You need to get a life.'

Waiting for the kettle to boil he stretched, coughed, then sauntered up the garden. It would be a fine day, despite what they say about a shepherd's warning. Anyway, he wasn't a shepherd. The sea looked fine, a bit wind but nothing to hinder his boat. He'd head out later and haul up the creels he had set the day before. He stood against the outhouse wall breathing in the tobacco, the glittering sea and the smack of air, till the whistling kettle from the cottage called him. Inside seemed gloomy after the bright outdoors. He brought down a tin mug, tea bags, sugar and an opened tin of Carnation milk. Last night's empty cans of beer littered the sideboard.

'Aye, that's what's seeing things.' He shoved them into the bin.

He dropped two tea bags into his mug and poured in the steaming water. The liquid blackened instantly. He fished a teaspoon from the sink. His porridge bowl was there from yesterday. He'd get round to porridge. First, sweet tea. Like tar. He took it outside with his second cigarette, the filter project abandoned.

Betsy Manson was pegging up sheets, making the most of a wind without rain. That woman was forever washing. Only last week one of her large vests had ended up straddling a whin bush a quarter-mile away. Rob lifted the stub of his cigarette and waved at her. She waved back. Had she spotted him earlier, dragging his black mood along the shore? Even from that distance Rob knew his neighbour was smiling. Her vigorous wave seemed to smile. Even her flapping white sheets seemed glad. 'A fine morning it is,' she shouted. Her cottage was a good fifty metres away. You couldn't throw a stone that far, but if the wind was in the right direction, you could throw a voice. At any rate, she could. He lifted a hand and nodded, ash tipping onto the sleeve of his gansey.

'If you've a lobster, later, Rob, I'll take it off you,' she called, breezy.

He could get good money for lobsters up at the pub. 'A crab more like,' he said, muttering more than shouting. Anyway, the wind was against him, and his voice out of practise.

'A fine thing this, being up with the lark, is it not?' she

shouted, still pegging away. Like him, she lived alone. He thought of her as old Miss Manson, but she was probably only fifty, or perhaps sixty, always busy, always annoyingly happy. She waved over to him. 'I've a loaf for you,' she shouted.

The porridge could wait. For all that Rob didn't hold with Betsy Manson's obsession with laundry, she baked a good loaf and he was hungry. He couldn't remember eating the night before. Rob set his empty mug on the bench and made his way along the track to his neighbour's cottage. She was still pegging up washing, all white, he noticed. Huge, billowy vests and tablecloths. Who used tablecloths these days? And why?

He leant on her fence post, smelling the freshly baked bread. 'What are you wanting with a lobster anyway?'

She came over, her empty peg bag, a yellow sock, slung over her arm. 'Oh, you know me Rob, a foodie. Always trying new recipes. If you could get me a langoustine or three, I'd be made.'

'Me too.'

'Or a lobster is fine.' She laughed. He'd never known such a woman for laughing. 'Wait there,' she said and waddled off towards her open front door. Two minutes later she was back with a loaf wrapped in a tea towel. He could hardly refuse her a lobster. Never mind he'd get £8 for a lobster in the pub. A loaf cost £1.50. He took the warm bread and smelled it.

'Thanks. Appreciate it. I'll see what the sea brings me.'

'A wife?' Smiling, she waved an arm towards the sea. 'You know what they say, Rob, plenty fish in the sea. A new start, and all that.'

He wondered if she was waiting for her own handsome fish to wash in with some tide.

'She was out here last night,' she said. 'Swimming in the moonlight, would you believe?'

'Who?' Rob guessed who.

'The beautiful stranger.' Betsy winked, 'who else?' Then she laughed again. 'Everything alright with you, Rob?' Like she asked at least once a week.

'Aye, fine, Betsy. How are you?'

She laughed. 'Oh, I'm fine, just fine.' She smiled at him. He knew the look, the pity. 'Well now, Rob,' she went on, still nodding sympathetically, 'it's a new year. Time to look ahead.' She patted him on the shoulder, then headed off, punching at her white sheets.

Despite himself, and knowing his well-meaning neighbour would probably be watching him from her kitchen window, he scanned the beach and up to the Hotel, teetering on the edge of the cliff. Then cast his gaze up in Heatherlee's direction. To forget the past, as Betsy was forever counselling him, it helped to put some imagined future in its place. The beautiful stranger, for instance.

The earlier drizzle had passed, and the low winter's sun was up, dazzling the water. Plenty fish in the dazzling sea. Except, there weren't anymore. Just like the young people in the village, the shoals of herring, that his dad used to call the silver darlings, had gone.

6

WHEN MR MACKIE got wind of the arrangement, he let it be known to everyone passing in and out of his shop that Lachie was taking a loan of 'the new lass,' as he now called her. The lass who seemed to possess no more than the pelt on her back. He would never have told her the way to Heatherlee if he thought for one second Lachie would be setting her to work carting stones. 'Let's face it,' Mackie added, 'clearing fields is hardly woman's work.'

But Mrs Crowther said, as far as she could see, the new lass worked like ten men, carting stones back and forth, and in this cold too. 'Where she comes from,' she said, knowingly, 'the women toil from morning till night in the fields.'

Lachie advised his new tenant and stone carter to ignore the damned gossips.

'They concern me not,' she said, milking the mystery voice.

Lachie frowned. 'Aye, well, I don't stick my nose in. This village is full of gossips, nothing better to do. The young leave as soon as they can and who can blame them. What's for them here? They get the hell out.'

Mairi stared at him, weighing his words against the many Izzy had ranted. Sticking his nose in, according to Izzy, was his speciality. And how, because he had caught her at Whaligoe Steps at night, a package in her hands, he had thrown her out of clan and county, his parting words a sting that lasted twenty-five years – 'you are no daughter of mine, you are no Gunn.'

'Mind you, I was wild by then,' Izzy had said. 'They couldn't handle me.'

'How do you mean, wild?'

'You know, boys, drink, stuff.'

'Stuff?'

'Yeah, selling stuff. Taking stuff. Parties. Staying out all night. Stuff.' – Izzy glared at her. – 'You know your problem?'

Mairi held her tongue. Her problem was having an ill, bitter mother who didn't let her daughter live her own life. She shrugged.

'You're too bloody naïve.'

'Though it is very beautiful here,' Mairi said, waving a hand through the air.

Her grandfather frowned at her, as if he'd long forgotten beauty. 'Aye, well, not everybody thinks so.' He fell into silence after that, not saying whether he thought so. He didn't even appear to wonder, when everyone else under the age of thirty headed south, why a young woman such as herself, dolled up, swanky as he put it, had turned up in the village, in midwinter no less, carrying one plastic bag! Several times he told her, 'Where you've come from is none of my business. Us Gunns are respectable folk, unlike some.' He told her she was doing a good job, and that, he assured her, was all that mattered. He would teach her dry stane dyking if she liked.

'What?'

'Mending the walls,' he explained. 'The dykes.'

Mairi smiled. 'Thank you. I would like that.'

Wind here seemed a living thing, slapping her, moaning, singing, sighing, biting, creaking, whistling, stroking.

Speaking; *Set me free.*

She remembered Mary's words, how the wind could do strange things. *Set me free*, the voice continued to hiss. Mairi heaved a round stone and pushed it into the gap in the wall, as if to silence the voice. *Set me…* She pushed further, shutting the whine of her mother up. It worked. She imagined walling up the phantom. Trapping it in the stones. She lifted another stone and jammed it into a gap.

She bent to lift a stone when a pebble landed with a ting on the other side of the wall. Mairi started back as another pebble flew through the air and hit the wall. In a rising panic she looked about her. 'Mary?' she called. There was no sign of her grandmother, but the next moment a fierce-looking woman appeared from behind a ragged gorse bush. 'Can… can I help you?' Mairi asked, as the woman, bundled in a thick coat and red headscarf, stomped across the field towards her, looking ready for a fight the way her jaw jutted and her beady eyes blazed.

'Aye, missy, yea can help me.' The woman almost spat the words. She drew close to the wall. 'Yea can help yerself,' the woman kept on, her voice low but menacing, 'help poor old Mary and Lachie too, help all o' us, by going back till wherever yea came from. We don't need a pot stirrer.'

'I… I can be wherever I like,' Mairi stammered.

'Aye, the further south the better,' the old woman snapped. It was Gladys Crowther.

Mairi tried to move away but the woman, more nimble than she looked, was through the gap in the wall in a flash. The cigarette smoke off her reeked. 'If yea ken what's good for you,' she hissed, 'you'll board the next bus south and quit swanning about. Let me tell you fir nothing, Lachie and Mary don't need mair hurt.'

'It is not your business.' Mairi wedged the next stone, trying to ignore the woman who was about two inches from her face. 'Is free world.'

'Free for what? Tae hurt folks who've been hurt enough? You don't know it, but you're stirring up two broken hearts, jist being here. As fir Rob doon the shore, he needs yea like he needs a hole in the head. That's three,' she lifted up three fingers and wagged them angrily in the air, 'three broken hearts.'

'I can be wherever I like,' Mairi blurted. 'What about my broken heart?' she wanted to yell but clamped her jaw.

'Fine, jist not here.' The old wife's parting shot, she turned and marched away, through the broken wall and over the field. Mairi, heart thumping and tears blurring her vision, watched till she disappeared from view.

7

IT'S A WONDER what three slices of fresh-baked, buttered bread can do, and two cups of hot sweet tea. Rob wiped a damp cloth over the kitchen table. Something about the sight of Miss Manson's washing had stirred him into cleanliness. Upstairs he threw the blanket over his bed, by way of making it, then got to work with a comb, but it wasn't having much effect. Back in the kitchen he rummaged for a pair of scissors. 'Right,' he said, yanking at his long hair, 'off with you!' He had to hack at it, but bit by bit his brown, thick and matted hair fell onto the kitchen floor. One act led to the next. The bath was full of fishing nets and random tackle. Rob hauled them out, dumped them in the outhouse, came back and ran a bath. The small bathroom filled up with steam.

As he lay soaking, Radio Na Gael blaring accordion music through the house, Rob tried to convince himself this sudden flurry of cleaning – body, and house – was not for the beautiful stranger.

Outdoors more than enough, he wasn't one for wandering the shore in the moonlight or star gazing, but as Rob lay in the bath that morning he reckoned a night-time walk, after the fishing, would be a fine thing. Why not? Might even get treated with the Northern Lights, or the Merry Dancers as his dad had called them.

That afternoon, out on his boat, the good feeling lingered.

The weather helped. It was one of those clear days, where the sky is stark blue and the low sun glints flashing coins off the water. He felt like the day as he leant over to haul up his creels. 'Right then,' he muttered, pulling up the first rope, 'let's be having you.' The World's End might take three, Betsy Manson wanted one or two, and the hotel down in Wick would take whatever was left. The hotel was one of the few in Caithness that stayed open over the winter. Mackay's it was called, and it kept Rob in beer, occasional company and steak pies.

For a small outfit such as the *Stella*, it had been a good catch. He lifted sixteen lobsters in all and a good few velvet crabs. When he'd stacked the creels, he puttered back towards the harbour. The two other boats there bobbed back and forth, their car-tyre fenders separating them from the wall. Old Stan Ross hardly ever ventured out nowadays on *Bonnie Blue* and had no son in the village to take it on. The other boat, by far the better boat, *Wishful Thinking*, belonged to Jake Henderson. Rob felt a knot in his stomach just looking at the boat. Old Jack Henderson had died and his son Jake, so rumours went, had returned to Ronester. But so far there was no sign of him on *Wishful Thinking*. His wife down in that Manchester, according to Gladys Crowther, had kicked him out. 'You lads can't wait to get shot of the place,' she had said, scorn laid on thick, 'but you all come running back here sooner or later, tails between yer legs.'

Rob hadn't seen Jake around yet. Nor did he want to. According to Mackie, Jake was busy making it in the rock music business. Rob could tell by Mackie's tone just what he thought of that. If it wasn't Country and Western, it wasn't music. So, the bay was left to the *Stella* and the seals.

There was no sign of Archie. As Rob manoeuvred his boat into the harbour and cut the engine, slinging his rope around the bollard, he caught a snatch of an old Scottish country dance tune drifting out from a house by the harbour. He had a sudden image of his dad sitting in his armchair, bent over the accordion, his foot tapping the wooden floor. 'Good for the heart,' his dad used to say, his fingers dancing over the black and white keys. Rob remembered how he had copied his dad, putting his fingers where he was shown, and working the bellows. The place felt full of life then, and even his mother, he dimly recalled, did a wee highland fling in the kitchen. She must have still been there, in this memory. Usually these memories disheartened him, for they just highlighted how changed everything was. He had only been back a year, shamed and with nowhere else to go, when his dad had died. Driven to an early grave, probably, by his ill-mannered son. Their black looks at the funeral said as much. Rob got well drunk that night. His dad had left Rob the boat and the tenancy for the house, for a fresh new start, he had written in his will. But he had taken the life and the music with him, and all semblance of order.

But today, for some reason, Rob felt the life might return. Thinking of his dad playing the accordion didn't leave him maudlin, like it usually did. Baked bread, white, clean sheets, the bright blustery January day, this sudden strain of music and the beautiful stranger. Together they were 'good for the heart,' and Rob's heart, well he knew, was sorely in need.

Archie was running down to the harbour. 'Sorry, I am late,' he yelled, as if Rob employed him.

Rob passed up boxes of lobsters and crabs. Archie screwed up his face at the still-alive lobsters as he laid them out in neat rows. 'Good catch,' he shouted, and Rob gave him the thumbs up. Sixteen lobsters, and thirty-two crabs, though not to be sniffed at, was never what Rob's dad would have called a good catch, but the emptying sea wasn't for Archie to bother about.

'You okay, Rob?' Archie shouted, as he reached down for the next polystyrene box.

'Yeah, grand, thanks.' Rob grasped the rusting iron ladder on the harbour wall and scaled it. 'How are you, my man?'

'I miss your dad,' Archie blurted, soon as Rob arrived next to him. This was something Archie often came out with, but today it seemed more heartfelt. Maybe on account of the accordion music in the distance. Archie pressed his hands to his small chest. 'I miss him so much. He took me out on the boat. We saw birds and dolphins and the selkie. I miss him so much.'

They both dangled their legs over the side. First Rob had heard about them watching birds and dolphins and the selkie. How old was the boy? Twelve? Thirteen?

'You miss him very much as well?' Archie asked, in his loud way.

Rob nodded, because right then he did, and the image of his dad out on the boat with wee Archie, pointing out seabirds and dolphins, and spinning his yarns about the selkie, caught him under the ribs. 'Aye,' he said, 'I do.'

The two of them sat, watching the sea. 'You going to marry someone one day, Rob?' Archie blurted.

Rob turned and grinned at him. 'No plans. What about you?'

Archie nodded vigorously. 'Soon as I'm sixteen,' he said, definitely. 'And I'll invite you, Rob.'

'Hey, thanks. I'll get the lobsters. It'll be grand.'

'No girlfriend, Rob?' Archie was persistent today.

And for once, Rob felt like talking. Wanted to tell him about a selkie he'd raised at Hogmanay, but instead told him about Shelagh, from years back. How she was good fun, and liked dancing and joking. Had long dark hair, so long she could sit on it. 'I suppose I thought we might get married one day, but it didn't work out that way.'

Archie nodded gravely like he understood. 'My gran says things work out the way they want to work out.' Then Archie jumped to his feet and patted Rob on the shoulder. 'See you tomorrow, Rob,' he blurted, then marched off up the road to the wee house he lived in with his grandmother.

Rob wanted to shout after him, tell him he wouldn't see him tomorrow. Tomorrow was Sunday. But Rob couldn't summon the strength of voice.

Rob slumped down on the bench by the harbour. He rolled a cigarette and looked out at the waves. Even in half an hour the sea had got up. Waves hit the breakwater by the harbour wall with regular thuds. Rob felt them work on his breathing, or maybe it was the cigarette, but he slowed, relaxed and grew half mesmerised with the rhythm of the waves. Which gave some respite from the replay of that fateful rig fire, that blot on his horizon.

But here, on the wooden bench, Rob wasn't dwelling on the rig fire. He blew smoke out towards the blue and white rolling sea. He liked that wee saying of Archie's gran's. He wanted to believe in things working out. He wanted to believe that, somehow, he wasn't forgotten in the great scheme of things. He envied Archie his sure, simple confidence.

'A penny for them.'

It was old Gordie, lowering himself onto the bench next to Rob. The old man was once a sailor, away for months at a time, as far as Greenland, so he'd said.

'Aye, Gordie,' Rob said, nodding to the old man who nodded back.

'Robert,' he said, a name so unfamiliar Rob hardly associated it with himself. 'Fine day for watching the sea, eh?'

'It is that,' said Rob, now blowing smoke away from Gordie, though the wind batted it back. 'Sorry.'

'Och, no need for sorry, Robert, no need at a'. Too many sorrys in this world.'

Rob turned to look at him. Gordie's eyes glinted. 'You know what I'm saying, Robert?' He fixed his bright eyes on Rob.

Rob found himself nodding, because part of him did know. Knew he'd been saying sorry for ten years.

'Live your life, grab hold o' her, for she soon passes.' Gordie rose to his feet then lifted a weathered hand.

Waves smashed on the sea wall with an echoing boom. The old man was gone. Rob wondered if he had ever been there.

Crossing the bridge Rob made it his habit to stop and look down at the river, marking a shift between the *Stella* and Seaview. Head down, he didn't see Jake until he practically bumped into him.

'How's it going, man,' Jake said.

Rob nodded. That was answer enough. He planned to walk past but the social culture was too embedded, even for a loner like Rob. So he stopped, rolled a cigarette, leant by the iron rail of the bridge and stared into the distance.

'Thought maybe you'd be giving us a tune in the hall.'

Rob lit his cigarette, cupping it close between his hands. 'I don't play,' he mumbled. He wanted to get at Jake. Wanted him to know the damage he'd done. If anyone needed to say sorry it was Jake Henderson.

'You were good, man,' Jake said. He was smoking too now. Not a roll up.

Rob hated the phony man thing.

'Fancy a drink, eh? For old time's sake?' Jake asked, looking at Rob who was looking at the sea.

'Not with you,' Rob said.

'Fine.'

'Na, it's not fine.' Rob crushed the dout of his cigarette between his fingers and put it in his pocket. 'Not fucking fine at all.' Then he did walk away, fast.

Jake leant over the bridge and stared down to the peaty water. 'Fuck you, Sinclair,' he muttered, flicking his half-smoked Marlboro into the river. Then he looked up, hearing the back door of Rob's cottage slam.

Later that afternoon, the brief light draining from the day, Rob loaded the iced boxes of crabs and lobsters into the back of his battered white van. It was a fifty-mile trip down to Wick and back, which ate into the slim profits, but Rob liked the open views over the North Sea. And he had Radio Na Gael blasting away for company.

Not too late to make a New Year's resolution, Rob vowed he would pick up the accordion again. Come Easter, he would have three tunes in his fingers. Or maybe two. Which had zero to do with Jake Henderson.

Down in Wick you could buy newspapers that were more or less up to date. In the newsagents to pick up tobacco, Rob scanned the headlines. His eyes landed on the photo of a man with a baby in his arms. The man looked distressed. Or, Rob remembered Mackie's word, dishevelled. Above him were the words 'Please come home,' and underneath, 'Shetland man appeals to missing wife.' But there was no picture of the missing wife. There was another headline about refugees arriving in Thurso. Where, he wondered, was the beautiful stranger from? Not one for buying papers he bought them both. And six cans of lager. A packet of Maltesers and a Lion bar.

'You got a sweet tooth,' the girl at the cash register said, grinning, 'and a thirst.'

'Happy New Year to you too,' Rob said, taking his change.

'Bit late for 'at,' the girl said.

'Never too late for a bit happiness,' he said, grinning back at her. On to the chandlers where he bought a canister of Calor gas, hefting it over his shoulder then lowering it into the back of the van.

Rob slowed down outside the hotel once his few messages were complete, thinking about Maggie, and whether she would be in the bar, and whether she would be alone. But he didn't go in.

On the drive back to the village he forgot about refugees and missing women. He forgot about Maggie. As he drove up the winding coastal road his thoughts wandered to the stranger. Would she be down at his beach when he got back? It was dark now and his headlights lit up ragged bushes, roofless crofts, a sign for a chambered cairn and miles of dark moorland. It was five o'clock when he bumped along the dirt track to his cottage. He left a lobster at Miss Manson's door, knocking before striding away. 'Thank you,' she called when Rob was almost home. He waved, seeing her silhouetted by her outside light, then he heard the snap of her door as she went in. Her washing would be down. He imagined the white wind-blown sheets spread on her bed, ready for her loveless night, and the white tablecloth smoothed over her dining room table. Ready for a fancy fish recipe. Saturday night dinner for one. Probably, Rob thought, she would light a candle. He wondered if she said grace, did anyone anymore. *For what we are about to receive…*

As he filled the kettle, the thought struck him what a beautiful word that was, Grace. Here he was, a week into the new year and thinking there were such things as beautiful words.

He felt a fool too. He hadn't even set eyes on this mystery

woman, not properly. But he recognised the feeling though it had been years. The light space in his chest. The elation, like a child excited about Santa. And his body, stirring. Aye, Rob Sinclair, he said, flicking his lighter then staring into its steady yellow flame, you're in love with a beautiful stranger you've barely clapped eyes on. You're an eejit, Robbie, a puffin. A right damn clown.

What would she be, he wondered?

An Avocet.

8

'AT'LL BE GOOD for fifty years.'

Mairi swung round to see Mary, out in her dressing gown and slippers, standing in the field, nodding. 'Or even a hundred. You've got the touch. A country lass at heart, I'm not saying you wouldna make a fine actress. But you do the walls jist right. You're strong, and Lachie said you've got the touch.'

'I am learning,' Mairi called back. It was the sudden way Mary tightened the cord of her dressing gown, as though belting herself in, that spun her back.

Perhaps even the dusty-pink dressing gown, near the end, had been the same make. Catalogues, Izzy had said, sneering, they got all their stuff out of catalogues. How Izzy had come reeling into the kitchen when Mairi was cleaning and smacked her hand on the table. 'Where's my ring?'

Mairi backed up against the sink. 'I don't know what you're talking about.'

'Don't give me that shit. Give it back to me. Where…?' Izzy swung towards her and Mairi ducked, 'is it?'

'You… had it on a chain. You said, I remember, it was too big. Maybe… it's in your bedroom.'

'You can't wait for me to kick the bucket, can you? Eh?' Izzy coughed, as if demonstrating how near the bucket was.

'I don't want your bloody ring,' Mairi shouted because sometimes nice girl snapped. 'Keep your bloody ring! Keep it!

I don't care about Gunns, and all those Elizabeths. They don't matter!'

Izzy lurched out of the room, pulling the cord tight around her dressing gown that to Mairi was the colour of misery.

'Stones last a long time,' Mary was saying.

So does bitterness, Mairi thought. She could feel her heart race, so loud she imagined Mary might hear. Izzy, she reminded herself, was dead, and the ring would be gone soon enough. She would rid herself of the family heirloom, free herself from this madness. Do the damn jobs. At any rate, return the ring to Heatherlee and scatter the ashes.

'You will catch cold,' Mairi said, rubbing her gloved hands to still the trembling.

Mary glanced down, as if suddenly noticing her clothes, or the lack of them. 'A book for you,' she said, like a magician conjuring one from the folds of her dressing gown. Mairi took it, glancing at the title and recognising it; *Folklore of the Far North*.

'Thank you.'

Mary did that harsh tightening of the cord around her waist again then hurried back to the farmhouse.

Mairi saw how thin she was.

Like Izzy at the end.

But also, not like her. Mary, her grandmother, had a softness that Izzy never had. Mary wore a wan smile on her face that Izzy rarely did. Mairi held the book to her, knowing every story in there, every myth, every superstition.

That night, in the starry dark, Mairi cast off her coat and dress, waded into the sea, crying out with the first shock, but stayed out there for two, three minutes, swimming fast. Strong urgent strokes. Her long hair fanned out. 'Mind your own business,' she cried to the image of the meddling old wifey. Mairi thrashed out, kicking back her heels. She hadn't come all this way to be banished like her mother had been. She kicked through the cold water and yelled.

No bully of an old wife in a head scarf was going to get to her. Though she had.

The peace that Mairi had begun to feel, these few days in the far north, had fled. She couldn't rid herself of the woman's threats. A seal, from further along the shore, moaned.

It wasn't only old Mrs Crowther who kept an eye on the beautiful stranger. That night Lachie watched her slip from the farm then followed her down to the beach. From behind a rock he watched her swim, the waxing moon enough to see her shape in the water. Like Rob, who was by the outhouse, watching her, he had been ready to save her, but she was only in there two, three minutes, then waded out, gasping, swaddling herself in the coat, stamping her feet on the sand. Lachie kept to the shadows, hurrying back up the track to Heatherlee. Rob called to her, but the wind was in the wrong direction.

No-one saw her drag her suitcase from the side-door of the hotel to the cliff edge, where she pushed it then peered over, watching the dark bulk of it tapsalteerie down to the sea. That's heading south, she thought, hearing a booming thud from far below, not me! She wanted to cast off more. She'd slough off her skin if she could. She didn't see the hoodie crow swoop low, but she cried out, feeling the tip of its wing brush her head as she came into the field by Heatherlee. The wind howled. From far below the waves crashed over the skerries and the voice in the whistling wind above her cried – *set me free...*

'Don't go catching yer death, noo,' Lachie said next morning. 'In this weather, I mean.' He stared into his bowl of porridge. 'You don't want the cold to seep into yer bones.'

'I like cold,' she said, hardening against him. This was the bully that banished her mother. 'Then I have warm coat.' Summoning Marlene Dietrich in some old black and white film helped give her voice the edge, and Mairi knew about old black and white films. And she *was* half Polish, wasn't she? Or Lithuanian. Or Selkie. The story changed all the time, but the half bit was consistent. She was half something.

'Am I half Polish?' she had asked, grasping for identity. For her people.

Izzy had stared at her coldly. 'You might be.'

'We don't want you taken by the sea,' Mary said, 'do we Lachie?'

'Of course not,' Lachie said, then focused on his porridge.

When he was at the door, putting boots on, Mary took Mairi's hand. Lowering her voice even more she murmured, 'Don't be waiting for boats now, Yulia.'

Lachie shook his head and looked at his wife, his expression a mix of pity and concern. 'Don't be daft. Don't frighten the lass. I've work to do. And Yulia has too.' He opened the back door and went out.

'Mary,' she began, reaching for words to connect them, but instantly the whining voice was back.

Don't say who you are, the voice of Izzy whistling in her head. *They banished me – I was too wild for them, and they never knew about you. Keep it that way.*

'Yes, dear?'

'I… I don't think you're… daft.'

Mary smiled wistfully. 'There's a lot he doesn't know.' She glanced at the door, as if checking he was gone. 'I was wild.'

9

SEAVIEW ONCE HAD a lean-to greenhouse where Rob's grandmother, who had worked for the estate and been given the cottage to stay in, so his father said, grew real grapes. Green sour ones. Never got more than a bowlful, his dad had told him. Not worth the effort. The notion of a grape in Caithness where hardly a tree survived seemed a small miracle.

The vine was dead now and the greenhouse caved in. Something else he hadn't seen to. And why should he? If the estate in all their glory wanted Seaview back, all they need do was serve him two months' notice.

Rob knew Ryder wouldn't do that. Ryder, like many others, felt sorry for Rob.

The rare visitors might have said the place was haunted. Rob might have agreed, though it didn't bother him. It was only the wind, or the ghost of his mother playing the piano, before she took off and left, and the ghost of his father playing mournful tunes on the accordion. Or at any rate, after Rob's mother took off, the tunes turned maudlin. These shadows were company of sorts and ghosts didn't mind dust on the top of the piano. Cups too. Ghosts didn't bother about overflowing ashtrays.

His neighbour was at the back door, saying she was off to Inverness for the weekend to see Sharon, and was there anything he needed from the big city. A cleaner, Rob thought. A life!

'Na, you're fine,' he called through to her. He was leaning

against the piano, rolling his first cigarette of the day. That was one thing the piano was good for, leaning against. But suddenly there was Betsy Manson, in his living room.

'Sorry, Rob,' she said, not looking about. 'But I wondered if you could bring my washing in if it rains.'

'Aye, sure,' he said, 'no bother,' popping the cigarette into his mouth. He flicked his lighter but paused, waiting for her to go.

'The house is open. Just dump it on the back of the sofa. No need if it's just a passing shower though.'

'Aye, sure,' he muttered again, his cigarette moving as he spoke. He nodded, thinking he should apologise for the mess.

'Bye, then,' she said, waving cheerily to him and backing out of the room.

Rob lit his cigarette, took a draw and wondered who Sharon was. He looked about, seeing the place as Betsy would have seen it. What a dump. There were charity shops down in Wick that would take the furniture. And face it, he thought, he would never get round to tuning or playing the piano.

Rob brought his cigarette and notebook outside. The day was breezy, bright and not freezing; six or seven, Rob reckoned. Practically balmy. He could see his neighbour's sheets billowing on the line.

He had a bench in front of the outhouse, facing the sea. He'd made it from a plank of driftwood balanced on stones. He sat there sharpening his pencil with his penknife. Life in the old pencil yet. He laughed, thinking the same of himself. If anyone had bothered to ask him that question a month ago, he'd have admitted Rob Sinclair was on the way out. That was before he had raised the selkie. He heard the cry of a curlew, beautiful and somehow terrible. He flicked to the C's. Cormorant. Curlew. A lonely cry, he wrote, wondering, not for the first time, if this jumble of words was more about him.

Rob had cut the picture of a curlew from a magazine then stuck it in his book. 'Draw the birds, son,' he remembered his dad saying. Rob was fresh back from Aberdeen then, and gruff. He'd been hunched over his notebook, then snapped it shut, telling his old dad to mind his own fucking business. 'Sorry, son,' his dad had said, that evening, 'I didn't mean to pry. A man's a right to his secrets.'

With a pang of guilt Rob tried to draw the slim and elegant shape of the curlew, its long, curved beak. Rob closed the notebook on his effort. He was no artist. It was high time this fisherman went to sea.

Rob cut the engine and let the boat drift. Soon he'd start on the business of hauling up his creels, and whatever lobsters and crabs were in them.

As a boy his dad had sometimes taken him in the boat. Then Rob waited for his dad to say something important, teach him something, but his dad was mostly silent, as though the habit of speech had left him.

Now, cutting the crackling radio, Rob wondered if he was more like his dad than he thought. Days could pass without Rob saying more than a few words.

Then, Rob was chatty. 'You're bending my ear,' his dad said and Rob thought that was funny, as he jabbered on about whales and sharks and especially gannets, these big sea birds, diving at ninety miles per hour after a fish in the sea.

Rob scanned the horizon. Far out at sea grey curtains of rain shrouded the alien monster straddled in the North Sea. Daft for a lobster fisherman to be hurrying back because of his neighbour's washing, but there he was, a few creels still on the seabed and him heading back to beat the rain and dump some sheets on the back of a sofa! Puttering towards the harbour, the watery sun lit up the brown nicotine stains on the ends of his fingers. 'Women don't like that,' someone had said, when he used to go to the pub.

'Well, too fucking bad,' Rob had said, back then. Now he studied his fingers.

Maybe he would try filters again. It couldn't be that hard.

After the wide-open space of the sea, and the clean freshness of his neighbour's cottage, Rob stood in his own small living room, feeling the sadness of the place wrap around him. Rain pattered on the window. He felt the ghosts of his parents, especially his dad. It was like he was still there, still sitting by the fire, watching him. Rob's gaze landed on his dad's accordion which sat in the corner. It was probably out of tune. He blew off the dust then hauled the straps over his shoulders. He'd forgotten how heavy the thing was. 'Just a wee tune,' he said, as if the ghost of his dad might hear. His right-hand fingers found the keys, his left-hand fingers found the buttons, his arms working the bellows. The accordion didn't sound as bad as he thought it might, and his 'Mairi's Wedding' wasn't terrible, and for a few minutes he was in the music, myrtle green and bracken brown.

After he'd set the instrument back in the corner he stoked up the fire. 'What you need to do, Robbie,' he said to the flames, as if the music had loosened the tongue in him, 'is play more.' He sat back and stretched his fingers. 'You're not dead yet. And the selkie might like a tune.'

Thinking he heard a cry, Rob bolted outside. 'Anybody there?' he cried. A seal moaned. Waves crashed. He took his torch and flashed it along the shore edge. He was sure something moved, kicking up water. The selkie was out there. 'Hello,' he shouted, the longing he'd been keeping at bay suddenly overtaking him. He wanted to run after her and hold her tight. This need frightened him, but he yelled out anyway. 'Hey! Are you there?'

He fell over a stone and a pain shot through his knee. He lay on the beach, breathing one... two... three. He stood up and battened down the mad longing, then took himself off to bed.

Tyne... Dogger... Fisher... German Bight...

10

THE SMALL CARAVAN stood behind the byre and had what could be called a double roof, to protect it from the relentless wind. An overhang from the byre roof covered half of the caravan, like a hen spreading a wing over a chick. Inside, huddled beside the wood-burning stove, her coat draped over her shoulders, Mairi squeezed face cream into her open palm. When she had worked the cream into her hands she fished the ring out and slipped it on. She would return it that night. Accomplish at least one of Izzy's requests and set her mother's spirit free.

By candlelight Mairi examined the strange engraving. IZZ. It wasn't well done. Graffiti more than engraving. Under the IZZ Mairi could make out the more ornate initials EG.

Except *that* isn't *this* Elizabeth Gunn, Izzy had said, jabbing a thin finger to her chest, wearing that sour look, her cracked lips pulled down. That fancy EG, she had said, was your grandmother, a right old cow. And before her was another Elizabeth Gunn. The sons got land and the Elizabeths got gold.

'Make sure he gets it,' Izzy said, the day she finally pressed the ring into Mairi's open palm. They can't get rid of me that easily. Izzy lay back and slept after that, like the effort was too much, but with the trace of a smile on her ravaged face.

'We're talking spirits,' Izzy had said, when Mairi said she didn't understand. How could you go back to a place when you're dead? 'You'll understand,' Izzy had said, an eerie smile distorting her face. 'Get to Ronester, lassie, and you'll see what I mean. The place is full of them.'

Mairi dropped the stolen ring into the pocket of the fur coat Izzy had given her. 'Call it your inheritance,' Izzy had said of the brown fur coat.

'Thanks, Mum,' Mairi had tried, but Izzy scowled.

'Izzy's the name.'

Beyond the caravan, a mournful bellowing was coming from the byre. Mairi felt like bellowing too. She stared into the flickering orange flames.

A knock sounded at the caravan door. She sat back with a gasp. 'Yes?'

'Just me, Yulia.' It was Mary. 'Just wondering if you wanted to come in and sit with us, dear, and watch the telly?'

Mairi opened the door. 'No, thank you,' she said.

The light from the stove spilled out, bathing Mary's face in a dancing yellow glow. 'Oh,' she said, peering up at Mairi, her expression eager, almost childlike. 'That's a shame.' She thrust something towards Mairi. 'Here, I made this for you, a wee lap blanket.'

Mairi took the bundle. It was hard to see in the fire's glow. 'Thank you. That is very kind.'

'Aye, now, it gives me something to do. It's brown, like your eyes.'

Mairi held the small blanket to her, feeling tears smart. 'The cows,' she blurted, 'what is wrong with them?'

'The calves went today.'

'Oh...'

For a moment the two women stood in silence, as if both picturing calves in a field somewhere behind a slaughterhouse. They'd be bellowing too. 'Well, they'll forget it by tomorrow,' Mary said, without conviction. 'Poor things.' Then she shuffled off, muttering, 'Nightie-night, dearie.'

But Mairi, cold with loneliness, called out to her. 'How do you mean, wild?'

She saw her grandmother pause, her small body silhouetted in the orange glow spilling from the open door of the caravan. She saw Mary turn around and take a few steps back towards the caravan. 'It was a long while ago,' Mary said, her voice chanting, as if she was about to tell a fairy story. 'I liked the old songs and sung them down by the shore. I wandered down there alone at night. I wasn't frightened, then. The selkie men liked the old songs.' Her story floated into silence.

'What are you saying, Mary?'

'I'm saying no more.' Her voice closed. 'It was another lifetime. Another story.'

She shuffled away, but singing as she went, her haunting song fading, but some words Mairi could make out; '*I am a man upon the land... I am a selkie in the sea...*'

Mairi stood clutching the blanket, feeling a pang of love and pity for her. Lachie had said she wasn't herself.

Neither am I, Mairi thought.

To distract herself from the bellowing Mairi reached for the folklore book, flicking through chapters about hand-fasting marriage customs, apparitions and the healing properties of seaweed. It was the same book Izzy had taken from a library somewhere, and never returned. And the same page was turned down; how selkie men seek human lovers on lonely shores. How Izzy had pointed to that page, stabbing a finger at the swirling artwork of a man rising from the waves. 'Your father,' she had said.

Mairi felt a shiver creep over her skin.

She looked up from the musty book to see the moon like a face shining through the window. Full, and a wolf-moon according to the book. Mairi pushed wild, lonely girls and dark-eyed selkie men to the back of her mind and slipped the ring onto her finger. This ring returning, well she knew, was no peace-making gesture on behalf of Izzy but rather a 'fuck you! I'm back! And I've scratched my bloody name all over your precious ring just to make sure you know that!'

Mairi planned to return the Gunn heirloom to Heatherlee that night, be rid of it once and for all. She would secrete it in the stone wall, not a great plan but the least hurtful thing she could think of. And if either Lachie or Mary ever found it, they would think it had been there for years, or think some bird had burrowed it there.

The TV inside the farmhouse was turned up loud. Mairi, even at that distance, could hear the babble of it. Curling up on the narrow bed she buried her face in the thick pelt of her coat. The bereft cows continued bellowing their loss.

At midnight, TV finally silent, Mairi left the caravan. With a wolf-moon to guide her she crept across the scrub of field, eased the clan ring from her finger and slotted it between two stones in the wall.

'You're back,' she murmured.

Probably not the kind of dramatic homecoming Izzy had in mind, but it was, Mairi convinced herself, better than nothing. The ring was in Heatherlee. Then she'd scatter the ashes on the sea and hopefully the vengeful ghost would go where ghosts go and leave her alone.

As for task number three, that didn't bear thinking about.

As she hurried back in the moonlight she imagined her mother, perched like a crow in the branches of the hawthorn tree, shaking her head and crying, *you can't do anything right. Can you? I tell you to give the ring back and you stick it in a fucking wall! You should have put it in the dresser, along with my photos!*

'Please, leave me alone,' she muttered to the hissing darkness. Then louder, like a fox barking at night. 'Leave me alone!'

ROB WASN'T ONE for frequenting the pub, but sometimes, if Maggie wasn't around, getting the crack with the barman made a change from silence. That night, Rob probably would have stayed home with his silence and cans, but Davie, a fisherman from further down the coast, had radioed him. 'A dram for the New Year, eh, Robbie?'

Rob liked Davie. He hardly ever saw him, but when he did he liked him well enough. 'Aye, well,' he heard himself say. The two men, out on their boats, each alone in a wide sea, kept their radios open. 'Jake Henderson's back,' Rob blurted, unaware till then how badly Jake being back in Ronester had been sitting on him.

'The one yea went to Aberdeen with?' Davie's voice, crackling, slapping waves a soundtrack. The screech of a gull. 'When yea got a job crewing supply boats for the rigs? Then he got into dealing? That bastard?'

'The same.'

'The one yea swapped shifts with, eh?'

'Aye, him.'

'Forget him, Robbie man. If yea see him tell him to back off.'

'He's a rock star apparently.'

Davie's voice came chuckling through the radio. 'Aye, right. An I'm Ewan MacGregor. How's the fishing?'

'Creels set. It's not bad. Mind you, Davie, only me here. If Jake Henderson takes his boat out, we'll be trawling the same beds. And you know what he's like, always gets the big fish.'

'It's your patch. Forget him.' Rob heard a racket of gulls coming through Davie's radio, then his voice; 'The World's End at five, a' right?'

Over and out.

It was easier to forget his own mother than it was to forget Jake Henderson.

In the small world that is Ronester, Rob was at the bar with Davie when Jake came in. Or maybe Jake had spotted him heading that way.

'That him?' Davie muttered, nudging Rob who was downing his pint.

Rob turned to look, then nodded. 'Aye, that's him.'

'Tell him, Robbie, yea tell him to back off wi' his boat.'

From further along the bar Rob heard Jake's voice. 'I'll take a Bourbon,' rock star American draped over highland vowels. Bourbon? Fuck the prick, who in Caithness asked for Bourbon? 'With ice.' And who the fuck wore a black hat to the pub, and it not even a funeral?

Rob, fuelled with three pints, didn't need Davie to nudge him on like a schoolboy. 'Jake,' he started.

'Hey, it's you again, Robbie, how ye' doin' man?'

Rob eyed him coldly. Aye, he looked the rock star part with his black clothes, blues man hat, the leather jacket, the drawl and swagger of him. 'Worse for seein' you.'

Jake caught the barman's eye and shrugged, laughed though it sounded hollow. 'Whoa, nice welcome home, eh? I must have got right ugly down south.'

'That's right.'

'Charming.' Jake pulled a wallet from the back pocket of his black jeans and waved a tenner at the barman. 'Maybe Robbie here wants a drink?' He nodded to where Rob stood. 'To cheer him up. Lager, I think, was his tipple, eh, Robbie?'

Rob glared at him. 'Keep your money.'

Davie, like a man at a tennis match, shifted his eyes from Rob to Jake, Jake to Rob.

'Hey, come on, Robbie,' Jake kept up the jovial tone, 'I owe you, man. And it's the new year.'

'Too fucking right you owe me. Ten fucking years you owe me. Money can't buy that back.'

Jake shrugged again, addressing the barman who was looking ready to flick a bar towel, his training in dealing with agro. 'Don't know what he's on about.'

'Swap shifts, Robbie, he said.' Rob too addressed the barman, who found himself the audience in some charged drama, with Davie in the side seats. 'Sure Jake, says me. So off he went with my girlfriend. And what did I get? One blazing rig in the middle of the North Sea, that's what, and one fucked up, lonely life. So get out of here, Henderson. Just go.'

'Och, come on, man. Past is past. How was I to know?'

'You knew I was seeing Shelagh.'

'I mean, the rig thing. Nobody could've known that. And you said you weren't mad on Shelagh.'

'Just go, Jake.' Rob was staring into the dregs of his pint.

'Aye now,' the barman piped up. 'I don't think Rob here's wanting a drink, so...'

Jake drank his Bourbon in one, lifted his hat to Rob, then left.

'Nice one, Robbie, nice one,' Davie said, patting him on the back while the barman got busy pouring more pints.

But it wasn't nice.

Later that night, staring into his coal fire, Rob knew it wasn't nice. Maybe Jake was right. Past was past. He drank to that, drank until the past was as raw and present as it ever was.

12

HEATHERLEE, IT WAS plain to see even for an untrained eye such as Mairi's, was hardly in its heyday. The few cows looked miserable, even more so now that the calves had gone, and the land was so stony little more than coarse grass grew there. Mairi tried to picture the lively farm Izzy spoke about. Spring was a riot, she had said. Wee lambs bleating and calves running about the place. Hens wandering into the kitchen. Yolks the colour of sun. What a blast!

'Not like that now,' Mairi murmured, as if the appeased ghost of her mother might hear. At least, Mairi hoped the fact task number one was done – in as much as the stolen ring was now back at the farm – was giving the ghost of her restless mother some peace. Twice she'd gone back to the wall to check. The second time she pushed mud in the hole to cover any glinting. No-one would ever guess a precious heirloom was propping up the crumbling walls.

Mairi, her face numb with cold and her arms aching, went in for lunch. The daily fare was mince and potatoes. The Gunns ate without talking, but there was more than enough noise with the sounds of chewing, coughing, swallowing and the radio's crackling drone.

Peter in Dorset wants to send birthday wishes to his beloved wife, Dorothy. Anything by Elton John, please.

But Mairi wasn't listening to Elton John. She turned over in her mind what she would say when Lachie left and it was just the two of them. How she would drop it into conversation – perhaps mention the wind, the weather and how did sailor men cope in storms. Did she know much about Whaligoe Steps? And about Sinclair, the sailor man, perhaps? Know where she could find him? Not to do damage to, but to talk to. To speak out the hurt and grief he had caused, and then walk away. Such was her plan, as vague as fog.

Lachie put his cap on and went out, to the fuzzy tune of 'Goodbye Yellow Brick Road'. Mairi began washing up, the congealed gravy sticking to the white plates and the water not hot enough to dissolve it.

'You'd make a fine film star though,' Mary said, putting the HP sauce back into the cupboard. 'I liked Elizabeth Taylor best,' she went on, and in a lowered voice added, 'I wouldn't have chosen that for a name though.'

'What name would you have chosen?' Mairi prompted her, the warm water gushing over the back of her hands.

'Rona. But I had no choice.' She stared into the frail mesh of her fingers.

'Why Rona?'

Mary smiled that faraway smile Mairi was coming to know. Her grandmother lost in some romantic long ago. 'Little seal,' she murmured.

'She would have liked that... she...' Mairi stopped, but Mary smiled wistfully, none the wiser.

'Aye, it would have broken tradition.' Mary glanced over at the door. 'But there was no question. Elizabeth it was.'

They fell silent, as if both listening for him, the tread of his boots, the click of the door. 'What... what happened to... Elizabeth?'

'Gone back to the sea.'

Mary was now pouring tea from the pot.

'Do you sing, Yulia?' Mary asked.

Mairi sipped at the strong brew. She shook her head.

'Bet you have a bonnie voice,' Mary went on.

Not what the casting agents had said. Or her mother.

'You sing though, Mary. I heard you the other night.'

As if just waiting for the invitation the old woman snapped off the radio, cleared her throat and set her cup down. 'I'll give you the old ballad. I was forever singing it to Bethie when she was little.'

Mary closed her eyes, and sang:

'In Nor'o lands there lived a maid…'

Mairi was transported into some magical, watery world, by this warm, soulful voice and the way her grandmother reached for the notes, poured heart into the words.

'Halloo-hallay…'

Mairi was vaguely aware of the door opening, but the strange song held her.

'I am a man upon the land
I am a selkie in the sea…
And when I'm far from any strand
I make my hame on Sule Skerry…'

Listening, a tear slid down her face. There were plenty verses, and Mary, it seemed, knew them all; about seals and golden chains and a gunner good.

But this gunner wasn't good. Mairi didn't understand all the words, but understood that. And Izzy had told her that. How, in the end, men are not good.

'He killed the son and the grey selkie.'

The haunting tune tugged under her ribs.

Lachie was standing by the door, his cap in his hand like a man at church. Mairi glanced at him then away. Enough to see a look of regret cloud his face.

'*And her tender heart did brak in three.*'

The song done Mary opened her eyes and smiled sadly. Lachie slipped outside, closing the door quietly behind him. 'Aye,' Mary said, reaching for her tea, 'it does the heart good.' She nodded to the door, 'and he likes a song.'

Mairi got up and kissed her grandmother on the cheek. 'I like it too,' she murmured. 'Thank you. It was beautiful. So sad.' But then remembered the bull-seal shot in the head. The mad story her mother told. 'Um… Whaligoe Steps? Three hundred and sixty-five steps built into the cliff side. They're famous, are they?'

The old woman's face paled.

The mood of the song was broken. The mood of grandmother and granddaughter was broken. Mairi bit her lip.

'We don't mention them,' Mary muttered.

Mairi hurried outside. Her mouth hurt, all the things she couldn't say. The things she couldn't mention. She'd scatter the ashes and be done with it. Job number two.

Later, picking stones from the field, Mairi thought about this mad third task. 'I'm handing in my notice,' she muttered to the wind above.

But the moaning voice of Izzy, as if responding to her defiance, hissed, *you promised. And I can't rest until it's done.*

Mairi stood up, easing her back, and looked out over the fields and down to the wide North Sea, feeling the weight of guilt on her. She'd scatter her soon, but Mairi had forgotten whether it was to be on an incoming or outgoing tide. She waited for the ghost to prompt her, but for once the ghost was silent.

13

THE GOSSIPS DIDN'T let up. From the slow queue in the local shop, where they always hoped the mysterious stranger might make an appearance but never did, they scurried along the street with their few bit messages and round into the Back Row, to huddle over Jean's kitchen table and sample her fruit slices.

Before Jean's huge brown teapot went cold, the three most committed gossips in the village had ten pounds each on the mysterious single woman with long, brassy-blonde hair and unnerving, furtive dark eyes as being nineteen, twenty-six, thirty-two. Another fiver on her background; somewhere in Eastern Europe, 'Poland probably,' said Mina, who lived three doors up from the shop and was, according to herself, a fine judge of character.

'A bounty hunter, likely,' Gladys said, polishing off her fruit slice and lighting up a cigarette.

'Or in hiding,' said Jean glancing out the kitchen window where she had a view of a few rusting old cars, and a handful of bleating, ragged sheep. And where a wronged husband might just make an appearance.

It was after dinner the next evening that Mary told Mairi about music in the pub.

'You could go, Yulia,' she said suddenly. 'There is a band

on. I saw it in the local paper. A lass has got to have fun. A bit freedom, eh?'

Mairi shrugged.

'I like old songs,' Mary went on, wistfully.

Lachie came in then, looking for a sugar lump to suck on.

'What will you wear, Yulia?' Mary asked.

Going into a pub alone was something Izzy would do. And had done, often. But never Mairi. 'My red dress,' she said, feeling the possibility of being someone who did things like that. Izzy was dead. Mairi could do whatever she liked.

Mary patted her husband on the back of his hand. 'Yulia,' she whispered, 'could do with a bit spending money.'

The farmer acted like he hadn't heard. 'Lachie,' she said, with more force than usual. 'Money for our worker.'

He fished in his pocket then brought out a ten-pound note. 'Here then.'

Back in the caravan Mairi lay down, exhausted. It was after nine when she woke. The notion of going alone to see a band daunted her. But why not? No-one knew her and the old wifey was unlikely to be there.

Mairi had hardly reached the road and already the fancy boots were caked with mud. She pictured Izzy wearing them, strutting down Tooting Broadway. Suddenly she wanted to yank the boots off and hurl them into the sea, to follow the gowns and tiaras. Two or three times she stopped to ease her feet and look up at the million stars. Izzy may have been wrong about her daughter reaching stardom, but had been right about the stars. They were like diamonds on black velvet.

Nearing the main village street, she could hear music, a drum beat, a twang of bass guitar. She followed it to The World's End pub. Outside the door she scraped mud from her boots, smoothed her wind-tangled hair, took two, three deep breaths, then pushed open the door. Adjusting to the noise, warmth and music, she pictured the farm-worker role exit stage left. Enter someone more glamorous. She cast her eyes around the busy place, deciding who. Marilyn had been Izzy's go-to, before drink then illness robbed her of curves. Pouting, Mairi hip-swayed her way past dancing bodies to the bar. People were laughing, shouting. Still wishing each other a Happy New Year though it was a good ten days into it. Some stopped mid-sentence to turn and watch her. 'Red wine,' she had to shout above the music.

The barman stared at her. 'Large? Small? Bottle? House? Or something fancy? And 'at's some coat by 'ee way.'

'Large glass, house, please,' she said.

A man at the bar laughed. 'Fancy coat and cheap wine, eh?' He leered at her, looking like he might slide off the bar stool. 'Fur coat and nae knickers.'

'Dinna mind Hector,' the young barman said, 'a couple o' drams and his manners fly oot 'ee window, eh? Hector? Keep it clean, a' right?'

Mairi turned to watch the dancers. No sign of that interfering busybody. Here, dancing, shouting, drinking, were young folks, who, according to Mary, didn't live here anymore, and would soon go back south. They didn't all gape like she was an alien, or not obviously. They kept dancing, drinking, joking. Mairi made her way to a free table at the back and slipped in, pulling off her coat and sitting on it. A Christmas tree in the corner flashed red lights on and off. She bit at her already broken fingernails, then drank, fast, watching the dancers, then the band. She still had six pounds and twenty pence left. She went to the bar and ordered another.

'Looks like old Lachie put his hand in his pocket.' The barman grinned at her. 'So, you're 'ee mysterious Polish

Princess.' He poured slowly, his eyes sliding from the wine to the woman. 'Eh?' She ignored him and turned to look at the band, cradling their guitars and thumping the drums. The barman tapped her on the shoulder. '£3.80.' Fumbling with the money, Mairi put four pound coins on the counter. 'Thought you lot drank vodka,' he said, pressing twenty pence into her hand. She frowned at him and took the drink, sipping from it as she wobbled her way back to her table. The boots were lethal. She squirmed under the table and pulled them off.

Leaving her glass almost empty she padded up to the small area in front of the band where people were dancing. Then people did look. For one she was dancing alone. For another, she was barefoot. Her arms circled in the air above her head and her curvy hips moved slowly from side to side. Her eyes were closed. Somebody clapped. Somebody else tried to imitate her. Somebody else said to leave her alone. In the flashing disco lights her long dress sparkled purple, then red, then black. Her hair lit up silver, then yellow, then gold. A drunk man danced with her, but she didn't notice him, and someone pulled him off the dance floor, shouting how she was a professional and he was a wanker. When the song finished some people clapped, but Mairi, thinking they were applauding the band, joined in. She wove her way back to her table and drained what was left of the wine.

She watched the dancers nestle up close. She had turned up in time for the end. The band were onto their slow smoochy number, about going blind, about walking away. The singer, eyes closed, embraced the mic, crying 'baby, baby, baby...' pouring everything into it. The song was like a fisherman's hook the way it tugged her. She wanted to love like that, to be wanted like that.

She went to the bar, grasping tables now as she navigated. 'Another red wine,' she slurred over the slow rift of guitar.

'Shiraz, was it?' The guy behind the bar, unlike her, didn't bother keeping his voice down.

She shrugged, then smiled at him. She only had £1.40 left. She pushed that across the bar. 'Sorry.'

The barman leaned over, handing her the wine. 'No worries.' He dropped the money into the till, not counting it. 'Hey, I saw you dancing. You're ace. Swedish, eh? See if I wasn't stuck here, I would have got you up to dance.'

'Thanks,' she said, taking the glass, the bar tipping like she was at sea. She reached out to steady herself. 'Do you know when that hotel opens?' she asked him, Eastern European accent gone over the side of the swaying boat.

The barman was the one to shrug now. 'Dunno. Owner's down in Edinburgh. Thought he would come up and open it for Christmas and New Year, but,' another shrug. 'Why?' He leaned over. 'What's it to you? You want a holiday there?'

Mairi shrugged. 'You know a man they call Sinclair the sailor man?'

The barman stared at her. 'God, you *are* a spy.'

She lurched away. Once in the dark haven of the alcove seat she lifted her glass, eyeing the bass player through it, blood-red and glass-curved.

The bass player was deep in a rift, the singer breaking his heart, plucking out his lovesick eyes, and the couples on the floor pressed up close. Some of them snogging. 'We're all looking for shomeone, eh?' she said to an older woman sitting close by. Her words slurred.

The woman made as if she hadn't heard. People on the dance floor were singing along. Everyone going blind.

Then, maybe it was the sight of her own daughter pressed up close to some young lad, the woman narrowed her eyes at Mairi and hissed, 'mind your own damn business.'

Which was when the song ended and her hissed, 'damn business,' rang out loud and clear.

Mairi lifted her empty wine glass to her eyes, distorting the angry woman through it. She laughed at the rounded, fuming face.

The guy behind the bar was at her side, ready to clear up the empties and dissolve any agro with his bar towel. 'Now, now, keep it clean, ladies,' he said, cheerily, as he whipped up the glasses, the bar-towel over his arm.

The woman was still glaring at Mairi. 'Who does she think she is? Coming here.'

Mairi wrapped her fur coat around her shoulders. 'Just...' Mairi hiccoughed, 'shetting the record straight. Helping me mammy.'

The band were waving to the cheering crowd. Mairi joined in the cheering and beckoned to the bass player.

'I mean,' the angry woman went on, raising her voice, 'who *is* she anyway?'

'She's a foreign dancer,' the barman said, helping Mairi on with her coat. 'Isn't 'at right?'

'Well, she can strip the willow right out of here,' the woman snapped.

That's when the bass player stepped forward. Dancers were returning to their seats or getting their coats and slipping off into the January night with whoever they had danced the last dance with. The band were unplugging, dismantling the illusion that for an hour or two they had American accents, transporting the weather-beaten inhabitants of this windswept North Sea coastal village over the Atlantic to some sun-kissed, easier and surely more passionate lifestyle.

'She's waiting for me,' the bass player said, fixing his smoke-crinkled eyes on her.

Izzy had said some of them were good looking. She wasn't wrong.

The barman backed off.

'Oh, hey, shanks,' Mairi said, trying to smile, the room spinning. 'You… God, you shaved me. I was drowning.' She laughed.

He put a cigarette into his mouth and his blues man hat on his head. 'Coming?'

She fumbled for her boots, but could only find one. She laughed, slung one boot across her shoulder then got to her feet, swaying and toppling against him, linking an arm in his, as if they were a couple. She was the girl with the band. His partner, even. 'Your place or mine?' she said, picturing the caravan, and the mess it was in, but it wouldn't matter. The air would clear her head. She'd light a candle. Then she hiccoughed.

The bass player leant in close, whispering in her ear, 'I was more thinking the back of my van.' He steered her through the crowd clustered around the doorway, buttoning coats, winding on scarves. He put a hand on her bum, the hand that had been cradling the guitar. 'It's got a heater,' he went on, manoeuvring her out into the cold and the dark. 'At least it has when I turn the engine on. Then it's hot.'

'Your hand?' she asked, giggling.

'Aye, that too. Just you wait. It's on fire.'

'Do you know, it'sh… a wolf-moon,' she said, pointing to the moon above them. She howled, then hiccoughed and stumbled against him, laughing. Others were drifting away, some turning back to stare at the barefoot drunk woman with Jake the bass player who had left a wife and child in Manchester, and who was making it in the music world.

'You're keen.' Then he kissed her neck, muttering and biting her ear, 'Bet you fuck like a wolf, eh?'

'Hey, Jake,' somebody shouted from the open door of the pub, cables wound round an arm. 'Hey, man, we need your help here.'

'Fuck's sake, Donny. Gie me five minutes, eh,' his accent breaking into pure highland. He waved his cigarette towards them. 'I'm gasping.'

He pulled the back door of the van open. 'Welcome to my love nest, you fucking wild thing.' Giggling, she fell in, dislodging cables and landing on a mattress, the side of her face pressed up against her high heeled boot.

'Ouch! Hey, you... you might know... Shinclair the sailor man?' She giggled then started humming her favourite film tune. *I wanna be loved by you...* thinking suddenly she could have sung that to her grandmother, the few lines she knew. *You... just you...* 'He went,' she hiccoughed, 'oops, fishing by Whaligoe shteps, at night.' He clicked on a torch. *I wanna be loved by you...* She brought a hand to her eyes. 'Ouch! You're blinding me.' But he kept the glare trained on her. She struggled to sit up, blinking. 'I would... go blind... Hey, what's this? The inqui... shin?' She hiccoughed again. 'God's shake.'

'Sailor man?' His ardour had cooled. He looked horrified. 'Sinclair?'

She hiccoughed, and giggled. 'Yeah, Whaligoe! Is it haunted? Is...'

'Sorry, but hey, you better go.'

'Why?' She felt soberness smack her. 'What have I done? What did I say? Haunted, is that it? You don't like that, eh? It's full of ghosts here. Or it's that Sinclair. You're scared of him, like everybody is.'

'I need to get back, help the guys.' He dropped the torch-beam to the ground.

'I'm not fifteen,' she muttered, but sheepishly now,

scrambling free of the cables.

'Look, I'm sorry.' Then he helped her out the back of the van and closed the door. 'Take care of yourself, eh?' Leaving her on the street he disappeared into The World's End.

One boot was still in his van, the other in the pub. She went down to the sea, swam the shame off her. But wading out and pulling on her coat she saw the shadow again at the cottage window. Then a door clicked open. 'Hey!' A man's voice called into the night. 'Hey! Don't run away! Please!'

She ran, fell, got up then kept running, up the hill like she was fleeing from a ghost. Not just one. Ghosts were everywhere. Breathless, her feet bleeding, she reached the caravan door then barricaded it with everything she could find.

14

HE STARTED TO picture her here with him, in the bedroom, the kitchen, the living room. For all that the place was draughty and old, it was a damn sight better than Lachie's old caravan. Though, Rob admitted, Seaview cottage wouldn't pass planning nowadays.

A hundred and seventy years ago, Rob guessed they didn't have such a thing, or the sea was much further back. Some days the front windows were so salt-smeared you couldn't see out. The bathroom window rattled in the wind. Wind snaked under the back door. Wind moaned down the chimney. Wind shook slates and had smashed the greenhouse. Not that the estate had bothered fixing any of it. The few visitors that ever dropped in kept their coats on and said he should get himself some of these draft excluder things that looked like giant sausages. Rob apologised. They stopped coming after a while, Rob telling himself it was because of the drafts, but guessed it was him. He'd forgotten how to be social. Anyway, he liked fresh air. It helped him feel alive. These few visitors also said he should get the damned landlord to fix stuff, but Rob shrugged. Broken stuff didn't bother him, and he didn't want to give Ryder an excuse to raise the rent.

It was easier without visitors.

But that didn't stop him imagining her in his bed, at his table, in his arms, brightening the place. Soothing him. Not a visitor but a stayer.

From the concrete outhouse that sat squat at the end of the garden, and had once served as a lookout for U-boats, Rob looked down on the beach and the sea. His dad had turned the place into his net store. It was still that, and a good spot for bird watching. It smelled of tobacco and seaweed, depending on tides and mysterious things like the shifting seabed. Occasionally sewage. There was also an undertow, if such things had smells, of loneliness. Of watching. Of waiting.

Rob sat on the crate that did for a chair and laid out a Rizla paper on the other crate that did for a table. He sprinkled tobacco over the paper. Placing the filter was not something he was getting the hang of. It kept rolling off. Probably because the crate wasn't straight, but Rob wasn't for trying and trying again. He rolled the cigarette minus tip, flicked the Zippo into life and lit up, taking the first drag of the day. 'See Dad,' he muttered, blowing out smoke and addressing the cobwebby ceiling, 'this black sheep gives up.' He took another draw, releasing the grey smoke slowly, 'Sorry to be the big disappointment of the clan.'

To stop his frequent peering out to see if the beautiful stranger was down by the shore, he tackled the knots. It was a job he'd put off for months. The place stank of seaweed and brine. Everything did. His whole life consisted of knots, things that needed doing, or undoing, things his dad would have sorted.

Despite watching from his window the night before, convinced he saw her, then running out to find nothing more than a dead seal, the light mood hadn't left him. He'd considered stealing up to Lachie's farm but hadn't. The Gunns weren't over fond of the Sinclairs, that was putting it mildly. Since 1586 the two hadn't seen eye to eye. Anyway, he wanted to happen upon her down by the shore. The romantic in him, that he thought had died, was firing him. He imagined them hand in hand. Snatches of forgotten poetry came back to him. *And I will love you still, my dear, till a' the seas gang dry.*

How he would show her his country. How men of his country could love. He hoped she did have a shady past. That would make them quits. They could start afresh together.

Now it was Sunday. Not that Rob was religious, but he wouldn't take the *Stella* out. No-one wanted fish on a Monday. He made a start teasing out the twisted ropes. A long job, but it was good to focus on something. Early afternoon and already dusk, falling.

'Working on the sabbath?' he could hear his father say, that hint of irony in his voice. 'Aye,' he would reply, 'your son's a terrible sinner.' But the old man would nod then get back to his own sabbath work, mending nets, cleaning the accordion, quiet stuff, he said, that suited the day. Then he'd strap the box over his shoulders and play a slow air; 'Fair me O'. Or, 'Abide wi me'.

Rob had a light rigged up in the outhouse, so could keep at this task for hours. He worked a thick knot, feeling the satisfaction when it came away. His gaze left the heap of ropes to look out to the shore, but it was dark now, and the moon not yet up. From where Rob sat, on a crate looking out the thick window, the world beyond, bar the oil rig, was utter blackness. He didn't even mind the rig tonight.

He worked at a double knot. It was like grappling with a thief, trying to claw back whatever the thief had filched. Something came free and clattered to the wooden floor, but Rob, absorbed in the task, didn't give the thing a second thought. Until the light caught it.

Retrieving the glinting thing Rob held it to the naked bulb. It was a piece of green metal, the sort of flotsam and jetsam his creels might dredge up. Peering closer, he saw it was a badge. Or, he turned it over, a medal. Winner, it said, in tiny, engraved writing. North of Scotland. 1995.

It came to him with a pang. It was his dad's medal. His one and only medal, he remembered his mother saying. Rob never knew if she was disappointed, or sarcastic. Now, holding the 'one and only medal' in his hand, thirty years on, Rob felt a lurch of sadness.

He had gone along with his parents. He was seven or eight, kitted out in his Sunday best, hair washed and all excited for the trip down to Wick. When they got there the hall was packed, and noisy. The morning had been loud with fiddles and accordions. The afternoon was a hushed nervous expectation.

'And the winner of the Accordion, is... Robert Sinclair.'

His mother looked ready to burst into tears. His dad – the winner – hung his head and stared at the floor. Young Robbie sat between his parents. Others in the hall had started clapping. The man with the medal was standing on the stage, beginning to look uncomfortable, waiting for the winner to come to the front and receive his prize, maybe even give a wee acceptance speech.

'Go on, Robert, up and get your medal,' his mother said, pushing him in his back. 'And say a few words for God's sake.'

But still Robert sat, as if frozen. His face had turned red. People were now shouting, 'Come on Robert! Come on Robert!'

Rob felt his dad's pained embarrassment. His mother looked flustered. The noise rose louder. Young Robbie wanted to tell them all to stop it. But he too was frozen.

'I can't, Jessie,' his dad muttered, 'I can't.' And for the first time, Rob understood, his own father was shy. Not just a little, but it crippled him. This big, bearded fisherman, King of the Sea, had no confidence in front of people. Yes, he could give them a tune, but as if the accordion protected him. Without it, or his boat, he was lost. It had hit Robbie like a punch and dislodged his almighty father from his throne. What was a man who couldn't stand up in front of people and take his prize? Not a proper man. And the realisation didn't end there. It wrapped Robbie in its arms too, squeezing the joy out of him. Like father, like son.

In the end his mother had hurried up to the stage, making excuses while the crowd laughed, then she practically ran back and banged the medal on the table.

Rob remembered his dad had got drunk that night and slept in the bath.

Rob looked at his father's one and only medal. He unclipped the pin which had rusted, but still worked. He fastened the medal to his sweater. His mother didn't stay long after that; a year or two, perhaps. Wanting more, wanting Robert Sinclair to be more.

He reached forward and tugged at another knot, remembering his resolution to pick up the accordion. As if on cue the seals in the bay called, their haunting, plaintive song.

It was that image that stayed with him as he sat in the outhouse, a jumble of net in his hands and the old medal now pinned to his jumper; his mother's face, red with anger. 'You're not man enough to go to the front and give them a few words,' she had shouted to the broken man who lay drunk in the bath, 'you hear me, Robert Sinclair, you're not a proper man.'

15

WHEN THEIR DRY stane dyke worker didn't appear for dinner, Mary left the farmhouse and went round the back of the byre. She knocked on the caravan door. 'Are you alright, Yulia?' she called, her voice thin. 'I have scones for you, fruit ones.' Then Mary was letting herself in, toppling the chair Mairi had used as barricade. 'And a woolly scarf. For the cold.'

Mairi got up quickly, her head reeling. She glanced about. Anything that needed hidden was under the bed. 'Um… sorry…' Fumbling, she righted the chair.

Mary was setting her gifts on the small work top, then taking off her coat. Mairi reached for the scarf and pressed it to her cheek. 'Thank you.'

'To keep you cosy,' Mary said. She glanced out the caravan window, then, as if assured the coast was clear, settled herself in the one chair. 'He doesn't like me going on about her, but he can't stop me.'

Mairi wound the scarf round her neck and waited for more, but Mary lapsed into silence. 'No,' Mairi said. 'He can't.'

'She wasn't all bad.' The old woman's gaze seemed fixed on some memory. 'She was like the wind. Wild, restless, and I said to him, you can't hold the wind, can you? You can't turn a gale into a breeze, can you?' She looked beseechingly at Mairi. 'Can you?'

Mairi nodded, then shook her head. Yes. No. You couldn't.

Mary sighed then looked at Mairi and smiled. 'Are you sure you're alright, dear? You look peaky. It's not right, you being here in winter. I mean, in this old caravan. If we had room...' she trailed off. 'Are you sure you're alright?'

Mairi drew one truth from the heap of lies. 'I drank some wine,' she said. 'Just a sore head. Not used to it.'

Mary nodded, as if she knew all about wine. 'It's the salt in the air, it puts thirst on your tongue.'

Even one small truth lightened her burden. Mairi settled on the bed, the fur coat over her legs. 'What was she like, this Elizabeth Gunn? Your daughter.'

'Restless. But the wind is too, isn't it?'

Mairi nodded. Her Izzy, the English, exiled, bitter Izzy, was restless, always flitting, but in the end couldn't bear a window open. As if the wind in her had been sucked out.

'But he was maybe right, you know, Yulia,' Mary went on. 'Drugs. The thirst for more. It was bad things and her out alone on a wild night. So young too, the wind howling and I was tucked up in bed with a hot-water bottle.' She looked deep into Mairi's eyes, and lowering her voice as if Lachie might hear said, 'I had my wild days too, but it was different back then. Safer. We had selkie men come ashore, yes, but not the bad things. Not the boats.' Mary sighed. 'You hope to have your child until they're eighteen at least, but after thirteen her spirit was gone from us. She was forever down the shore. Or on the cliff tops. Or out I don't know where. It got that I didn't want to know where.'

'Or out at sea?'

'Oh, maybe. Nothing would surprise me. She said it was our fault for living on the edge. What did we expect? Anyway, it was another night and her too long away and me fretting, then Lachie gets a call and he's away, into the night and not saying a word, but a face on him like thunder. I knew this time she had gone too far. There was nothing I could say. Do you understand, dear, nothing. It would have made no difference.'

Mairi nodded.

'He was right,' Mary went on. 'It would only end badly. He was right to take her south for a fresh start. She fell in with a bad crowd here. I cried for weeks and barely ate. He suffered too; I know. Something was broken in him. But,' a faraway smile came onto the old woman's face, 'as a peedie thing she was a joy, running, laughing, playing with the lambs and her dolls. And the hens. We had hens then. I want to get hens now, a bit life about the place, but Lachie says they're too much for me. Ach.' Mary wiped tears from her eyes. 'You never know which way the wind will turn, do you?'

From the farmhouse there came the sound of a door creaking. Then Lachie's voice, 'Mary!'

Mary bundled her coat into her arms and stood to leave. 'I blame myself and my own wild frolics down the shore. I was warned.' She spoke quickly now. 'Stay away from the shore at night, the other girls warned me. Or you'll birth a wild creature. But I couldn't stay away.'

She opened the caravan door. 'I think Lachie knew. That's why he was hard on her. He knew she wasn't his.'

When Mary had gone, Mairi sunk onto the bed and wept fat, salt tears.

Mairi didn't stray from the farm for three days. She did her work, clearing the field of as many stones as she could find and piling them by the walls, and though the sea called she couldn't bear the shame of bumping into the bass player. She wasn't keen on coming face to face with the meddling old woman either. Plus, that man she had heard calling her when she was down at the shore had unsettled her. Ronester seemed to be conspiring against her. She wasn't going to be hounded out, though couldn't stay much longer in the caravan, she knew that. It was cold and damp. The small stove took the edge off, but she often woke in the middle of the night, a tightening in her chest. She looked out over the bleak fields. Where next? Ronester was the end of the road.

And there was the question of the sailor man. Izzy's voice, screeching in the wind, had grown louder, more insistent. *Do damage to the bastard Sinclair the sailor man. Push him down Whaligoe Steps!*

Mairi had been nearly two weeks in Ronester by now, and had been nowhere save beating a path like an animal from farm to sea and sea to farm. But now she forced herself to return to the small village shop. She hoped she had enough money for a can of Coke, then, in passing, she'd ask about this Sinclair. Show the restless ghost of her mother she was at least doing something.

Head buried in her fur coat, she pushed on along the village street. No harm in asking, she convinced herself. Could say she had a message for him, which was not a lie. She slowed down, trying to see through the shop window. Empty would be preferable. She clutched the three pound coins and entered, bell clanging above the shop door as she did. Her luck was in, only the old-fashioned shopkeeper was there, neat in a brown apron, and beaming at her.

'Hello, hello, it's you again, and how are you today?'

Mairi forced a smile. 'Fine,' she muttered. Her eye fell on the newspapers on the counter, as if the monster Sinclair might be making headlines. Or – precious ring discovered in wall!

The shopkeeper went on, 'And how are you liking village life now?' Hope they're not working you too hard.' He waited for a reply, his face, Mairi noticed, scrubbed clean.

'Um,' she began, nodding, forgetting her voice. 'Coke,' she

said, flustered. She read the man's shifting expression. Not quite so beaming now.

'The drink, not the drug, I hope,' the shopkeeper said, then laughed, though Mairi could tell it was forced. He was uncomfortable, she could see that. But his discomfort gave her confidence.

'Sinclair, the sailor man,' she blurted. Just as she had done with her grandmother, as if blurting the name was the only way to get it out of her throat where it festered.

The shopkeeper placed a can of Coke on the counter. 'Ninety pence,' he said, then shook his head. 'Aye, now, I see the Gunns have been burdening you with their tale of woe. Pay it no heed is my advice. None at all.'

The bell clanged. A gust of cold wind and old Mina blew in. Mairi took the Coke, dropped the coin onto the counter and hurried out.

Out on the street she stared up to the racing clouds above. I tried, she muttered, the wind clawing at her tangled hair. You can't say I didn't try.

But back the spectral voice came, like so many school report cards – *you didn't try hard enough*. Mairi hurried down to the hotel and round the back to the cliff edge. She wrapped her fingers around the chilled metal of the Coke can and hurled it over the cliff.

The next day it started to snow, flakes swirling past the caravan window like waltzing ghosts.

'There's plenty ghosts here, you know,' Mary had told her.

Mairi could believe it, especially now, the mesmerising way the snow swept around. She began to wonder whether that old woman, flinging pebbles and telling her to get a bus south, had been a ghost. Here, the veil between this world and the 'Other' was thin, so it said in the folklore book.

Mairi stretched her fingers and eyed the small webs between them. Her head reeled.

Ladling lentil soup into bowls that evening, Mary looked, Mairi thought, utterly lost. As if she had stepped from the kitchen into Tir-nan-Og; another mythic place from her folklore book. Mairi saw how frail her grandmother's hands were, how she hardly ate and how her eyes kept drifting to Mairi, then away. Mairi wanted to break the spell, imagined a hundred ways of spilling the beans – Surprise, surprise! Hey presto! You're not going to believe this… Sit down while I tell you something. I'm your granddaughter. And Elizabeth is dead.

But the habit of secrecy had muted her. And the voice that harangued her to silence scared her.

That voice wasn't mute, no matter the ring had been returned. If anything, the disembodied voice grew louder. *Set me free. Don't dare let on who you are. I'm watching you.*

But she had heard somewhere, on some TV programme, how the voice of a dead person can sound on long after their passing. That's all it was, she tried to convince herself, the echo of the dead.

After washing up, Lachie and Mary invited her to sit with them and watch television. Mairi excused herself, saying she wanted to be out in the snow. It looked so pure and white and lovely, she said. 'Some young folks,' Lachie explained to his wife, slowly making his way over to the TV, 'like the great outdoors.' He switched it on.

'Well, it's not safe,' Mary muttered, her voice drowned out by voices from the television.

'I like snow,' Mairi said. 'And I have good coat.' The accent wavered. She didn't care anymore. And they didn't seem to notice. They were outside of society, like her. They rarely saw anyone, went anywhere. Their world had shrunk to the size of a few ragged fields, a byre, a kitchen, a few moon-eyed cows, a television screen, and eight fading photographs. It had been a very long while since Mary Gunn had frolicked by the shore.

'Aye, you want to watch, swanning about with that swanky thing on your back. Don't see them these days. Where did you get it anyway? Must be worth a bit.' A long speech for Lachie, and nosy for a man who never pried into anyone's business.

Mary was staring at him. Mairi too, who said nothing, but thoughts ran through her, how the luxury coat was all Izzy had had left. Izzy said she felt protected in it, said it had the wild in it. Said it reminded her of the stranger who came ashore.

'It's a bonnie coat, dearie, and it'll keep you warm.' Mary said.

'Aye, well, don't tarry out there long, will you now,' Lachie said, but his face, expressionless, was turned to the screen. 'We can get fierce blizzards up here.'

'Awful fierce,' Mary added, also turning to the screen.

By now the room was loud with American accents. Someone started shouting. Mairi was hovering by the kitchen door. 'Yulia,' Lachie said, turning now to look at her, 'far be it for me to be telling you what to do and where to go, but...' He hesitated and turned back to the TV, as if he might find the rest of his sentence there.

'But what?'

Lachie continued staring at the TV, his face shut.

Mary looked round at Mairi. 'Just look after yourself, dearie,' she said, 'and don't be waiting for any boats now.'

Mairi left them staring at the flickering screen. Outside the world was quiet and the snow falling steadily. The fierce wind of earlier had calmed. She hurried round to the caravan where she put on her fur coat, took the silk-wrapped box from under the bed and stepped outside. 'Time to let you go,' she whispered to the box.

Mairi put her one glove on. She'd lost the other. She slipped into her wellies and made her way, in the winter dusk, down to the shore. By the time she reached the beach her hair was white, the fur coat too, like a snow leopard. She tipped back her head, stretched out her tongue and caught a snowflake.

The snow fell heavy now, vanishing into the sea, wiped clean with each wave that rolled in and ebbed back.

Gladys Crowther was probably watching the crying, screaming sisters in America too, because she didn't see the beautiful stranger drift through the snow and skirt the shore, then open the box and scatter her mother's ashes over the sea. Where the tide wasn't coming in, it was going out.

16

ROB WATCHED THE snowflakes from his bedroom window. He liked that winter dusk time when the light drained from the sky. The shadow time, his dad had called it. Rob thought he saw something moving down by the shore. A stag? A grey seal? The mysterious selkie? Or a trick of the failing light. He took up the binoculars. Though the snow blurred vision he was sure it was the woman. She was bending, some kind of scarf flapping in her hand. He ran outside, bolting up to the outhouse where he had a better view, then, hardly knowing what he would ever find to say to her, took off across the slippery stones. 'Hello,' he cried out. The woman flung the box into the sea then fled like a startled deer. 'It's alright,' he shouted, 'hey, sorry, it's alright. You don't have to run off. I'm a good man.' But she had vanished into the snowy gloaming.

Fuelled suddenly with the urge to get a note to her he hurried back to the cottage and rummaged for a sheet of paper. *Sorry. I didnt mean to give you a fright,* he scribbled. Then signed it, *Rob fisherman at the shore.* But it needed more, some invitation, so added, *Drop in. for a cup of tea. Don't be a stranger.* He put on his heavy wax jacket and slipped the letter into his pocket. Rob didn't stop to think. If he had, he would have thrown the paper into the fire and opened a can of beer.

He ran up the track. The snow was swirling, for the wind had come up. 'Christ,' he muttered, pulling his jacket against him. She was a fast runner, unless she had slipped off the track. Sure he had seen her head towards the village, he kept going, leaning into the swirling flakes, reaching the main street where not a soul stirred. Curtains were drawn. Fires on. Feeling like the last man on earth he pushed on up the hushed street, then up the winding track to Lachie's farm. He wasn't welcome there, he knew that, but Rob didn't care. He had to find her. She had become a lifeline to a drowning man.

Approaching the farmhouse he kept into the shadows, saw a lamp glow at a window. As he stood, blowing on his fingertips and the snow falling on him, he wondered what he would do now. Push the note under her caravan door? Knock and introduce himself? He felt foolish. What would he even say? Was she alright? Had she lost something? I saw you down by the shore and wondered if you were looking for something? Someone? I didn't mean to frighten you.

What had seemed a fine, urgent idea twenty minutes ago now didn't, but Rob's footsteps were bolder than his mind. They skirted the farmhouse and made their way to the byre. In the snow-fused dusk he could make out the bulky shapes of Lachie's cows, huddled round a bale of hay. The smell off them was comforting. So were the sounds, the way they shuffled, chewed, breathed. He might be a fisherman, but Rob liked farms fine. Afraid the cows would start bellowing he carried on, past the byre, to Lachie's old caravan.

Rob smelt the smoke from her fire. He fumbled in his pocket for the letter, his fingers numb with cold. There was no obvious place to leave a note. He stepped up to the door and knocked.

No-one answered, but inside, he glimpsed through the window, the stove was on, an orange glow. He knocked again. Then he heard a sound, but not from the caravan. It was old Lachie himself barking out into the night, 'Who's there?'

Probably, Rob thought, suddenly feeling like an idiot, the woman was inside the house with them. Probably she hadn't been down at the shore at all. Or probably she was back in her selkie home under the sea. It wasn't the first time he had imagined things. He thought to run off but next moment a lurching torchlight swung its glare up by the byre. 'Yulia?' Lachie called. 'Is that you?'

Was that her name? So, she wasn't with them. Rob stood outside the caravan door, as if frozen to the spot. 'What the hell are you doing here?' Lachie trained his torch light on Rob's snow-dusted face.

'Nothing,' Rob blurted.

'Rob bloody Sinclair,' the farmer hissed. 'Doesn't look like nothing. Yulia!' Lachie shouted. 'Yulia! Are you alright?'

'She's not here,' Rob said.

'Aye, but you are.' Lachie stepped closer, blinding Rob with his torch light. 'You bloody well are, and I'm not scared of you.'

'Fuck's sake,' Rob muttered, shielding his eyes.

'What have yea done to her?' Lachie growled. He stepped closer, menacing. 'I never trusted yea, Rob Sinclair. If yea've laid a hand on her, I'll break your neck.'

'Look,' Rob shouted. 'I don't even know her.'

'So... just thought you'd come snooping about, eh?' Lachie held the torch like a gun, pointing it into Rob's eyes. 'Nice night for a wee visit, eh?'

'No... I...'

'Just like you drew our Bethie into the devil's own work. If it wasn't for you, she'd never have touched these damn drugs, you hear me? Never! Now beat it and leave this lassie alone!'

'You might want to talk to Jake Henderson on that score.'

'What's that? What?'

'Forget it.'

'Aye, just like your dad, eh? A clipe, a right damn interfering Sinclair, eh? In about our business, think you can lord it over the county, well beat it.'

Rob felt the bile rise. He clamped his jaw tight. 'Leave my dad out of it.'

'Pity he hadn't thought of that himself, eh? Then we might still have her.'

Rob heard the old man's voice break. Saw how old he was, and hurting. He felt a twinge of pity. 'That's nothing to do with me,' he said.

But the old man's face hardened, a look of hatred etching his face. 'Blood is blood, and don't forget it. Now get the hell out of here, and don't come back. You hear me? I don't want the likes of you up here. Yea think you're a hero, Sinclair, but by God, your copy book's blotted on that score. Now beat it. I'll have no Sinclair darkening my door, yea hear?'

A call came, high and shrill from the farmhouse door. 'Lachie. Is she alright?'

'Beat it, Sinclair,' hissed Lachie. 'Aye, fine,' he called back to his wife.

'You're not her dad,' Rob shouted, then he turned and ran, hearing Lachie's curses behind him as he belted down the track.

Rob stopped when he came to the hotel. Above him the sign creaked in the wind. The place, usually so dark and lifeless during the winter, looked, snow-draped, like something from a fairy tale. Sheltered in against the door Rob drew out his pouch of tobacco, and his undelivered letter.

'Bastard,' he spat. Rob was the first to know just how blotted his so-called copy book was. He kicked at the snow. 'Bastard,' he cried. His own father had never seen eye to eye with Lachlan Gunn. It's the old fisherman-farmer war, his mother had said, by way of explaining the hostilities. That, and the old clan feud. Now here was the gripe, passed down to the fisherman's son. That, and the fact Rob had broken Lachlan Gunn's cousin's nose in some drunken brawl in Aberdeen. And the fact that their wild and wayward only child, Beth Sinclair, went, as his dad put it, 'completely off the rails.'

Blood is blood. Rob crumpled the note that invited the woman to come and have a cup of tea, and tossed it into the snow. 'Grumpy old bugger.' Rob rolled a cigarette. He smoked fast, then threw the stub into the snow, after the letter, and was ready to head out when he thought he heard a noise, like a door closing. He glanced up. The sign was creaking, but the sound came from inside the closed hotel. Or he thought it did. He could hear waves wash over the skerries. 'You're hearing things, Robbie Sinclair,' he muttered, and pushed off into the snow.

Up at Heatherlee, Lachie kept the lamp glowing. When his wife called him to come to bed, he said he would sit up awhile and read the paper. He wasn't tired, he told her. He read the same page over and over, his ears alert for any sound. He put on the outside light and peered into the night where the snow was thick on the ground, but had stopped falling. He took a couple of sawn logs from his own fireside and crept round by the byre. The bastard Sinclair's footprints were there, heading right up to the caravan, but, bar these, none other. She wasn't back yet. He set the logs down by her door and hurried round by the byre and back into the warmth of the farmhouse. He returned to his lookout by the window and read the piece in the paper he had read five times now. Shetland man pleads for his wife's return. For a man who didn't care about anyone else's business, Lachie found his thoughts returning to Yulia. Could this runaway wife be her? And was she still out in the snow, and what the hell did that no-good Sinclair want with her anyway?

'Should we not phone the police?' Mary appeared in her worn, pink dressing gown, her face drawn with worry. 'Should we?'

'We're not her parents,' Lachie said, remembering Rob's parting, galling shot.

Mary's eyes welled up. 'But... she might be... she... it could be her,' the woman said, sobbing, smiling, shaking her head.

'She'd be a lot older than Yulia. Our Beth is dead and gone.'

'Don't! Don't say that. She's not dead.'

'To us...' He looked as if he might say more but stopped and nodded to his wife, patting the back of her shaking hand. 'Go back to bed, Mary, go on with you now. This is not our business.'

It was after one in the morning when Lachie heard a faint cough from outside. He crept to the kitchen door and opened it, alert as a hunted fox. The cough came again. It was her. There was no laughter. No whispered voices. No boys. He heard the sound of stamping feet then the caravan door opened. Lachie pictured her, shaking snow from her boots, perhaps brushing snow from her swanky coat. Then he heard the caravan door softly close. Sound travelled easily in the snow-thick night. Had she noticed the logs, he wondered. Did she pick them up? Lachie turned off the outside light, switched off the lamp, and padded through to his bedroom. 'Is she home safe?' his wife murmured.

'Aye,' Lachie assured her as he climbed into bed. 'Go to sleep now. Everything's fine.'

17

ROB TOO SAT up till long after midnight, several times stepping out into the snow, shining his torch along the beach. A thick blanket of the soft, silent stuff lay everywhere, except over the sea and the salted fringe of the bay. Rob went inside, stoked up his fire and drank two beers. It was a night for letter writing. Rob, never one for writing anything that wasn't on sea birds, pulled another sheet of paper towards him, because the words wanted out. He could write to his cousin Doug, over in Kinlochbervie. Or to Davie down in Wick.

Dear Doug, he began, then scored that out.

Hey Davie…

But knew this wasn't for sending. *Dear Mum… Maggie… dear Betsy, Sandy… curlew, cormorant, dear anyone…*

How she had got under his skin. How she was like a selkie, the way she swam, then vanished. How maybe she was a selkie. Her hair was long and blonde. How she could be some magic thing he had summoned with the whisky sprinkling. How she had sparked the sleepy village into life, and him too. And how, Christ, he wanted her. How he thought that longing had died in him, along with everything else, but it hadn't. Whoever she was, she was bringing him back from the dead.

He screwed the paper up and threw it into the fire where it blazed blue, then died. He didn't want to love like that. He wanted his love to burn on and on. But the writing, at least, had taken the raw edge off his need. What had she been up to anyway? And why did she run away? He dragged his chair closer to the fire. A fur coat would help, he thought, because no thought was far from her. Yulia, Lachie had called her. Not a million miles from Julie Christie after all.

Yulia what, he wondered?

For all that the night had been a failure, in terms of meeting the woman, Rob felt exhilarated with the running through the snow, daring to knock on her caravan door, shouting at Lachie, then the fright at the door of the deserted hotel.

Owls, he thought. Nesting in the eaves. Or bats. He thought of his note crumpled in the snow, hit with the thought some busybody might find it. Gladys Crowther, God help him. Then he'd be the laughingstock. Bad enough he was already the solitary man by the shore who needed to take things easy. Rob considered making his way back up to the hotel to retrieve the pathetic, scrunched-up, love note. But it was late. And cold. And finally, he was tired.

Rob woke late the following morning. Looking out the bedroom window he saw the snow, marking the tide line. For all that it was winter, the sea had her own seasons and snow made no difference. As Rob busied himself making tea, he remembered his dad's stories about seas around Finland that froze over and how boats ploughed through the ice. Seldom here. Except in 1963, his dad had told him, then the boats were frozen in the harbour. 'Now son, thon was a sight to behold. I was just a laddie.'

Later that morning, Rob took his boat out. The lettering was faded now. Not for the first time Rob thought about changing the name. Yulia? Baiting his creels it came back to him; the way Lachie had barked at him. And the desolate emptiness of that old caravan. The smell of unfamiliar wood smoke. Who burned logs in this treeless county anyway? And the sadness that sat over that farm. God, he could give her something better.

Out on the open sea his pet gull wheeled above him. Sometimes the gull vanished for days. But here it was. Rob threw a bacon rind. Then he set his creels, marking the spots with yellow buoys, the herring gull hopping up the rail, as if to inspect. Rob lifted creels set two days before. Fourteen lobsters in all he brought from the water, twenty big crabs and a handful of velvets. Worth the trip to Mackay's Hotel in Wick. 'Not bad, eh?' he said to the gull, who gave a cry then flew off.

After Rob had loaded his catch into the van he went inside and called Maggie on his land line. He had chucked his mobile into the sea in 2023, and didn't miss it. He called her, partly because the beautiful stranger had stirred an ache in him. And partly because he hadn't seen Maggie since early December. She was good for him. Like whisky was. It felt fine at the time.

'Are you free later?' he asked her.

She didn't answer right away.

'I'll be in The Camps,' he said, looking up at the kitchen clock. 'Around 4.'

'Aye, alright then, Robbie,' she said.

'Right then,' he said.

'Oh Rob,' she said, as he went to put down the phone. He brought the receiver back to his ear. 'Happy New Year.' It was a good fortnight into it, but the greeting was good until spring.

'Aye, Maggie, Happy New Year.'

On the slow drive on snow-ploughed roads down to Wick, it wasn't Maggie Rob thought of. It seldom was. Rob wasn't the only one who went to Maggie and he knew it. He knew she knew. Probably half of Wick knew. 'We'll keep it uncomplicated,' she had said. That was three years ago. And Rob had agreed, he wasn't looking for anything more.

'I keep you warm,' she told him, 'and you buy me a drink or two, and you put £40 in my purse when you leave, more if you're feeling flush. That way it's uncomplicated. Get it?'

Aye, he got it.

'We can call it our arrangement,' Maggie said. 'Or deal, if you're a card playing man.'

For once a month or so, that's how it went. Better than nothing. And he wasn't fit for more.

But now Rob wanted more than an arrangement. Wanted someone to hold in the night. To wake up and her be there, next to him. Was that too much to hope for? He drove the familiar road in the unfamiliar white landscape. The road had been ploughed and gritted. Even so, the weather brought the average speed down to fifteen miles an hour. The landmarks seemed to take forever; Freswick, Auckengill, Nybster, Keiss, Reiss, Staxigoe. It was half four and dark before Rob arrived in Wick, where the streets were deserted. Half the shops looked shut, not counting the boarded-up ones that always were.

He parked up by the tradesman's entrance then carted his boxes containing still-live lobsters and crabs into the hotel kitchen. The place, like the streets, was empty. The chef, bent over a small pan, looked up as Rob entered. 'Sorry,' the chef said, 'boss said we only take one lobster today. For his dinner. Nobody in. No bookings. He tried call you.'

Rob shrugged. Imagined his old phone ringing at the bottom of the sea.

As he spoke the chef looked into the small pan, rather than at Rob, all the usual bustle of clattering dishes and swinging doors absent. 'Can I get you hot chocolate?' the chef asked, nodding to his small steaming pan.

Rob sighed. He had over two hundred pounds worth of shellfish in his boxes. He set them down on the large steel worktable. 'Ok.' Above the polystyrene boxes orange claws bound in elastic bands squirmed. 'What a bloody waste,' he muttered.

The chef poured the steaming hot chocolate into big mugs, decorated with the hotel logo. 'Maybe,' he said as he filled the mugs, 'you free them back in the sea.' The chef pushed a mug towards Rob, then, before drinking his, filled a large pan with water. He set that on a gas ring, then came to the table. 'Cheers, to you,' he said, 'a Happy New Year!'

'Anybody in the bar?' Rob asked.

'Boss closed it. Dead. Everywhere dead. Just ghosts. They don't pay.'

Rob finished his drink then got up. He handed one bound lobster to the chef who let it drop into the pan of boiling water. The chef quickly put the lid on then held a towel over it, but that didn't muffle the squeal. 'Not good bit,' the chef said. When the squeal died away, he took the empty mugs over to the sink.

Rob carted his remaining crabs and lobsters back to the van. Betsy Manson could have one. Two even. Maybe he would take one himself, but, like the chef, Rob didn't like that bit either.

'Know what I'll do,' he spoke to the spared catch behind him as he drove north, 'I'll throw you back in the sea. Betsy Manson can eat beans on toast. It's your lucky day.'

Rob was halfway home when he remembered Maggie. 'That arrangement's over,' he told the shellfish. The headlights lit up the white, flat world. Sometimes, on a hairpin bend, his lights swept over the black open sea like a lighthouse beam.

18

MIDNIGHT, AND STILL the snow dropped, like small feathers drifting through darkness. Mairi sat huddled by the stove, feeling the weight of the promise on her. She thought about her failed mission to the shop for information. How old-fashioned the shop was, and how the shopkeeper had stiffened at the mention of this mysterious sailor man. Part of the Gunn's story of woe, he had said.

From the shopkeeper's reaction she concluded this Sinclair was real, and was somebody people didn't like to talk about. Scared to mention his name. But where was he? Who was he?

Mairi stood up and went outside. She needed to be in this magic. She sat on the snowy step by the caravan door and turned her face up. Snowflakes landed gently on her cheeks, her forehead, her nose, her chin. They trickled like tiny secret rivers down her neck. Out in the snow everything faded. The nagging voice of her mother, the ache of pretending, the memories, even this mysterious Sinclair the Sailor Man slipped away. Her breath rose and fell with the night air. She breathed deeply, filling herself with the purity of it all.

In the distance an owl hooted.

A few times, after dark, the beautiful stranger had been spotted wandering the shoreline. Once she had been seen hanging about the hotel, even though the place was closed. Something shady about that one, if you ask me, Gladys said, finger to her nose but not saying what, exactly. Gladys also admitted she couldn't be sure, being night and all, but it looked as though the lassie went into the sea. The gossips, hanging on Gladys's every word, said she was likely a winkle picker. Or pearl diver.

'Aye, a tink, now that might account for it,' said Jean.

The others thought for a moment, as if here was a thing they hadn't considered, and Jean might very well be right.

'Either that,' continued Jean, 'or she's lost something.'

'Aye, that's clear,' they agreed, 'her marbles.'

If she'd been party to their gossiping, Mairi would agree, she *had* lost something. Though lost implies you had it in the first place. Her own life was what she wanted. Wandering the shore, breathing in the clean, cold air, swimming in the sea, heaving stones back and forth, she was trying to find it.

That night Mairi walked along the beach in bare feet, letting the cold water run over her feet and ankles. She needed the brisk shock of it, the sucking sound of waves breaking then dragging back. There was one lone seabird out there, bobbing on the rippling water.

By the time Rob reached home it was dark, the moon not yet risen. He pulled on his head torch. From the back of his van he tipped a lobster into a large bucket, prized off the rubber band that bound its pincers, then picked up another and freed that too into the bucket. But the lobsters attacked each other. While they lashed claws, Rob ran over the pebble beach down to the sea. Near the water's edge he tipped the bucket onto its side. In the beam from his head torch the warring creatures scuttled off. He watched them disappear into the black water. Far out in the North Sea the oil rig, lit up like a monstrous Christmas tree, held Rob's gaze. He steadied his breathing, then turned back for more lobsters.

Will you, won't you, will you, won't you, won't you join the dance?

One of his mother's party pieces came into his head. Strange, he thought, how people's voices live on after they've gone. His mother's voice, tripping fast, like a ghost in his ear; *oh, will you, won't you, will you, won't you...*

Rob wanted a cigarette, and a drink. He wanted to stoke up the fire and sit with his feet up. He wanted to shut the door on the ghost voices. Caithness might appear empty but it was thronging with ghosts and right now Rob needed to silence them. But if he went inside and sat down, he'd likely not finish the job. And if he didn't, the remaining lobsters and crabs would be dead by morning.

He kept going, each time dropping one large lobster into his bucket, tipping it out, then watching the creature scuttle forward. He set the crabs free and they lurched like they were drunk then side-stepped to the sea.

He shoved the last lobster towards the water with the toe of his boot, struck with the notion that here he was again, giving more offerings to the selkie spirit. Whisky. Lobsters. Crabs. What else does she want?

'Move on,' he called to the scuttling foam. 'You're alive!'

As he reached for the tin bucket Rob noticed the fur, draped over a rock. His heart thudded. He heard a splash. His last lobster, he thought, hurling itself into an incoming wave. He approached the pelt. Flicking his torch beam over it he recognised the fur coat of the mystery woman. Part of him felt the dull ache of loneliness. Hardly aware what he was doing he lifted the fur, pressing the luxurious coat to him. He looked around, his beam of light lurching over the sea and beach. He couldn't see her.

Warmth seeped into him as he grasped the coat tightly.

'Hey!' he shouted into the dark. 'Hello!' panicked suddenly that she was in trouble. It was a calm enough night, but it was January for God's sake. The water was freezing. What if she had drowned while swimming? Or killed herself? Or got pinched by a confused lobster. He snapped out of his dad's old stories. This woman was no selkie, no fanciful sea-spirit. She was a woman, down on her luck, living in a damp caravan. A refugee perhaps. A displaced person. 'Hey!' he shouted again.

Had she forgotten the coat? That seemed unlikely but Rob held to the thought like he was holding to the coat, picturing her in a warm bed. And how he would take the coat up to her come first light. Lachie wouldn't lay a finger on him. He wouldn't dare. Still pressing the coat to his chest Rob called again into the night, 'Anybody out there?'

No answer. Just a shrill cry from an oyster catcher along the shore. Rob burrowed his face in the thick pelt and the musky scent of it rushed into him. When he lifted his head the beam of light from his head torch lit up a wild, marvellous creature, wading out of the sea. Rob gasped. Long hair clung to her body and strands of seaweed half hid her nakedness. She cried out and shielded her eyes. She wanted to run away, he could tell, but she wanted her coat. She was in the shallows now, coming towards him, her hands trying to hide her nakedness. In the glare her eyes were black, her eyebrows too, startling against her small face that seemed ghost white. Her mouth was open, eyes, wide and startled looking, fixed on him, water beading like lace round her ankles. She reached for the coat.

'I… I found it,' he blurted. 'By that skerry.' He gestured to a sloping rock.

'It's mine,' she cried, taking a hesitant step closer.

'You must be bloody freezing,' Rob said.

'Not with that coat.' She held out one arm, the other pressed to her body. 'Give it back to me!'

But Rob didn't. He held onto the thick pelt. Rob's mind raced, like, where was her accent from, and how beautiful she was and strange. And my God, she was naked, though he tried not to look, tried to keep his eyes on her face. And she was trying to tug seaweed over her and cover her breasts with her long hair. In his distraction of thoughts, she lunged forward, pulled the coat from him then drew back, wrapping herself in it. Hurriedly she slipped her feet into wellington boots. Rob hadn't seen those. She moved away from him, along the shore.

Rob followed her. 'Sorry!' He needed to keep her there. 'I was looking after it for you. Hey, must be freezing in the sea. You must be... strong... I... was worried about you.' He laughed. 'Thought I was seeing things. Christ, thought you were a selkie. But, you're the woman who arrived at New Year, eh?'

'It is so fresh,' she said, now twisting the long rope of her hair, wringing it out, and gesturing to the dark sea. 'Makes me feel born again.' She turned up the collar of the coat.

'Cocoa?' he blurted.

She looked back at him, shielding her eyes.

'Sorry.' Rob fumbled with the head torch and shoved it into his pocket where it glowed. 'I live just there. Um... I can get a fire going. Get you something hot to drink. Heat you up. You wouldn't get me in the sea.' Words rushed out now. 'I can make you cocoa. You know, hot chocolate.' His mind leaping to his kitchen cupboard and did he have whisky to lace it with. He did, he thought he did. 'Do selkies drink cocoa?'

There was just enough moon to see her nod.

She didn't smile, or speak, but warily followed Rob up the stony beach. He kept turning round, waiting for her, wanting to help her over the stones, to say something, to let her know he might look a bit rough, but he was a good man. But the rush of speech had left him.

In the cottage she sat in the chair he offered, hugging herself in her bulk of coat. He hurried to twist old newspaper and stack a tent of sticks. In moments flames had taken. He dropped coal onto the kindling. She leant towards the fire, her hair so close Rob was afraid she would burn it. Then she'd go up in flames.

'Sit back,' he blurted. 'Please.'

She turned and stared at him, but did shift back.

'I mean…' he shrugged, 'don't want you out of the water, into the fire.' It sounded lame but she nodded then looked about. He saw the place through her eyes. What a tip. Jackets, boots, papers, cups, lying everywhere. She turned back to the fire, gazing into the flames through the steaming curtain of her hair.

'Whisky with it?' Rob held up the whisky bottle in case she might not understand. She looked at him and for the first time, smiled, briefly, but enough for him to see a gap where a tooth should be. It made her, he thought, look interesting, quirky. He took in her dark eyebrows, chiselled features, flushed cheeks and eyes tinged with fear.

'You are very kind,' she said.

No-one had called him that. Except wee Archie, and wee Archie didn't know what Rob was.

He handed her the mug of cocoa, with milk in it, and sugar and whisky. Her eyes, he saw, darted to his scar, the red slash from ear half to chin. He caught the flash of fear. 'Cheers!' he said, pulling hair over that side of his face. 'Hey, I won't hurt you,' he blurted. 'I'm a quiet-living man.'

Was he? Did this half-life, going nowhere, seeing no-one except gulls, living in a tip and drowning his sorrows in beer, amount to a quiet life? He wanted more. Saw how she clutched the mug to her. 'It was a wee car accident,' he lied, resting his hand there. 'The roads round here are mental, but I'm not.'

That rang truer. It had been three years since he'd punched anyone. He wasn't mental. Just lonely.

She cradled her hands around the mug and sipped, glancing at him over the rim. When he tried to meet her eyes she lowered them, as if she might read her fortune in the steaming liquid.

Rob brought a wooden chair through from the kitchen and set it by the fire, across from her. 'So, where is it you're from?' he asked, his voice low, encouraging. 'Not from round here then, eh?'

She stared into the cocoa, not answering.

'Um... I know the place is a mess,' he went on, 'but... I've got a spare room. I mean if you want it. Must be freezing in that caravan.'

Suddenly she rose and placed the empty mug on top of the littered piano then moved quickly towards him. Rob felt a jolt of fear. But she moved past him and was gone.

When Rob reached the back door she was nowhere to be seen. He pulled the head torch from his jacket pocket, training the beam of light up the track, but she had vanished. He thought about running after her, but hearing a spit of coal from inside went back into the living room. Retrieving the ember from the sheepskin rug Rob knelt for a while, not knowing what to do, where to go. He thought of going up to Lachie's farm, but didn't. Instead, he sunk into her chair. Already it was that, her chair. Gazing into the flames he turned her words over – you are very kind. And the tone of her voice, low and shy, hesitant as if she struggled to speak. And her face, sad and beautiful.

This was it, the something good, something new. It was because he had ended things with Maggie. And because he had freed the crabs and lobsters. And maybe, because it was time.

As he reeled into sleep, he pictured his lobsters out in the dark sea. His dreaming mind followed them, hundreds of them, fighting, scuttling. And a woman with long hair threaded with seaweed among them. *Will you, won't you…*

In his dream he swam under the sea and found her. He kissed her then held her in his arms. He nestled into the crook of her neck, then brought her up to the surface. By the rock he kissed her again. She felt warm and soft. 'Where is it?' she murmured, between his hundred kisses planted on her face, her neck, her shoulders. 'Where is my skin? My coat? Where is it?'

'Don't you worry, my love,' Rob was murmuring as he stroked her cheek. 'I am protecting it for you. Like I will protect you.'

Rob woke, moonlight streaming into his bedroom. But she had her coat. He hadn't stolen it. Though he had, for a split second, thought that, by keeping something of hers she would be bound to him. But it had been a fleeting thought. She had run off wearing her fur coat. Who was she? Where was she from? Some unease had slipped in. Rob began to wonder whether he had dreamt the whole thing. It wouldn't be the first time. And when he slid again into sleep, the sea was on fire and men were on fire and they were screaming and leaping into the boiling sea and one, with a halo of flames, was waiting for Rob to look at him, but Rob was thrashing at the blankets and shouting – 'No! No!'

19

THICK STRANDS OF kelp snaked around her legs as she swam in the winter's dusk. Slowing her. Salting her. Like something wilful it wrapped around her naked body and clung to her. She expected to be repulsed, and was, but only for a moment. It excited her. She was caught up in it, slimy ribbons, or long exploring fingers, tongues, stroking her belly, licking her breasts.

Gasping, she swallowed salt water and looked up, straight into binoculars.

It was the man again. He stood in the moonlight, his lens trained on her, on her cry and glow, her naked body still tangled in seaweed. She stared at the lenses, letting him see the kelp slithering over her skin. For the briefest moment she let herself be seen.

He was standing on a rock that jutted out to sea. He looked a strong, rough creature, wild like the ocean.

Still staring, she lifted a hand from the cold water. Then dived under, kicking to free herself from the seaweed.

And there he was, at the water's edge. He was holding her fur coat again, waiting for her. She waded from the sea, seaweed trailing from her skin and hair.

She reached for her coat, but it was his hand that reached for her. He touched her shoulder, tentatively, as if checking for the substance of flesh. He stroked her arm. And she let him touch her. She felt him tremble. He picked a strand of kelp from her hair. 'Cold,' he said, his voice little more than a hush. He placed the fur coat over her shoulders, murmuring, 'Come, selkie. You don't need to be in that cold caravan. Come with me. I'll keep you warm, I promise.'

Waves crashed on the rocks. Somewhere in the distance someone was shouting. Or was it a gull screaming? For a moment Mairi let herself lean into him. The man felt strong and good. Until the thing out for revenge was back. Mairi gasped. She pulled away. *Set me free,* the voice wailed. Mairi batted at the air. 'I... I can't,' she cried, turning from him and racing along the beach.

At the end of the beach, she stopped. The voice had stilled. She laughed. It was only wind. He had promised to keep her warm. And he was strong, and he was good.

Rob hurried back to the cottage where he downed a whisky. His heart raced. What just happened? He reached for steady things, the table, the worktop, the tap. Things to anchor him. Two, three times he went to the window. He left the door ajar, set a lamp at the window. He counted to thirty.

In the bathroom he ran a hand through his hair, splashed cold water over his face. He rubbed his chin and the image of jaws he had broken flashed into his mind. Like the Russian sailor who was drunk in Aberdeen, and others egging him on, and Johnny Murray boasting how no-one could go the length with Robbie Sinclair. It was like that then, folk pushing him on to fight, he hardly knowing why he did it. Some blind oblivion from the nightmares, perhaps. With this one he saw the drunk sailor stagger towards him, push him onto the pavement. Then saw a boot coming for his head, ducked, jumped to his feet and broke the jaw of whoever wore that boot, then beat up the drunk sailor as well.

But with the selkie he would be tender.

He would be loving.

He was pouring another whisky when the door opened.

She stood just inside the kitchen and said nothing, eyeing him from under her heavy, wet fringe. 'Come in,' Rob said, almost dropping the bottle in his hand. 'It's good to see you again...' He felt embarrassed for what he had done, touching her. But he couldn't stop smiling. She had returned. 'A drink?' He pulled back a seat at the kitchen table. 'The place is a mess, sorry, but, hey, take a seat. Make yourself at home. It's great...' He wanted to touch her again.

Wondered whether touching her at the water's edge had been another dream.

'How did you know?' she said.

'Um... know what?'

'About caravan?'

He shrugged. 'Oh, hey, small place. I heard you...'

'How?'

'In the shop, they...'

'Can I live here?' she cut over him. 'You said.'

Rob touched the sleeve of her coat. 'Um...'

'You didn't mean.' She pulled away from him and made for the door. 'A joke.'

'No! I mean, yes, you can. Sure. It wasn't a joke. Yes, great, of course you can. Please...'

She hovered at the door. Rob set the whisky bottle on the kitchen table and again beckoned for her to sit down. Slowly, she did. 'Thanks,' she mumbled. 'I am grateful.'

Rob wanted to put an arm around her, kiss her, take her up to his bed. Go on with what they had begun. He wanted to touch her everywhere. But it had been so long. With Maggie it was clear. The arrangement. But this? What was this? What even was she? 'So… a whisky?' Brushing her sleeve, a jolt shot through him. He fumbled for two glasses, rubbed them on his sleeve and set them on the table. He brought his chair up close to hers, but seeing her wary expression drew back.

'Where is room?' she asked. Eastern European again. Exotic and mysterious.

'Room?'

'For me.' She coughed and held her chest.

'Right,' said Rob. 'Yes, um, I'll clean it up. It's not fancy, but better than Lachie's old caravan.'

She wiped her eyes with her one glove. 'Thank you. But caravan was fine. They are kind.' She made the effort to smile.

'Right. Whatever you say. Hey, that glove. I've got the other one.' Rob was pouring whisky now. 'It was in the river.' But the glove was up in the outhouse and he didn't want to leave. She seemed the kind of woman who would vanish. 'I'll get it later,' he said, 'but, hey, that's a bit of coincidence, isn't it? Me, having your glove.'

'I have little things,' she said. 'It is for short time till hotel opens.'

Rob's mind raced. He recalled Mackie saying she was supposed to get a job in the hotel. Where was she from? Was she on the run? And had she suffered some kind of breakdown? She seemed anxious, and wild somehow. And that coat, something like that must cost thousands. Hundreds, anyway. She looked like she was waiting for an answer. Rob smiled at her. 'Hey, sure. Yes, you can stay here till the hotel opens.' He offered her a glass of whisky, but she got up and made for the door.

Rob followed, reached out and touched her arm, feeling the thick bulk of fur. 'I'm Rob, by the way. Um… are you alright?'

She pulled her arm away, tugged open the back door and

headed outside.

'So… when are you moving in?' he called after her. 'You can come anytime. Like tomorrow? Or tonight even.' He could hear the desperation in his voice. 'You don't need to be in that shit caravan. I'll start cleaning right now.'

The light from the back porch fell on her as she slowly turned round. 'Thank you. Tomorrow or day after then is good. Thank you.'

'You're welcome,' Rob called out to her as she hurried along the shore track. 'You're very welcome, Yulia.'

From the snow-silvered dark she called back; 'My name is not Yulia.'

20

ROB CAME TO in the dark and cold, trying to work out where he was. With his lighter he snapped the living room into a flickering glow. Groggy with whisky and sleep, he padded up to the bedroom and fell onto his bed. The mystery woman was moving in with him. A warm glow stirred his body. He moaned her name, until, spent like waves foaming on the skerries, he remembered that wasn't her name. Fuck it, whatever her name was, she was beautiful and she was coming to him.

Rob was up early, whistling an old accordion tune and filling a pail with water. He hadn't washed the floor in years. Swept, yes, but never dragged a mop back and forth over the kitchen floor. Like his mother had done every evening. Back then the stone floor had been gleaming, crumb-less, dust-less. Now it was inch-thick with grime.

Would the woman, he wondered, as he bent to push the mop under the table, notice clean floors? Would she be like his mother? Would she leave like his mother had? And would Rob, like his dad, be too shy for her, too stuck in his ways? Not enough?

That halted him. The truth of it squeezed his heart. He had been 'not enough to save the men on the burning rig.' He had been 'not enough to hold down a relationship.' He had been 'not enough for his mother.' In the end not enough for his father either. And now this; something good coming to him, something loving he had summoned by sprinkling the whisky on the sea.

For this would he be not enough?

Rob smoked, drank a black coffee and turned his music up loud in an effort to drown out all these 'not enoughs' as he tried to clean the floor. Kris Drever helped. Phyl and Ali helped. Julie Fowlis helped. But for all their musical aid the floor ended up messier than before he started. He soaked up pools of grey water with towels, picturing the mysterious woman who would soon be his, what? Lodger? Girlfriend? Lover? Wife? Rob looked about the place. What a dump. If there had been space on any surface, he could have written a love poem in dust.

There were only a few things in the room Rob liked; the sheepskin rug that lay in front of the fire and the wonky coffee table he had made from driftwood. On the wall was one watercolour painting of a fulmar in flight he'd found in a charity shop, and next to that, his drawing of an avocet. He'd done loads but this one he was, more or less, pleased with. At least enough to pin it up. On the mantelpiece above the fire sat a carving of a sea-eagle (another charity shop find) and a photo of his dad on the *Stella*. Those were his things. Everything else was inherited and worn: out of tune piano. Guilt-inducing accordion. Teak sideboards, a brown sagging sofa and by the fire one brown, tattered, but too comfy to get rid of armchair.

Back then his mother put great store by cleanliness. Next to Godliness, she said. She seemed always to be cleaning. She cleaned for the Ryders, then came home and cleaned Seaview cottage. 'We don't want nasty germs, do we Rob,' she said.

Rob laughed. Here he was, trying to do as his mother had done, and making a right pig's ear of it.

Half an hour later Rob was pegging up the towels. Not exactly what his mother would have called a good drying day but if he hung them in front of the fire that would just add to the damp and steam up the windows. Betsy Manson spotted him.

'Fine morning,' she shouted.

The sky was grey, snow still lay on the land and it was cold. 'Aye, tis that,' Rob shouted, grinning. He should tell his neighbour. She would find out soon enough. Christ, it was rare Rob had a visitor, now here he was having someone, and not just anyone, he was having the 'mystery stranger' moving in with him, plus it was bursting in him, this need to come out with it. He sauntered over at a pace. By the time he reached her cottage she was at the gate with a freshly baked loaf in her hands.

'Good morning, Rob,' she said.

He took the bread, thanked her then blurted, 'You were right about her, about the woman, the one you saw down this way, and… um… she'll be around a lot, just for you to know.'

'Congratulations,' Betsy said, smiling widely. 'I had a feeling this one was for you, Rob. When I first spotted her wandering along the shore I thought, there's a woman for Rob. Well, I wish you every happiness.'

'Thanks.' Rob couldn't wipe the smile off his face. He waited but Betsy didn't ask – where is she from? Who are her people?

'I am happy for you,' was all she said.

She was jumping the gun, and so was he, but so what? Rob practically flew back to his house, appetite enough to devour a whole loaf. He sat in the cleanish kitchen, for once with no dirty dishes in the sink and started in on Betsy's fresh bread, aware as he slathered it with butter and bit into it that he hadn't started on the spare room. If he went in there it was to dump things he didn't know what to do with. For all the excitement Rob had for his new lodger, the task of cleaning that room seemed Ben Nevis-like.

Of course, he wanted her to sleep in his room. In his bed, that he had made from driftwood. It was one of the few things he was proud of. The spare room, on the other hand, was a room of shame. Though as a boy it had been his bedroom, with his shark posters on the wall, and his CD player, and his bird books. What bird, he wondered, would she be?

Mairi blinked awake, trying to push away the dream where her wrists had been bound with a gold ring to the bitter ghost of her mother. She sat up, her breath visible in the cold air, slipped into the fur coat which had served as an extra blanket, then set about building the fire. A few twists of newspaper, sticks, three lumps of coal, like the man had done, then she struck a match. She huddled close, staring into the flames and thinking of the man. She wasn't used to people wanting to help her, but he did. And he wanted her. That thrilled and scared her. He was older. Rough somehow. Broken. But so was she. And he had said he was good. She clung to that.

She looked about the old, cold caravan. For nearly three weeks it had been a refuge, but it was time to move on. Not south, as the old biddy had suggested. And not far from her grandparents. But into a cottage by the sea half a mile away. He was a good man.

Good men, Izzy had frequently reminded her, don't exist.

Mairi gazed out the back window to the white fields. It looked magical. She slipped her feet into the Wellington boots, wrapped the scarf round her neck, then opened the caravan door, toppling a wedge of snow. She stepped into the white world where the usual mud-rutted tracks and bits of broken tractor were gone. The world looked beautiful. A white stage, where there were no jobs to do, no parts to play.

'Hello, Yulia, you're up then.' It was Mary, up too, though still wearing her slippers. She was hovering just outside the farmhouse. 'Come inside for porridge,' she called over. 'It's so cold.'

'I'm not hungry,' Mairi lied. 'I... I will come... but later... I want to walk in snow.' She took a few steps towards the old woman who was gripping her shawl. 'I will be moving on,' Mairi blurted, looking away rather than into her grandmother's pained expression.

'But you just got here. You can't go.'

Mairi said nothing.

'I can ask him to give you more money,' Mary said, on the brink of tears. 'More coal. And I'm knitting gloves for you. You must stay. Come into the house. You can have her room. It's time.'

Mairi shook her head.

'I said he shouldn't set you carting stones and mending walls. I said, the very notion, she'll leave, just like...' her voice trailed away. Mairi took her grandmother's trembling hand and gently squeezed it. The old woman shook her head then pulled away.

'What the hell do you mean?' Lachie asked her later that afternoon, his hands on his hips as if he was ready to draw a pistol. 'Eh?'

Mairi stood framed in the doorway of the caravan, looking down at him. It was four in the afternoon, dusk already. Melting snow dripped from the broken guttering. 'I will complete the last wall tomorrow, then go,' she repeated, slower and louder this time, as if Lachie was hard of hearing. 'It is all simple.' Splat, went the snow-melt.

Lachie looked stunned. 'Go where, Yulia? Where exactly?'

She didn't answer.

'You can't just...'

'I can,' she said, now giving Lachie the staring treatment and with the advantage of two steps. Lachie seemed to shrink.

'But...' he looked down. 'But...'

'Thank you for your kindness,' she said, bookending her visit with the same phrase.

Lachie pulled an old handkerchief from his jacket pocket and wiped his brow, as if it was a balmy summer's day and not this chill late January afternoon. 'I'll need a forwarding address,' he said, 'and Mary, she's taken a fondness for you, knitting like there's no tomorrow. She's taking it bad, you announcing you're going off like this. It'll likely tip her over. We had a girl,' he blurted, but to the tackety boots on his feet, 'our only child and she went off…' Still he stared at his feet.

Here was her chance.

'Will you come and visit, at least?' Lachie asked.

Mairi shrugged. She smiled sadly.

'But you're not saying where you're going. Did you find a house? Did you?'

Secrecy had become a habit. She couldn't even remember the awkward-looking man's name. Lachie didn't approve of him, that much she guessed. She changed the subject. 'Just a few stones to be set, after your walls are strong for fifty years more.' Smiling down at him she closed the caravan door, leaving Lachie shaking his head, his arms limp by his side.

'She'll come back and visit us,' his wife said, as they took their morning cup of tea in the kitchen, while outside in the slush Mairi positioned the last few stones. Mary patted the back of her husband's hand. 'And she's done a grand job. The walls are so neat-looking now. Who would have thought a woman could do something like that, eh?'

'Tell me where you are going, dearie?' Mary asked, when it was her turn to stand outside the caravan door while Mairi tidied up. 'I haven't finished your gloves.'

'Not so far, Mary,' Mairi said, coming to the doorway with

the rug, then stepping down, away from Mary. She wore her green dress, and wellington boots.

A gust of wind blew the dust backwards and Mary coughed.

'Sorry,' Mairi said. She smiled apologetically at her grandmother. She rarely smiled. It showed the missing tooth. The one her no-good husband had punched out, according to Lachie. The violent husband she's running away from, according to Mary.

'You'll always have a place here,' Mary said, handing her a final bag of scones. Her eyes filled with tears. 'I am your friend, dearie. Don't you worry about him.' She nodded towards the farmhouse. 'You can see me whenever you want. I would like that. I could get on a bus and come to visit you.'

Mairi couldn't imagine her coping with a bus. Anyway, where Mairi was going she wouldn't need one. The prospect of keeping in touch with Mary lightened something in Mairi. 'You could sing to me,' she said.

Mary nodded. 'I will,' she said, pressing the girl's hand. 'And I can teach you a song.'

Feeling a lump in her throat Mairi went back into the caravan where she set about clearing out the stove. Mary stood by the open caravan door, peering in.

Mairi tipped the mound of grey powder into the ash bucket. Outside, as she emptied the ashes into the ash pit the women stood, side by side, watching the wind lift and billow them. 'Ashes to ashes,' Mary murmured then headed off towards the farmhouse. Mairi watched her grandmother go, her shoulders slumped, her steps hesitant.

'Mary,' Mairi called.

Mary turned, her face lit up like a child's. 'Yes, dear?'

Mairi stared at her sad, eager eyes, her worn face. She glimpsed Izzy there. Even herself. Here were her people, faces

scored with disappointment. 'Thank you. I *will* visit. I would…'
Mairi broke off, aware her voice was breaking. Aware too that
part of her reason for leaving Heatherlee was this pain of being
so close to family yet sworn to secrecy. She blinked back tears
and continued. '… I would like that.' Then she hurried back
into the caravan and closed the door, murmuring the word she
longed to speak out: 'Grandmother.'

Mairi had little to pack except her other dress, a bag of fruit
scones, underwear, t-shirts, her scrapbook, lap blanket, scarf
and a toothbrush. Shame she hadn't kept the blue jumper. It had
been in the suitcase with Izzy's costumes, but good riddance to
the rest. She pictured these outfits for all the plays she would
never be in rotting in a ghostly theatre at the bottom of the sea.

Lachie said he would drive her, wherever she wanted to go.
But Mairi said no, thank you. She made the goodbye short and
they stood at the gate, watching her leave, in her fur coat and
wellington boots, carrying her plastic bag. At the end of the
track she turned and waved. Then she murmured the locked
words, a whistling wind between them. 'Bye Grandmother. Bye
Grandfather.'

She murmured her own name; Mairi Gunn. And threw out
the name Mairi Whyte.

Izzy had told her about Rob Roy MacGregor and how,
sent to hang their heads in shame for being law-breaking
MacGregors, them that wanted to rid themselves of the clan
shame chose a new name, Whyte. No history with Whyte, Izzy
said. A clean slate. Start fresh. It's the name for them that want
to cut links with the past. The old sergeant major dragged me
from Whaligoe Steps, hurled the packet I was holding into the
sea, then drove me to Glasgow, didn't say a word the whole
journey, except to un-Gunn me. He took my name, Izzy said,

her face twisted with bitterness, he wiped my identity. Then she lifted the ring on her finger and sneered. 'Except you can't do that to me. My wild spirit is up there. And that's not going to die.'

Spooking herself with memories, Mairi glanced up. The sign for the closed hotel swung, dimly lit by the orange glow of a streetlamp. The sign creaking. A voice in the wind – *I'm watching you.*

Mairi pushed away from the hotel, picturing the warm cottage down by the shore. A mug of cocoa. A flickering fire. And perhaps he would gently touch her again. He was, she repeated, a good man. A strong man. He would help banish this ghost, though as she clomped down the sloping track towards the beach she knew she was clutching at straws. She knew nothing about this man, but he was offering her a room for free, and she liked the idea of living close to the sea. And there was something about him she felt drawn to. Some quiet strength. And he was real, not a wailing voice on the wind.

She stopped to breathe in salt air. She pulled off the wellington boots Lachie had insisted she keep. The waves rolled in with a soft crash, then back with a sigh. And the wide sky was studded with stars. 'Ronester is beautiful,' Izzy had said, stretching her arms in that cramped kitchen to describe the endless sky. 'You should see them fucking stars.'

Then Izzy had laughed, saying she could die happy knowing her ashes would be scattered over the sea on an incoming tide. 'Banished no more,' she said, making a V-sign in the direction of north. 'Ghosts thrive up there, you know.' Mairi had laughed, then stopped when she saw Izzy wasn't.

Gazing at the stars, Mairi tried to picture a beautiful Scottish mother not ravaged by drugs, drink, bitterness and finally cancer. Elizabeth Gunn. Bethie. A mother not grown sour with a thirst for revenge. Not embittered with banishment. Not cut with a broken heart. A mother whose ashes had been scattered on the outgoing tide. Only a half mistake, Mairi realised. The other half was a desire to send her on her way.

Mairi carried on barefoot down the track that led to the fisherman's cottage.

21

'I TOOK A wee wander up to Lachie's farm,' Mr Mackie told Mina as he fetched her Caramel Wafers. There was nobody else in the shop, so they had no need to whisper. 'I hadn't been out in days. Seeing as how there was a bit thaw, well, I thought I'd take a wee dander. Check his walls.'

'They're looking good as new,' Mina said, for she too had taken a wee dander up in that direction. 'Takes some skill to mend a wall, mind. I heard Lachie showed her how. Wonders will never cease.'

'She could be a Romanian shot-putter. You know, one of these ones on steroids?'

Mina frowned as she considered this. 'You might be right, Mackie. Maybe she's defected.'

Mr Mackie wasn't sure whether people still did that but told Mina he would find out. He wasn't even sure defected was the right word. Didn't that mean not the full shilling? Mina cackled and said anyone mending walls in the snow was doubtless that too.

'Anyway,' said Mina, dropping her wafers into her coat pocket, 'she's cleared out and mark my words, next thing we'll have the whole family up here, cousins and all, taking our jobs.'

In came Gladys for her pack of twenty, catching the tail end of their gossip. 'Let's just say,' Gladys said, knowingly, 'I brought her into the picture. And she's taken my advice and gone back south.'

Mackie and Mina waited, all ears. 'What picture?' Mackie asked, when Gladys wasn't forthcoming.

'I let her know how the Gunns have suffered, how any change could tip them over and how she wasn't doing them any favours. I'm surprised you sent her there in the first place.'

Mackie looked chastised. 'Aye, maybe you're right. I wasn't thinking. But I told her not to get caught up in their sorrow.'

The two women stared at him.

Mackie nodded. 'Aye, she was here wanting another can of Coke. She didn't even wait for her change. Old Mary's been storytelling. I told the lass to ignore it.'

'Did you? Well,' went on Gladys, 'I let her know our poor Rob is back here to take things easy. And swanning past his place looking like some nymph of the sea is not what he needs. Anyway, she's cleared off now.'

Her audience looked disappointed.

'Gone where? That's what I'd like to know,' Mackie said, and Mina admitted she'd sorely like to know too, but didn't. Not yet.

They'd work it out soon enough.

Mairi had arrived at Rob's door at eight o'clock, her long hair dripping wet.

Rob had the fire on and had made a pan of leek and tattie soup. He had actually found his mother's old tablecloth and laid it over the wooden table that he had brought through from the kitchen, thinking it looked cosier in the living room, close to the fire. He had candles for electricity cuts, and one now flickered, cheering up the middle of the table and dripping wax into a chipped saucer. Around the candle he had set two bowls, two spoons, and a slate with Betsy's quiche, local cheddar and oatcakes.

The back door creaked open and there she was, in the kitchen, in bare feet, looking smaller and younger than he remembered. She clutched a plastic bag. A pair of green wellies stuck out the top. 'I came, like I said.' Rob could smell the sea off her and couldn't stop the smile on his face. 'I am here,' she went on, 'but I ask you, please, ask me no questions. That's part of deal.'

Rob couldn't recall any deal but didn't care. She could have asked him to dance the highland fling and he would have sprung about the room. 'You're here.' Rob moved towards her. He wanted to carry her up to the bedroom, their bedroom, where he had made the bed and lit another candle. But she stood in front of him looking wary, her arms folded. Up this close she smelt of seaweed.

'Didn't know it was raining,' he said.

'It's not.' She circled around him. 'It is fine night.'

'Ah, right. Swimming again, eh?' He'd better get used to that. Maybe he would learn to swim. Maybe now he'd do all kinds of things he'd never done. Buy a wetsuit, why not? 'I can get you a pair of socks. If you want. These stone floors are cold.' Rob was reluctant to leave her, but she nodded so he bolted upstairs, rummaged in a drawer and was back in seconds, breathless, offering her thick woollen socks. She took them and moved away. Rob gestured to the armchair by the fire.

'You'll be hungry,' he said. The smile pulling at his face had a will of its own. He hadn't felt this good in years. The mysterious selkie was in his cottage, sitting in his armchair, pulling on his socks. He gestured for her to come to the table, noticing she still clutched her bag, and wore her coat, like she wasn't staying.

She sat on the chair Rob had pulled out for her. She cradled the bulky plastic bag in her lap where it bumped against the table.

'I can take that from you,' Rob said, nodding to the bag. 'And your coat. Put them somewhere, so you can eat. Be more comfortable.'

Mairi tightened her grip of the bag and shook her head.

'You're fine,' he said, reassuring.

'He's fine,' she thought, her heart thudding, drumming in her ears. He had brushed up, she could tell. Clean white t-shirt, light blue jeans. Maybe he wasn't fifty. He was strong, fit, she could see that. She coughed as if she might say something, then drifted into silence. After some minutes she set the bag between her feet and rubbed her hands together.

'Please, stop,' she said.

'What?'

'Staring.'

'Sorry.'

One of Betsy's courgette and feta quiches sat on a slate beside the pan of soup. Rob saw how his fingers trembled as he cut a slice. 'I'm not used to having guests,' he blurted, almost cutting himself. 'Certainly not…' he laughed nervously, 'beautiful ones. Sorry.'

She stared at the food on the table, sometimes glancing down at her bag. Like a polite, uncomfortable child, she spoke when spoken to, in one-, two-word answers, her voice stilted. She agreed that, yes, the quiche was tasty, and that the soup could do with more salt. She liked salt, she told him. After Rob offered her an oatcake he struggled to open the vacuum pack of cheese. She sat, oddly silent and still, in her fur coat. Occasionally she smiled shyly at him, but the missing tooth had put a damper on smiling. So had life. Rob took the pack of cheese over to the cutlery drawer where he fished out a pair of scissors. 'That's better,' he said, snipping the pack open.

'Can you borrow me these?'

'Borrow?' He laughed. 'Sure.' Rob was ready to give her whatever she asked for. The moon. His heart. A red, red rose. She got up from the table, where she had hardly touched the soup, and took the scissors from him. She lifted the plastic bag.

'You have bathroom?' she asked, looking about.

She sounded, Rob thought, like a spy in a James Bond film. 'Aye, sure, upstairs.' Rob pointed to the ceiling. 'You can't miss it.' He had spent at least an hour cleaning the bathroom, glad he had made the effort. 'That pink towel can be yours,' he called out. He heard her steps on the stairs, then heard the bathroom door click. He went back to the table but couldn't eat. He cut her a slice of cheddar and laid it on an oatcake. She was up there a while. He hovered at the foot of the stairs, listening. He couldn't hear anything. With a sickening jolt he wondered if she had slit her wrists. Shit, who was she anyway? Who knows what mess she was in? He rushed up the stairs and knocked on the door. 'Hey, you alright in there?'

There was no response. He was about to knock again, or kick the door in, when the door opened and she stood in front of him, her hair shorn, spikey and black, still wearing the fur coat, still holding the bag.

Rob stood staring into the bathroom. Long strands of blonde hair lay scattered across the bathroom floor. He'd guessed it was dyed. But it was still a shock.

Rob closed the bathroom door and followed her downstairs. 'Hey, well, that's a change!' Back in the living room he stared at her, then laughed nervously. 'Hey, right, I've got lager. Do you like that?'

'You have wine?'

'I'll get wine in tomorrow,' he said, apologetically. 'Whatever you want, just ask.'

'Red,' she said, hardening herself against him. Izzy's advice; that way you don't get hurt.

She laid the scissors on the table and went back to her supper, nibbling at the oatcake and cheese, sometimes glancing at him, then away. A few more wisps floated down. She ran her hand through her hair. She looked like a boy, he thought, or an elf. He would get used to it. She was still beautiful.

Crumbs fells onto the tablecloth. 'I don't usually have this,' he said, stroking the stiff, white tablecloth, suddenly embarrassed about it. She said nothing. 'Lachie called you Yulia,' he went on, then reached over and touched her thick fur sleeve. 'What will I call you?'

She didn't answer but let him leave his hand there. Her silence unnerved him. 'So, hey, can I take your coat?' He looked flustered, his hand lifting, gesturing a question. 'You warm enough now? Are you, mystery girl?' He laughed nervously. 'Selkie.'

She looked up then, a crumb of oatcake on her lower lip. Rob could see her eye colour now, glinting in the firelight and the candle glow. Brown as earth, almost black.

'I am fine,' she said, stroking the coat. 'Yulia's is gone.' She laughed wryly, like she had just cracked a bad joke. 'Have you coffee?' The name may have gone but the accent strayed east of the Brandenburg Gate. Staring at her Rob wondered, again, if she was suffering some kind of breakdown. Or was on the run. She stared back. 'Do you?'

He got up and put on the kettle, keeping the door between kitchen and living room open, his mind racing to place her accent. Not Shetland, that was for sure. But she didn't ring true, though maybe it was him, forgetting how people are. Waiting for the kettle to boil he rolled a cigarette and offered it to her but she shook her head.

Rob stepped back to light his cigarette, drew on it then breathed out, batting smoke away. 'Sorry, um, I've got filters,' he glanced about, as if they might materialise in the air, 'somewhere.'

'So much fresh air here,' Mairi said then stifled a yawn. 'I'm bloody knackered.'

Rob was having to readjust his picture of his mystery woman, fast. 'I bet you're knackered,' he went on, 'heaving stones about for old Lachie. It's not right. Hope he paid you well.'

'I am actress,' she suddenly declared, as if responding to the way he was studying her. 'Between jobs at moment.'

That made sense. The fur coat. The aura of mystery. The sultry foreign voice. 'Wow,' was all he said. 'Should I know you? Sorry, I'm not nosy. Just wondering if... you know, like, on the telly?'

She shrugged.

'Give me a clue. A film?' He nodded to the old TV in the corner, which he had cleared of envelopes and cups. 'You been in anything I would know?'

'I said, I am now between jobs.' She laughed again, a strained sound that threatened to spill into crying. 'Do not ask more. I was supposed get job in hotel. Bloody hotel closed. That's what actresses do, no? They get job in hotels between films. I got wrong information. So here I am, a traveller now.'

Rob nodded, like he knew all about actresses between jobs. 'Yeah, he shuts it for the winter. Like a lot of places up here. Shut from October to Easter.'

'Yeah, for me shit. So, I come all way for shut hotel.'

For me, he wanted to say. A silence fell over the room. He

thought of her in the sea. What madness was that? 'Cold, in the water,' he said, trying not to sound questioning.

'You are close to the sea,' she said.

He wasn't sure what she meant. The cottage was. Too close sometimes in storms and spring tides. 'Aye,' he said.

The kettle was boiling, its whine demanding. He brought out cups, coffee, sugar. He had told himself that afternoon, while he cleaned and changed the bed sheets, and made soup, and searched for a tablecloth, that he wouldn't pry. He didn't know much about films, or actresses, but doubted she was one. She was cagey, that was for sure. If she had some murky past she was trying to get away from that was none of his business. She wouldn't be the first coming to the end of the road, trying to shake something off.

And who was he, the pot calling the kettle black? Aye, they could both start afresh. They would be good for each other.

But out it came before he could stop himself. 'Where is it you're from again?' He came through from the kitchen and set the cups on the table. 'I just wondered,' he added when she didn't answer.

'I'm here now,' she said, looking up at him defiantly. 'That is where. Ronester. In this house. You said was fine for me.' She scraped back her chair. 'I can go.'

'No, stay. Please, it's great you're here.' He sat down and smiled at her. 'So… hey… if Yulia's gone, what do I call you?'

She clutched the cup. 'Sophia,' she said, and for the first time since arriving she sat back and smiled at him.

'Sophia, what?'

She frowned. 'Questions,' she said and put her finger to her lip.

'Ok, fine. Sophia.' The image flashed before his mind, of a woman in the sea, drinking the whisky he sprinkled there.

He blinked, trying to steady himself. Hurriedly going through his practise; table, chair, bowl of soup, candle, woman. He breathed. Normal woman. Down on her luck. That's all. Selkies don't exist. 'Fine,' he said again, and managed to right the tilting boat of his shaky reality. 'Great.'

'Good soup,' she offered and took the spoon.

He watched her for clues. How she held the spoon, slurped the soup.

'Salty enough?' A question but she didn't bat it back. Didn't answer either. 'Maybe you like to eat fish?'

She looked up at him, then laughed. 'Yes, fish is good. Maybe I eat seaweed also.'

Now he laughed. She was teasing him and he liked it, whoever she was, wherever she was from. 'Great you're here, Sophia. I mean it, and I'm not nosy like half the people in this village.'

'You said.' She sipped the soup from the spoon. Her intense look softened.

She looked up at him and he smiled back, suddenly not minding the boyish haircut, the mystery of her, if she was a selkie or not, or the mess in the bathroom. He would clean it up. It didn't matter what her name was or where she was from. Why was that such a big deal anyway, to know where someone was from? To know who her people were? Selkie women liked fishermen, he'd read that. His dad had told him that. His quiet father had probably had his own selkie, now Rob thought about it, on some rock out at sea, him serenading her with his music and sharing his flask with her. Rob smiled, picturing it. This one was here, with him, and she needed his help. Encouraged by her smile he went over to her. He'd almost forgotten about the spare room. Perhaps she had too. But as he bent towards her, she hastily put her spoon down and drew back. 'I go now to my room. I am tired.'

'Bloody knackered?'

'Yes.' She flashed him that wary look.

'Right, then,' Rob said, pulling back.

'Where is?' She bent to pick up her bag.

'Upstairs,' Rob said. 'I'll show you.' He made his way up the stairway to the small upper floor of the cottage, intensely aware of her behind him. 'Sophia what?' he asked, turning round and smiling when he reached the top of the stairs.

She paused three steps below him and frowned, looking like she might turn and go, head out into the wind and the night, clutching her little bag.

Rob shrugged. 'Hey, sorry, I...'

'No questions, please,' she said, peering up at him. 'I need space, is all.'

'Sure, sure.' He vowed to give her all the space she needed. His dad had said the same of him when he came back from Aberdeen like a broken man. He just needs space, he had told the concerned villagers. My son has had a shock. Seen things no-one should see. Give him space. He'll be fine.

Rob batted the image of his dad away and blinked at the woman now standing in his bedroom. Her bedroom. If she guessed the room with the double bed and the candle burning and binoculars by the window was his bedroom, she said nothing. He hovered by the door and she smiled shyly at him. 'So, goodnight, Rob,' she said, then stepped back and closed the door, leaving Rob on the landing.

He went to the bathroom, his mind a whirr. Should he knock on the bedroom door and go in? What was he supposed to do here? She seemed to like him. Maybe a bit shy. But then again, he was out of practise. Love, he reckoned, was probably a lesson in reading signs. He could read the sea, the wind, the tide, the flight of a gull. But not women. His dad had failed to read the needs of his mother. Rob guessed he was cut from the same cloth. He turned off the tap and listened for sounds of her but could hear nothing. Maybe it was that simple. Maybe Sophia, whoever she was, was knackered. Maybe she was already in his bed, fast asleep. She'd been hauling stones out of the earth, after all.

He stood in the bathroom, until he felt cold and tired himself. He paused outside his bedroom door and softly put his hand on the door handle till he remembered the way she had looked at him. Warily. He drew his hand back and went downstairs. He fished out the old sleeping bag from the cupboard, wriggled into it, tried to make himself fit on the sofa, couldn't, but it didn't matter. He lay on the sheepskin rug in front of the fire, imagined tracing a finger over her skin. The fire crackled. He pictured her in his bed. An ache of loneliness swept over him. He yearned to go to her, but something stopped him; shyness, lack of practise, or the deliberate way she had shut the door on him.

So he counted the alphabet of seabirds; avocet, black backed gull, cormorant, dunlin, eagle, fulmar, grebe, heron, ibis...

By J he was asleep.

22

MAIRI CAME TO, wondering where she was. The caravan was her first sleep-drenched thought. Blinking, she glimpsed the end of a wooden bed frame. The light here was different. The air too. Not the caravan. London? Her throat tightened, but this was not Tooting with its cigarette smoke and stale air. She rubbed her eyes and light streamed in. She sniffed the salt tang of the sea. Wherever she was, she could breathe. And Izzy was dead. Izzy's ashes were scattered over the sea. Izzy's stolen ring was back in Heatherlee. Not in the house as instructed, but near enough.

And ghosts do not exist.

Filling her lungs with this fresh sea air, she reminded herself that she was in the fisherman's cottage, where she could hear waves lapping, wind blowing and the sound of a man, whistling. And he was a good man. He sounded happy, carefree. She couldn't remember his name. She knew nothing about him, but she was lying naked in his bed. She slipped out of the stranger's bed and into the fur coat. Seeing the wide ocean out the small window she gasped. The sun was a red glow on the horizon. She wanted to run into the sea and merge with it. She ran her hands through her hair, wondering where it went. Then remembered.

Opening the fur coat, she looked down at her body, so white, round and somehow, so alien. She placed a hand on her chest and pictured the fisherman. His hand on her skin. Then hugged the coat to her and opened the bedroom door a crack. Seeing the coast clear she padded across the small landing to the bathroom. The whistling was coming from in there. Mairi was about to retreat back to the bedroom when the bathroom door opened and the man stood in front of her, his hair wet. He smiled at her and she smiled back, still hugging the coat about her. On the floor behind him she saw strands of blonde hair.

'Hey,' he said, 'did you sleep OK?'

She nodded but couldn't meet his gaze. 'Yes, I did,' she said, trying to gather up her lost accent. Even her name. What did she tell him?

As if reading her desperate thoughts, he came to her aid. 'You want some coffee, Sophia?'

That's it. She was back, collecting her lines, her Loren cool. 'You have it real?'

The man grinned. 'I'm real,' he said. She slid past him, needing to pee. She closed the door on him and his realness, his salt-blue, hungry eyes. She leant back against the door, seeing no lock. She snatched in deep breaths, only now realising her rashness, madness, or plain eagerness to belong in Ronester, with someone. Anyone. She knew nothing about this man. Couldn't even remember his name. He had a scar on his face. He smoked, and drank, and as far as she could see, was dirt poor. Was she out of her mind? She clung to his words, I'm a good man.

She stood on the hair, fanned out on the linoleum floor, and studied her tired-looking reflection in the mirror, imagining she saw Izzy's face there, like a mask over her own. 'Leave me alone,' she whispered, 'you hear me, get out of me.'

For two days she slept, only getting up to shuffle across to the bathroom. For two days Rob sat alert in the living room, or the kitchen, hovering often in the bathroom. The sea was calm. Good conditions and Rob had creels to lift. Just once he took the boat out, but with no mind for the catch. Hurriedly he hauled up the creels and turned for Ronester where he hastily packed the few lobsters in the cold store.

Rob strode along the pier, his rucksack slung over his shoulder. Archie ran after him. 'Rob, Rob, wait for me.'

Rob kept walking, quickening his pace. 'Rob, wait.' Archie was wailing now.

Rob swung round. 'It's okay, Archie. I'll see you later.' He waved, then broke into a run. Soon he was at the bridge. He didn't look back. If he had, he would have seen Archie staring down at the *Stella*.

Mostly Rob made time for Archie but not always, like when the dark mood came on him or when he was in a hurry, like now.

From the age of five Archie had been out daily at the harbour helping Rob's dad bait the creels and lift the catch. When Rob took over Archie was part of the inheritance. Rob's dad called Archie that before he died. Inheritance. Be good to wee Archie. The *Stella* means a lot to him, he had said.

Rob resumed his vigil in the kitchen, cup of tea and cigarette for company, all doors open. He cursed Lachlan Gunn for working her so hard. The poor girl was exhausted. Several times he went upstairs and knocked on the bedroom door, asking did she need anything. On the third day she answered, her voice small, like a child's. 'Red wine.'

Rob was reluctant to make even the short trip up to the shop, but she had asked for wine, so he went. 'Didn't think you were a wine man,' Mackie said.

Rob forced himself to meet his eyes. 'Folk can change.'

But when he took a glass up to her, she shook her head and

yawned. She looked small and helpless. He couldn't believe this sleeping beauty had ever said 'bloody knackered.'

'Tea then?' he asked, at her bedroom door fifteen minutes later.

No answer. Rob opened the door and looked in. She was asleep. The tea went cold as Rob stood by the door watching her. She had spread her swanky coat over the brown woollen blanket and was buried under its bulk. He could only see half of her face. The soft daylight fell on her. She looked tired. Under her eyes were shadows and, in her sleep, she made small whimpering sounds. How old *was* she? Early thirties? Perhaps even younger. Twenty-seven, -eight. It was hard to tell. Something fretful tugging at her features, dark patches under her eyes.

She stirred. Rob stood by the door, waiting for a word, some giveaway, some strain of an old selkie song. But she gave nothing away. Rob stepped back and closed the door. He took the mug of tea back down to the kitchen, poured that down the sink then sat by the fire and started on the wine. Aye, he thought, raising a glass in the direction of the village, he could be a wine man too. He could change. He could be a lover. A husband.

A real man.

He turned over in his mind the few things he knew about the woman in his bed; that she said she was an actress, she had a strange accent he couldn't place and she had wanted a job in the hotel. He knew she was strong enough to heave stones, strong enough to swim in the cold sea. She was a liar, or at any rate easy with names. Yulia. Sophia. He doubted she was any of these. She didn't seem crazy, not more than most folk. She was surely hiding something. Relief swept through him.

Because so was he.

After two glasses of wine Rob fished out the dusty old

accordion and set it on his knee. He wanted his music to drift upstairs, waft into her dreams. He wanted her to love the old tunes, through them to love him. He wanted to do something she could admire. His fingers found the keys and he pressed a C major chord. The familiar music, like the sound of warming up before a ceilidh, brought a pang for his father. The accordion was in tune, to his out of practise ear, at least. He pressed the chord again, working the buttons, fanning out the bellows. He picked out notes, relying on finger memory from lessons his dad had given him, decades back. 'Step We Gaily, On We Go,' sounded, at least, recognisable. Rob was in the music, hardly believing he was making these sounds. Music was another thing he thought had died in him, but here they were; music, love and glimmers of happiness, coming back.

He was so lost in the music he didn't hear the wind tug the window. He played on, amazed the way his fingers found the old keys. When the window banged open he stopped playing. 'Who's that?' he shouted. When there was no answer, he set the accordion down and went outside. A slate had come loose and had fallen to the ground. Rob looked up to see his lodger leaning out of the window.

'What happened?' she called down.

'The wind,' Rob said, lifting the slate and holding it up like an offering.

'So much wind here.'

'You can say that again.'

'I love wind. I can breathe.' As if to demonstrate she stretched her arms and sucked in a great lungful. Then she peered down at him in the fading afternoon winter light, rosy cheeked and beautiful, like a Juliet on her balcony. 'You play music?'

He shrugged, looking awkward. 'I'm out o' practise.' He

smiled up at her. 'I'm what you might call, out o' practise in a lot of things, like speaking tae women.'

'Play to me.'

'Aye, when I've put in a bit practise. Then I surely will.'

'No, no.' The strangeness of her seemed to have washed away with three days sleep. 'Please. I heard you. Wind heard too. Play to me.'

And he wanted to. He didn't want to be this awkward, shy man the way his father was. 'Aye, well,' he said, 'I will then, but dinna laugh.'

'Of course I won't,' she called down.

He hefted the old accordion outdoors, taking the weight of it on one knee and resting his foot on the window ledge. He gave her 'Mairi's Wedding', the wind tousling his hair. When he had got through the tune she clapped like a child.

'More,' she cried. 'You are good. I could listen forever.'

He played the same tune again. Of course she knew it. Thought it was her tune the few occasions she had heard it growing up. Then she wondered if, somehow, he knew her, and this was his way of telling her.

But how could he?

No-one in Scotland knew of the existence of this Mairi.

Just when he thought the music had bridged something between them, and he was ready to run upstairs and into her arms, she yawned, said goodnight and disappeared from view. He heard the window snap shut.

But the woman in his bed liked his music and liked him. He was sure of that. And she had called him good. She said she could listen forever. He clung to that.

23

ROB BROUGHT THE accordion back inside and sat by the fire. He was unsure what to do, wired tight picturing her in his bed. Wind whistling down the chimney, and dark now outside, he worked his way through the bottle of wine. The drunker he got the more his aching heart ran on, planning a life for Rob and Sophia. They could hide out here together, in this place time forgot. He would take her walks along the beach. She could sing her selkie heart out to the seals in the bay. She'd never feel homesick with a fisherman for a husband.

By the fifth glass of wine he was lost in the selkie myth, convinced that's what she was, and glad this was the way love had found him. He was so outside of normal life no everyday woman would want him. But this unearthly one did. She had come to him, swum to him. He, like a magician, had summoned her.

He had an urge to tell her all about him, about the oil rig and the burning men he couldn't stop seeing, and hearing, and the one he was too cowardly to look at, the one with the halo. The one he had let down. She would understand. Then she could tell her story. He'd be her counsellor; God knows he knew the talk. *Take your time, when you're ready, just tell us what happened, and how you felt, no-one is judging you...*

He bolted upright, the wine rushing to his head, stars spinning behind his eyes. He held the table to steady himself. The house was a boat in a swell, but he cast off, determined to make a lurch for the stairs. Beer didn't go to his head so fast, the way wine did. He stumbled on the first step and grasped the wooden banister, sucking in a few breaths, to steady the storm. He would slip into bed with her. Fuck it, it was his bed anyway. If she thought his bedroom was the spare room, he was going to set that notion straight. And fuck Lachlan Gunn. Who the fuck did he think he was? And fuck Jake Henderson, back in Ronester to stir it all up. It was bad enough having a fucking oil rig out his fucking window, lit up like Blackpool illuminations, now he had Jake to remind him too. Rob hauled himself up the stairs, drink coaxing him on. This was *his* bedroom, and *that* totally fucking ace bed had been made by *his* own hands, oh, and these hands would hold her and stroke her and love her. My God, he lunged up three steps at once, he would show her what these hands could do. They'd done some damage, but they could do some passion too.

But he missed the top step and fell backwards, bump, bumping, crying out, thudding then landing in a heap at the bottom, wedged against the front door. As he lay there, in a kind of twisted foetal position, he scanned his bones. He had been here before. He knew quickly whether anything was broken. His head throbbed. His shoulder felt weird. Dislocated. Like he felt dislocated. What was real? Was he? This pathetic heap of love-hungry bones? Was she? Jolted sober he shunned the mad selkie story. What an idiot. He tried to move but couldn't.

'Oh, you hurt yourself?' A small voice from the top of the stairs.

'Na,' Rob mumbled, then let out a yelp as he tried to get up. 'I tripped,' he managed to say. 'I'm okay.'

'Don't look okay,' she said, coming down the stairs and crouching next to him. She wore nothing but a skimpy t-shirt and knickers.

She took his shoulder and gently moved it away from where it was wedged between his head and the bottom stair. It was excruciating but the feel of her touching him pulled in the other direction. He could bear any pain when she was there to hold him. She squatted down, threaded her arms under his oxters and slowly helped him up. 'Can you stand?' she asked.

'I'm... dislocated,' he said, a crying laugh. Then an ouch, Fuck! At least the spinning feeling had gone. He could stand but wanted her to keep holding him. His shoulder was in agony, as if it was in spasm. She brought him back through to the living room and lowered him onto the sofa, but he kept hold of her as he slumped back, the empty wine bottle at his feet. 'Just hold me,' he murmured, 'please.' And she did, letting him wrap his one good arm about her waist. He burrowed his face into her neck and before he could stop, tears streamed down his face, onto her neck.

'You will be okay later, Rob,' she said and for maybe ten minutes they stayed like that, bundled awkwardly on the sofa, him feeling like a child. What had earlier been desire melted into a rush of neediness. 'Sorry,' he said, between gulping sobs, 'sorry.' He felt a fool but couldn't stop. It had been years since he had cried and once he started he felt he would never stop. All the things he wanted to tell her, but couldn't say anything more than sorry. Sorry.

Eventually she pulled away from him and he lifted his sleeve to his wet face. He felt wrung out. 'Sorry,' he said again, hiding his face for shame behind his shirt sleeve. She was standing now, staring at him.

'Don't be,' she said, 'you gave me your bed.'

Rob felt sorry about that too, as if he'd been found out lying. 'It's nothing,' he managed to say from behind his sodden sleeve. 'You're good for me, thanks.'

She cast her eyes about the room. From his place on the sofa, with his shoulder throbbing and a pain flaring in his forehead, Rob saw her take in Seaview Cottage. The old piano that hadn't been played in years. The stains on the coffee table. The burn marks on the rug. The overflowing ashes in the bucket. Overflowing ashtray. The bag of coal by the fireplace with the shovel sticking out the top. About the floor, the scattered mugs of soup and cups of tea he had been supplying her with. And his sleeping bag, torn and ancient looking under the table. A book next to it, *Seabirds of Scotland*. And an empty bottle of wine. This was his life. He wanted to cry again. It seemed so pathetic. But he wanted to tell her why. She turned back to him and smiled. 'You can walk, yes?'

'Aye,' said Rob, nodding and wiping the last of the tears onto his sleeve.

'Then you can walk upstairs, uh? You can manage this? Up to your bed?'

'With you?'

She smiled and nodded. 'With me to help.'

She helped him upstairs. He couldn't stop repeating his apologies. 'Tonight, we swap, okay?' she said, nudging open the bedroom door and guiding him into the bedroom. She helped lower him onto the bed, and all he could do was let himself fall, and try not to cry out when she propped a pillow behind his painful shoulder, and not to weep like a child again when she touched his arm. 'Sleep good,' she said, her coat draped over her arms, her plastic bag in her hand. 'It's very comfortable bed,' she said, smiling at him.

'Thanks,' he said. 'I made it.'

'Wow. Nice, you are clever. It is the best bed I saw. Best bed I slept in. And you made it?'

'I mean, the frame.' Rob tried to touch the frame, but

couldn't. He let out a small yelp again, then covered it with a cough. 'Ouch... yeah, it's from driftwood. An old boat washed up here. And I... you know, sanded it and made this bed. It took a while... I... when I came back... from...'

'It's good,' she said.

'Thanks.' It was one of the few things Rob was proud of. 'It's made to last.' Like us, he thought. Stay, he wanted to say, but gently she closed the door.

What strange beginning was this? She should be here in his arms. He reeled into sleep and despite his pain and the dull head after wine, he slept for hours without the nightmare to break his night.

Now it was her sitting by the fire with her knees to her chin, staring into the glowing embers. Sophia, she murmured, as if trying out the name. She picked up his bird book and flicked through it. Avocet. Fulmar. Guillemot. Oyster catcher. Shearwater. Skua. A note on the woman he would love, and how she would be an avocet. His drawings, and his scrawled notes, which birds found mates, which didn't, and how there was a love-sick Albatross, gone off course. And how maybe that was him.

She got up and drank the dregs of a cold cup of tea. '*I want to be loved by you...*' she sang, going through a little dance routine in the middle of Rob's small, sad looking living room, moving her hips and shoulders, turning the empty cup into a microphone... '*nobody else but you... just you...*' Films had been a big part of her small life. Her and Izzy, cooped in dismal flats, lost in old Hollywood movies. Izzy saying there was no film like Ronester.

Mairi draped her coat over the sheepskin rug, wriggled into the man's sleeping bag and laid herself on her fur coat, in front of the fire. She thought about him and this see-saw, changing beds, dancing about each other. He was strange, surly, but so what. She was hardly Miss Normal. If Izzy was to be believed when she was drunk, she wasn't even human!

She flicked through the book again, touched that so much in his notes was about love, finding a mate. And how he hadn't. Wrote how some birds never did. How Avocet was the beauty. She traced a finger around its elegant head, the old song still singing softly in her head... *just you... yes you...* Puffin was the clown. Black-backed the bully. How a lost Albatross was looking for love among gannets on a remote Scottish island. Eyelids drooping, she let the book drop, its pages of love-sick sea birds folding in like a fan.

It was the strange fisherman she thought of as she sunk under the waters of sleep.

And she thought of him in the morning, setting the radio on the bottom step. She turned it on and folk music drifted upstairs.

It was the music of the sea soothed her. At first light she was up and out. She draped her coat over a rock and waded into the icy cold water. Waist deep, she tipped forward and swam, gasping then swimming in long, strong strokes, pushing against the incoming tide. A seal lifted its head and watched her, then dipped under and was gone. Oyster catchers set up a racket of piping cries. She flipped round and swam back, swaying fronds of seaweed wrapped around her legs. She thought of the way it had aroused her. Now it was him she wanted.

But she needed to nurse him first. The folklore book said how seaweed had been used to treat almost every ailment. Wading back to the shore she gathered armfuls of the slippery stuff; kelp, dulse and bladderwrack, according to the book.

The patient was still asleep. In this light he looked younger, less troubled. She crept across the bare floorboards but whether it was the stench of seaweed, or the vivid presence of her, he opened his eyes. Just in time to see her press a wad of seaweed against his shoulder.

Falling down the stairs was worth it for this. 'In the bad old days,' Rob murmured, still fuzzy with sleep, 'they burned folk like you at the stake.' But she went on layering the slimy brown and green fronds across his now swollen shoulder. Emboldened by his night's sleep and the tender way she was ministering to him, he reached out with his good arm. 'A kiss?' he asked.

'One,' she said and bent over. Her lips reached his ear. Rather than kiss him, she whispered; 'You lure me into your net, fisherman.'

He tried to lift himself onto his elbows, wanting to pull her to him, but he was helpless. His shoulder, still throbbing, felt numb. So he gazed up at her, drinking her in. 'I didn't lure you.' But maybe he had. The way he and Betsy jumped the gun, imagining him married off and all he had offered her was a place to stay, one small rung up from the Gunn's damp caravan.

She did kiss him then, like a butterfly landing briefly on his cheek then lifting off. She stepped back and stared at him. He couldn't read her expression. It could have been desire. It could have been distrust. It was probably pity. 'Don't go,' he said, trying to stretch towards her but unable to, and now a weight of seaweed pressed down on him. 'Hey, I never meant to lure you. But… it's just… you're lovely. And a man gets lonely.'

There. He'd said it. He felt vulnerable, admitting something so shameful as loneliness. But it made her pause. 'I know,' she said, then coughed, breaking the moment as if it hung too heavy. 'Rob, there is no spare room,' she said. 'This is your room.'

'There's another one, downstairs. I'll clean it. I'll sort it. Honest.' He could feel tears. Again. It seemed like once that tap had been unwrenched the slightest thing brought them on. Again, she had found him out, saw how weak he was, a hoarder, a trickster, a pathetic needy child. 'Please, don't go. I… I won't hurt you, honest.'

Here he was, the man who had hurt a good few folk, promising he wouldn't. 'Please,' he cried out, trying to lift onto his elbow, 'you can trust me. I'm… not bad. Really. Not a bad man.'

She thought of how Mary had said the same of Lachie.

'I… I love you…' He slumped back with the effort, whimpering, like an injured animal.

She shut the door and hurried downstairs where she grabbed her coat and ran outside. She ran along the shoreline, skirting the waves, letting the foam curl over her feet. From her window Betsy Manson watched her.

Far out at sea the fulmars were drifting. They had seen to their nesting ledges. The lonely Albatross was still looking for love among the Gannet colony off the West Coast, and back in the bay the resident oyster catchers were pecking at limpets.

Mairi bent to pick up pebbles. His rushed, shy words repeated in her, like the waves breaking over her feet. I love you… love you…

He couldn't. He didn't know her, she who had, through the fact of being born, 'ruined her mother's life.' Who couldn't land even the lowliest of acting jobs. Barely knew who she was, or what was real, what wasn't.

The tide was out, showing skerries she hadn't seen till now. That was the word Rob had written in his bird book – for these flat, large rocks that jutted into the sea; skerries. A seal slipped into the bay from the edge of a skerry. A moment later, from the water, it turned and gazed at her. Then it lowered its head and was gone, only to reappear seconds later. Its gaze seemed warm, kind. Life would be so much simpler, she imagined, being a seal.

Or a selkie. In this thin place on the edge, she could almost believe she was.

She thought of the story in the folklore book. Those magical seals that took off their seal skins, that found their way into the marriage beds of lonely fishermen. Those creatures who were of land and sea. In-between creatures. She thought of the haunting song her grandmother had sung.

Maybe her father really was a selkie man? The notion was mad, but she couldn't shake it off. Up here anything seemed possible. London, with its cars, shops, offices and fashions, tubes, crowds, noise, pace and ambition, felt like another universe.

The man's words, even though she couldn't believe them, thrummed in her veins. She thought of that first night on the shore, how he had touched her, his warm skin on her cold skin, as if to check she was human. Or?

'Selkie,' he had murmured.

She padded upstairs, opened the bedroom door without a creak, then stood by his bed, watching him sleep. The room stunk of seaweed. A pungent, briny smell that she liked. His head to the side on the pillow. The slow rise and fall of his Adam's apple. His scar, like a sickle moon, shining out from dark stubble. The quiet ruffle of his breathing. The sight of him, unravelled like that, stirred her.

Mairi stepped closer, her leg brushing the blanket. Still he slept. She bent over, putting her lips to his forehead. He smelt of warm sleep, and sea. She pushed a strand aside and kissed his shoulder. He blinked open his eyes and stared up at her.

'Hey, selkie nurse, it's you.'

She put a finger to his lips. 'Shh.' She let her fur coat fall behind her. Wearing her long green dress, she climbed up onto the bed next to him. She curled in behind him, slid her arm over his chest, and slotted her knees behind his. A good fit, she thought. 'Just this,' she said. 'Just holding.'

'Holding is fine,' he murmured, reaching for her hand then pressing it to his chest. 'Hold me as much as you like.'

As she burrowed into him she dislodged more of the seaweed. Strands draped over her arm. She moved with his breath, and felt how he shook slightly. How his whole body trembled. 'It's alright,' she whispered.

After lying like that for the length of two tunes drifting up from the radio, the trembling stopped. Accordion tunes they were; a jig then a lament.

Pressed into him like that she felt herself unwind. Some deep need in her wanted to stay holding this man for hours, weeks, years.

Until a faint wind started up, whistling in the room, banishing the quiet. Trying to ignore it she held him tighter.

Set me free.

Izzy was back.

Mairi rolled off the bed, scooped up her discarded fur coat and crept towards the bedroom door. 'Sophia, hey...' Rob murmured, 'you are...' but she closed the door on his murmurings, not hearing what she was.

'Haunted,' she whimpered, reaching the bottom step.

'You won't spoil this, just because I'm living my life,' she muttered, to the wind moaning down the chimney, because that's where she imagined the ghost of her mother, lost in the restless wind. In the living room she started humming... *I wanna be loved by you...* partly to get Izzy out of her head. And partly because she did... she was. Loved. He had said it. *You... just you...*

While Rob slept she made her way back to Heatherlee, approaching via the cover of gorse bushes. From there she spied Lachie trudging across the field. He stopped, looked around. She drew back. For an hour or more she hid, waiting for Mary to step outside, but she never did. Nor did Mairi knock on the door and say hello. It was enough, for now, to have grandparents close by.

Spying on a life that could be hers but wasn't.

Not yet.

Later she headed back to the beach. She could belong here, in this place, with this sea, under this vast sky, with this awkward, lonely fisherman.

She could be his selkie.

Two days later, the seaweed dry on his shoulder, she went to him. She pushed aside the remaining strands of seaweed and pulled off her long green dress.

'Hold me,' she pleaded, clambering onto the bed next to him.

'Sophia, honey,' he sounded brighter, 'know what? I'll never let you go.' He rolled round to face her, pulling her to him.

'Then we starve, you and me,' she said.

'Darling.' He kissed her ear, then whispered, 'you can drop the accent.'

Though his breath in her ear stirred her, she stiffened.

'Tell me who you are?' he persisted, 'I mean... really.'

For a moment she felt the possibility of that, and the weight that would fall from her if she broke the oath.

'I am... a traveller visiting north.'

'Traveller come ashore?' Rob kissed her neck, in the dip under her ear, then ran his hand down her back. 'Pleased to meet you,' he murmured. He seemed stronger, more confident, as if the seaweed, and her ministerings, had emboldened him.

She put a finger to his lips to shush him then kissed him on the chin, felt the roughness of him. 'Fisherman,' she murmured, and kissed his warm neck.

Gently he slipped his hand from the small of her back round to her belly. Tentatively, he pressed his hand over the mound of her stomach then drew a finger slowly from her belly button to the dip between her breasts. Her nipples hardened, like they did in the cold sea. He brushed a fingertip around one nipple, then slowly traced a path down again. Her skin rising to his touch.

'Like a musician,' she murmured and stroked the tight muscle of his thighs. 'You play me.'

'Aye, I play you,' he said, his fingers achingly slow now, down to her triangle of black hair. She felt him tremble. His touch so light she wondered if he held a feather. Her ran his fingers down the inside of her leg. 'What tune?'

'I don't know.' Something fast, she wanted to say, something wild. But this slow lightness was wild. He was so close, so real, and the way he stroked her skin turned her into someone other. Someone softer and wilder. Someone free. Selkie.

They kissed then, both hungry, eager. Their mouths wet, tongues like fish, moving fast. She felt him grow hard against her.

'This tune?' he murmured, his breath coming faster now.

'Yes.'

'Is it safe?'

'Yes,' she moaned. She'd had a coil fitted two years earlier, though precious little need she'd had for it. 'Yes.'

And in moments he was inside her, and they moved together urgently, he thrusting deeper, she dissolving in this ocean of her and him, into this merging, until too soon his tide was coming in. He cried out. She felt the spasm roll through him. She felt his trembling cease. His body collapsed on her. 'Sorry,' he said, panting, smiling, rolling his weight off her, withdrawing his cock, slippery, spent. 'Sorry. I came too...'

'Shh,' she said, 'it's alright.'

'We'll get better.'

'Shh...'

He slept then. She lay by his side, the haunting voice of her mother silenced.

She listened to his breath. Sometimes gently stroking his skin. Listening to waves lapping over the stony beach and gulls crying. She thought she heard the low calling of a seal. She folded an arm across his back, felt that if he could just keep holding her she wouldn't dissolve.

It was afternoon when they woke. The patient rolled out of bed and stood up, naked and smiling. He flexed his shoulder. 'You've healed me. You are amazing. Whoever you are, wherever you're from, you are totally...' he stopped, seemed to reach for the word, the sense that no word was good enough, 'lovely.'

He lifted a strand of seaweed and draped it over his shoulder. 'It's you, Sophia. You are bloody good for me.'

Set me free...

Mairi got up and pulled on his old gansey. 'Tea?' she said, forcing brightness into her voice as she made for the door. 'And biscuits?'

'And you,' he said, grinning. The locals, grown accustomed to his sullen moods, wouldn't know this smiler.

While the kettle boiled, the ghost voice grew louder. It had followed her downstairs, swirled about the living room, now hovered like a droning insect in the kitchen. She reached for a cup but it shattered under her tight grasp. She cried out. Shards fell and a trickle of blood pooled in the palm of her hand. A sudden memory of Izzy falling against her, knocking out her tooth, spilling blood. That was what this was all about; blood.

Suddenly he was there next to her, tugging her gently to the sink, rinsing her hand, binding it with a bandage. 'It's alright, love, it's alright.'

But it wasn't.

The ghostly voice was back, *Settle the scores. We're blood, remember?*

She glanced at him, to see if he had heard it too. But he was kissing her hand, and trying to make light of it, saying he needed new cups anyway. New everything.

With the kettle shrieking, Mairi buried her face in his chest. She clung on, but the kettle was a banshee. Izzy was in that wailing. She pulled away from him and ran outside. She needed to breathe, to fling this thing from her. She lurched across the grass and down the stony beach. With her good hand she picked up stones then flung them into the sea. 'Leave me alone,' she cried. She grabbed another, and another, volleying stones into the rippling water. 'Let me breathe!' Then she sunk to her knees and sobbed.

She didn't hear the neighbour. Wasn't aware of her until the woman tapped her on the shoulder. 'I have some ginger cake for you and Rob,' she said, offering her a tissue. 'Or I will have soon. It's in the oven. I'll put it on the doorstep in half an hour. Look out for it,' she went on, cheerily, 'we don't want the greedy gulls tucking into my good ginger cake, do we?' The woman walked away, then stopped and looked back. 'Whatever it is, lassie, that is so heavy on you, it will pass.' Mairi nodded, a look of hope on her tear-stained face. 'Robert Sinclair is a good man. Don't let anyone tell you otherwise. He saw things he never should have seen, that's the trouble, but love can heal that.'

Mairi felt a punch to her chest. 'Sinclair the sailor man?' she blurted, already knowing it was him. Because her mother could move her like a pawn in her game. Already had. Easy for a ghost. *I'll be watching you… remember!*

'Some might say.' The woman smiled kindly at Mairi. 'He has a good heart, but it broke.' She saw the bandage then and came closer. 'Now, lassie, what happened?'

'A cup broke,' Mairi managed, 'He… helped me.' He. Sinclair the sailor man.

The woman nodded her approval at the bandage. 'Many the times he's helped me.'

Mairi's body started shaking. The ghost of her mother had steered her exactly where she wanted her. This man she was falling in love with was the one she was to nudge over Whaligoe Steps. *Eye for an eye.*

For a long time she stayed, stunned, on her knees, the waves breaking behind her, gulls crying above, and the crushing knowledge that she was trapped, enthralled to her mother's ache for revenge. And that this would go on, and on.

You can't exile ghosts, Izzy had said. Often.

'Stop it, please, stop it!' She had cried as a child, when her mother's ghost stories got under her skin. 'I'm frightened.'

That fear crawled over her skin now.

'Sophia,' someone called. Mairi glanced behind her. Was there someone here called Sophia?

She jolted back to the role she was caught in. And there was the handsome fisherman, standing by the outhouse, lifting an arm, waving at her, and her suddenly patting the sand and pretending she was searching for cowrie shells. 'Tea time,' he called, 'and tae go wi' it, the best ginger cake in the far north. Your luck's in.'

But she couldn't find a lucky cowrie shell. Her luck was not in. She sunk to her knees, ran her fingers frantically through the sand and glanced up at him.

He was happy. She could see that. Anyone could. It frightened her how happy he was. *But so was I,* the voice cried in the wind, *and they banished me.*

24

IZZY'S STORIES OF Ronester varied depending on whether Izzy was sober or not. Sometimes men were rotten, pot-bellied bastards there. Sometimes they were handsome as fuck. Sometimes the place was as exciting as a committee meeting in the church hall on a Tuesday morning. Other times there was no place as wild and wonderful on the face of this earth. But whether she was waxing lyrical about Ronester, or cursing it, all stories ended the same; 'The bastards banished me. One in particular. The grasser.' In time, all her venom focused on him.

When Mairi tried to move out Izzy got ill. Or iller. So she stayed. 'You're all I've got,' Izzy whinged, collapsing onto tattered armchairs, cheap, lumpy beds. Mairi felt the rooms of their existence move in closer. In her nightmares she gulped like a landed fish.

Days merged into each other, while life, that glory of immense possibilities Mairi had seen in films, shrunk till she was a seal trapped in a net.

Tooting Bec was the last flat. Smaller than the rest. Mairi slept on the sofa and was woken up when Izzy came in from her work in the bar, around 1am, usually drunk, smoking, hating the windows open. Though Mairi had tried. When Izzy was out Mairi wrestled with the windows, but they seemed to be painted shut, as if the air of Tooting was a foul thing.

'I'm dying, for fuck's sake,' Izzy said, 'fucking lung cancer just in case you've forgotten,' when Mairi mentioned trying to get a window open. 'And it's winter.'

'And I'm suffocating,' Mairi thought but would never say. 'Sorry, Mum,' she tried but Izzy glared at her.

'Izzy's the name.'

That was in her bad days, when her mood was dark, and Mairi's existence was to blame for their sorry lot. There were some good days, when she brought home sparkling white wine and let Mairi have a drink. When she put on a Dolly Parton CD and her red wig, and danced about the room. Or when she sat curled up in her chair, got out the Scottish folklore book she had never returned to a Preston library, put on her storytelling voice, her *once upon a time in Ronester* voice, and brought into that sad London flat beautiful selkies dancing in green waves. Oh, it was wild and free up there, she said, so wild the wind would near enough rape you. How seals hauled up on large, flat stones and how cliffs were lethal, loud with seabirds nesting on ledges. How spirits wandered free up there. How the far North was like nowhere else. How there was a hotel called The Aurora, how Izzy used to work there. How after work she'd hurry down to the beach. And how a man came ashore and found her. How she was wild.

'That's where we made you,' she said.

'What was he like?'

'Handsome as fuck and fucked off back to the sea soon as I told him I was up the fucking spout. Dark eyes, long black hair, strong and wild. Everything up there was wild. Like me, fuck it, I was the wildest thing there, but he didn't come back. So then I got even wilder. Then I got banished.' She laughed like it was a sick joke. 'Who the fuck gets banished, like it's the 18th century? "You're a Gunn no more." That's what the bastard said after the Sinclair bastard grassed on me. And you know what, Mairi, I loved that farm. And the sea, the cliffs, the wildness of the place. I fucking loved it. And that Sinclair bastard shot my selkie man.'

When Mairi suggested they go back, incognito, Izzy's gaze hardened. 'I'm not going where I'm not wanted.'

'But... who would know?'

'I would.'

Her mood soured after that.

Mairi gathered the good nuggets and cherished them; the soothing waves, her father's dark eyes and cheek bones, stars like diamonds, the hotel on the cliff, the wind fresh and the sea wild and blue. And the seals lying on flat, grey stones. And how her father was handsome. And how it was all so wild and beautiful. And free.

At other times her father was a waiter who worked in the hotel. Izzy couldn't remember where he was from. 'You might have been made in a hotel cupboard,' she said, dancing about the room like a tipsy Ginger Rogers, 'or the beach. Take your pick!' She laughed and spun faster. 'Choose your story.'

London winter turned into spring. Because Izzy suggested it, Mairi had dyed her hair blonde. Good actresses, she had assured her, had blonde hair. But there was little time to go to auditions. Or anywhere. Even if there had been, Mairi knew she was not a good actress, whatever her hair colour. She didn't have the natural confidence for it. Spring blossomed into summer, and Izzy, her condition too advanced for treatment, got worse. 'Anyway,' she said, coughing blood, 'I've about had it in the vale of tears.' She laughed. 'I'd rather be a ghost.'

Mairi handed her a towel to spit into.

'Aye,' her mother went on, wiping her pale lips, 'I'll go back to Ronester.' Izzy smiled that thin smile that pulls the lips and doesn't reach the eyes. 'That'll suit me. Home at last.'

Mairi felt a shudder crawl over her skin.

'The Sinclair bastard,' Izzy choked. 'He ruined everything,' she hissed, holding her chest, 'your life and mine. Don't forget that.'

How could she? It seemed Izzy's wrath grew with time, as if it was easier to hurl every accusation at this sailor man. Time didn't heal, it etched.

Asking questions was never easy, but sometimes Mairi got an answer. Izzy reeled off his sins. 'The Sinclair bastard never liked me, always wanted rid of me, as if I was some kind of disease the county was better off without. Shot my selkie lover too. There was I, waiting down by the shore for him and what washes up with the tide but a bull seal shot through the head. Sinclair did that. And Sinclair shopped me and got us banished. And he's got to pay, simple as that.'

Simple as a wee nudge off a cliff side, Izzy said.

Mairi felt sick.

Izzy hadn't meant to knock her daughter's tooth out but fell against her with a glass in her hand. The glass fell to the floor where it broke. Blood spurted out and Izzy stared, mesmerised at the bright red colour running down her daughter's chin. She reached out and touched it then stared at her smeared finger. 'So that's what my blood looks like,' she said. Gunn blood. It was Mairi who said sorry. Said it didn't matter.

London brightened up. Summer came to Tooting. Flowers came out, though precious few around Magnolia Road, despite the name.

The kitchen window was clean, because Mairi had cleaned it. The sun streamed in, illuminating the haze of smoke that hung like a permanent grey cloud in the flat. The one tree in a nearby back garden was in full leaf. Mairi leaned over the sink.

She had been working to loosen the window for weeks. This morning, with one mighty effort, she succeeded in breaking the paint seal and freeing the window. She opened it as far as it would go and the effect of fresh air rushing into the room was like… breathing summer in, and letting London, the cigarette smoke and smells of illness, the metallic whiff of pills, the acrid stench of urine, the cloying stink of bitterness… go. Mairi wasn't sure how long she stood there, leaning over the sink, her face as close to the open window as she could reach, gulping in air. She didn't hear the front door click.

'What the fuck?'

She heard that. She swung round and banged the side of her head against the tap.

'Shut the bloody window. It's freezing in here. Well seeing you're not paying the bills.' Izzy collapsed into the tattered armchair while Mairi rubbed her throbbing ear then drew the window down, leaving an inch of air space.

'I said shut it.' Izzy groaned. 'God, you'll be the death of me.'

The impact of breathing in fresh air, and summer, broke something in Mairi. Tears pricked her eyes then ran down her cheeks. Izzy had already made it clear she didn't like cry-babies, but Mairi couldn't help it. 'Please,' she whined.

'Christ, what a fuss,' Izzy snapped, lighting a cigarette. 'I'm the one dying around here. Look at me, I'm skin and bones.' She waved the cigarette around then spoke to it. 'Got me in the end, eh?' Then turned back to her daughter. 'Last thing I need is a fucking draft.'

'I need to breathe,' Mairi managed to say, between gulping sobs. She nodded to the window, to outside, to the world beyond the flat.

Mairi watched her mother through the blur of tears, witnessing some change in her face, some cruel light of an idea.

'You want to breathe, do you?'

Mairi nodded, feeling the desperation. It was never far away. My God, more than anything, she needed to breathe. Mairi gestured to the window.

'You can do a few wee jobs for your mother in a place with loads of fresh air.'

Mairi wiped her face with the sleeve of her red dress. 'What?'

'I said,' a twisted smile on her grey face, 'wee jobs.'

But it was the word 'mother' that had stunned Mairi. Having a baby at sixteen, Izzy hated the word. It aged her, she said, when Mairi was old enough to understand. Izzy's the name. Sometimes, when they had been out in a park, or on the street, Izzy had told people the little girl trotting behind her, trying to catch her up, was her annoying little sister.

'Aye,' Izzy was looking excited now, almost a fever in the way her eyes glinted. 'Do these wee jobs for your mother then you can breathe all the fresh air you like.'

Mairi wiped her eyes and nodded. 'Yes, Mum,' she said, and for once Izzy didn't wince at the word.

Izzy crushed the stub of her cigarette into the pot of a withered spider plant.

'What jobs, Mum?' Mairi asked.

A joyless smile tugged at Izzy's painted lips. 'Oh, getting even jobs, you might say.' Her strange smile grew. 'Never too late to settle scores, eh?'

Unsure what to say, Mairi nodded. Izzy was on the throne of her armchair, weaving her spell. 'Do these jobs for me and you'll be setting my spirit free. I never could rest, never could forgive the sergeant major, especially the bastard Sinclair who shopped me, and then there was that fucking Hendo nutcase that set me up and it was likely Sinclair the sailor man who shot the selkie man. Shot your father. Sinclair hated seals. Hated how they ripped into his fucking creels.' She stared at her daughter and nodded. 'You're my blood. You can get even. Then the ghost of your poor old mother will rest in peace.' She smiled a terrible smile. 'Know what I mean?'

Mairi didn't. She nodded.

'Good.' Izzy lit another cigarette. 'That's a load off my mind. I always knew I'd get back there and get even. I couldn't face going myself. I knew it would kill me.' She laughed. 'Which is kind of funny.' Then she started coughing. Mairi got up hurriedly and patted her back, feeling the bones. When Izzy had recovered from her coughing fit she slumped back, looking exhausted. 'Christ, be a shame to kick the bucket now, and you not knowing what them wee jobs are.'

So, while Mairi knelt in front of her, Izzy told her.

25

MAIRI GOT UP slowly, like someone had punched her in the gut. A fist gripped round her heart. Robert Sinclair? She felt sick. Sinclair the Sailor man? The one she was to do serious damage to because he'd sniped on her mother, bringing about her banishment? And maybe he'd shot her father if she was to believe that mad story. She swayed like she was drunk. She didn't know what was real and what wasn't. She felt like she was trapped in one of her mother's old films. Was he job number three? Struggling to breathe, she knew he was. Izzy had power, like she threatened. Here was Mairi, the blood puppet, moved exactly where Izzy wanted her. First to the grandparents, then Seaview cottage, all to carry out revenge, get back into clan and county.

Checkmate!

And there he was, waving to her. 'Betsy's baking is amazing,' he was shouting. She nodded and made her way over the pebbles, every step like wading through a swamp. She glanced down, hoping for just one cowrie shell. Then she'd give it to him, press it into his hand and pray it acted like a charm against Izzy.

But there were no cowrie shells.

Shove him down Whaligoe.

This Sinclair the sailor man was, according to Izzy, one of the chief bastards who had ruined her life. He had been out on his boat that night and spied her waiting at the foot of Whaligoe Steps, Izzy had told her, one drunken night in the small flat after her shift, her eyes slitted and her words hard with hurt. She had woken Mairi up to tell her, like it was weighing on her and needed out. How the Sinclair bastard radioed word to her dad to come and catch her red-handed. How that Sinclair cunt had always hated her, being a Gunn. As if it wasn't enough, he had killed her lover. He never liked wild Bethie Gunn. Always had it in for her.

So her dad came running. The packet of cocaine worth twenty thousand pounds, that Hendo had thrown to her at the foot of the steps from a boat, was snatched from her at the top of the steps and hurled into the sea, with such force Izzy thought her sergeant major of a dad was going to hurl her after it.

'And you were inside me,' Izzy had said, hitting her stomach, her words slurring, 'not that the sergeant major knew about that.' He dragged her into his jeep and drove her home, then, after giving her long enough to pack a suitcase, and steal a ring, he drove her to Glasgow, letting her know she should never darken their door again. Ever. She was, from that moment, a Gunn no more. 'Banished from the clan, cast out from the county,' Izzy had said, downing the last of her vodka then laughing a joyless cackle of a laugh. 'For my own good, he said! Banished? Ha! Like we're back in the dark ages. So, know what I said to him?'

Mairi shook her head, though knew because Izzy had already told her.

'I banish you!'

'He just left you on the streets in Glasgow?' Mairi had asked. 'Pregnant?'

Her mother scowled. 'He didn't know about that. He didn't know about you and he never will. He banged me up with some churchy cousin and his wife in some cold room on the outskirts of Glasgow. He paid them six months' rent, telling them he hoped I would fare better out of bad influence. Then off he went without a cheerio, his shamed face shut to me like I didn't exist. I nicked that rent, which was mine anyway, and two days later left old Bonny and took a bus to Carlisle. Me and you, girl, we were on the run.' She broke into a short tuneless rendition of Bruce Springsteen's 'Born to Run'.

A gull swept low, squawking. Mairi ducked, in case it was Izzy, out to sink her talons into her skull. Mairi looked at the man in front of the cottage, the handsome sailor man. It seemed forever that she walked up the beach towards him. She wasn't going to be a pawn for her dead mother. She didn't need to be part of this sick revenge. There was something so eager in his smile. She didn't want to hurt him.

But in the next moment the thought slammed through her that, if it wasn't for this Robert Sinclair her mother would still be in Caithness and her father would still be alive. He would have given up the sea for the land, and for the love of a woman. They would be a proper family and Mairi would be part of this place, and know exactly who she was. She wouldn't have spent her life trailing after her mother from one seedy flat to another, being her carer, listening endlessly to her stories of banishment, Hollywood her babysitter.

But in the next breath she wanted him. If there was someone out there who could keep her from dissolving into madness it was him. She wanted to slip into bed and press her aching body to his. She wanted to kiss his scarred cheek, soothe his loneliness, soothe her own.

Because she wasn't banished.

She wasn't dead. She wasn't Izzy Whyte.

And some promises are better broken.

She scooped up one last stone and hurled it into the sea. She would peel this shade off her. Live her own life.

'The cake's still warm,' Rob was calling. 'Tea or coffee?

'Real coffee,' she shouted up the beach.

'You coming now?'

'Now,' she called back. But she needed to silence the voice first. She grabbed more stones and volleyed them into the water.

In the cottage he refilled the kettle. Waiting for it to boil he lit a candle, banked up the fire and turned the radio on. He didn't have any real coffee, wasn't even sure what it was.

By the time she came in half an hour had passed. The coffee was cold, and he was slumped on the sofa, the blanket huddled about him. He had half a slice of Betsy's good cake next to him, but not the stomach to finish it. He was too churned up, with desire and confusion. What was going on? Did she not know he was waiting for her? Had something upset her? Was it breaking the cup that set her off? Or his too eager love-making? But Rob, already sucked into her web of secrecy, said nothing.

'I don't mind cold,' she said picking up the mug from the table and taking it back to the fire. Did she mean the water, coffee, or his mood?

'What happened to your tooth?'

She tapped a finger to her nose. 'Questions, questions,' she said, chidingly.

'I just wondered.'

'A fight with a wolf.' She sipped her coffee then made as if to roar, putting the gap on display.

'Same wolf you've got on your back, eh?'

She stroked the coat. 'You might say.'

'I better watch myself then, eh?' He grinned. 'Wild girl.'

'Yes, mister Sinclair, you better watch out for wild girl.' She held up her bandaged hand to shush him. 'We made pact,' her spy voice was back, 'no prying.'

Rob didn't remember any pact, or telling her his name. That felt strangely vulnerable, her knowing his name, and him not knowing hers. 'How's your hand?'

She nodded. 'Salt is good for cut.'

'This shoulder's totally healed,' he said, 'thanks, you're good for me, you know.' He wanted to pull the fur coat off her. But she slipped from his reach and seemed suddenly distant.

'Another kiss for this lonely fisherman.' He moved towards her, but she stepped back. She wasn't the same Sophia who had been up there in his bed, holding him tight.

'She make real cake,' she said, reaching for a slice of Betsy's ginger cake. 'But you make shit coffee.' She held up her mug and frowned.

'Coz, I made it ages ago. And it's cold. Now, you said.'

'No need to snap. Coffee is not real, is what I mean to say.'

'Sorry,' Rob murmured, unsure whether he was apologising for instant coffee, or his getting angry about it, the scar, or everything; the mess, his loneliness, his premature ejaculation. All the inadequacies. Here she was with her fancy fur coat, and her taste for real coffee, in Rob Sinclair's hovel by the shore. Something had changed in her. He knew that look of distrust, because some things he could read. 'In Scotland we...' his voice trailed off. We drink instant, he was going to say, or tea, but it sounded pathetic. And he wanted Scotland to be attractive to her.

'How much?' she asked.

Rob frowned. 'Um... for what? Coffee?'

'The room. How much rent?'

'It's fine. Nothing, honest. I mean, it's hardly the Ritz.' Rob tried again to approach her. 'Hey, Sophia, come on. I... I'll be good to you, honest. The bed's a grand bed, and you and me, we're right together, eh? I mean, I'll get better...'

She looked at him warily, cake in one hand, mug of coffee in the other, both held up like shields. 'I supposed to get job in hotel.'

'You said, it's alright. Shit happens, it's okay. You can stay here with me.'

'I have five pounds. Not alright.'

Rob reeled his desire in, imagining how it might feel, to be her, lost, far from home, down on her luck, vulnerable, no job, and now living in this old cottage with a lonely fisherman. Maybe she really had lost her seal skin? That's how it went in these old stories. The selkie is stuck on land because she lost her seal skin. He batted the daft notion away. Maybe he'd only imagined making love. He felt the room tip. He held the table. Breathed, one... two... 'Fine. Yeah, the room upstairs can be yours, for five pounds a month.'

She set the mug and remains of the cake down on the table. 'Five pounds? Ha – like 1970s here.'

'Yeah, you're not joking.' He smiled at her but kept his fingers curled around the table edge, kept grounding himself by listing the real things; table, fireplace, window, woman. 'And five pounds can pay for good coffee.' Sheepskin rug. Beautiful stranger. Selkie.

'And you?'

For a moment he hoped she might be inviting him up to the bedroom, but there was something in her steely gaze, her stiff body language and suspicious eyes that made it clear she wasn't. Something had changed.

'Where you sleep?'

'Whoa, what is this? Third degree? You were up there, in bed with me, weren't you?' Table, chair, drawing of an avocet.

'Weren't you?'

She looked down. 'Yes.'

The world steadied. 'So, you're acting like I'm this stranger. You only like me when I'm lying in bed ill, is that it?'

'I don't know you,' she said, moving towards the kitchen door.

'Jesus, where did this come from? It's me doesn't know you.' He went after her and held her arm. She didn't resist, just stood staring down at the stone floor. 'Listen,' he said, 'I don't even know where you're from. Traveller, you said. Like, what's that supposed to mean? You want to know me? I'll tell you. I'm from Ronester, went to Aberdeen for work, crewing supply boats for the rigs, and so it was us did rescue stuff, saw some bad stuff that I couldn't stop seeing, and now I'm back here, living quiet. Do a bit lobster fishing in my dad's old boat. That's about it. As far as life stories go, this one's pretty shit, but it could get better, Sophia...'

'I can leave. Go another place.'

'No, please, stay. Really. I'll sort the spare room out. It'll be fine.' We can get to know each other, he wanted to say, but there was a chill in her that silenced him. He let go of her arm. Was this what sex did? Bloody excited cock. 'Sorry,' he muttered.

She looked up at him. 'Ok.'

'Great,' he said. 'That you're here, I mean, it's just great.'

Mairi pictured Izzy rubbing her hands, and muttering, *aye, sailor man, just great.*

26

HE COULDN'T STOP looking at her. In certain lights; mist, candlelight, when the embers were low in the fire, she looked ethereal. She'd be stunning in a black and white photo, coming out of a room, suddenly noticing the camera too late, before she adjusted her face. Rob thought of buying a camera, just to keep her image, should she go. Because she would go. Someone like her did not stay with someone like him.

If he wasn't looking at her, he was thinking about her. On his way to the shop for milk and bread he thought of her touch, her soft skin. Two ate more than one and his usual once a week shop wasn't enough. He took his time and paused outside the Aurora Hotel. From here he could look down to his cottage. Sophia was in there, in bed. Probably still asleep. She slept a lot. When she wasn't swimming, or mooching around the shore, gathering shells or gazing out to sea.

Since that one time, she hadn't touched him, if she ever had.

Seeing Lachie's jeep pull up by the hotel, Rob drew back, then slipped round the side, dropping his cigarette and squashing the dout under his boot. He heard Lachie get out of the car, shut the door, heard the heavy tread of his boots then the rattle of the front door knob of the hotel. It was then Rob stepped into view. 'Looking for something?'

Lachie started back. 'Christ.'

'No, just Rob.'

Lachie's face darkened. 'It's none of your business.' Lachie peered through a window of the hotel.

'It might be.' Rob took a step towards Lachie.

Lachie turned and glared at him. 'Don't come the hard man with me, Sinclair.'

Rob clenched his fists and breathed deeply. Lachie hurried round the other side of the hotel and Rob followed him.

'She's not here, Lachie,' Rob said, but not in anger. More like a statement. Sophia wasn't, Beth wasn't. Nobody was.

'What do you know?' Lachie hobbled past him. 'You don't know. You don't know anything.' He sounded desperate. He tried the side door. It gave and he lurched inside, into the dark cupboard.

Rob felt a clutching round his heart. 'Lachie…'

'Leave me alone, Sinclair.' Lachie practically spat the name. 'Just get the hell out of here.'

Rob sauntered across the road, looking way more nonchalant than he felt. He carried on down the dead-end street that led to the shop, not looking back at the old man on the brink of tears. Mackie brought him a jar of coffee and two pints of milk. 'Got company?' the shopkeeper asked, and Rob, sick of the secrets gave him a curt – 'aye.'

'Aye, well,' continued Mackie, knowing exactly who the company was, despite the change in hair style, 'that damp caravan was no place for her. Where is it exactly she's from?'

But Rob acted like he hadn't heard. He gathered up his few items and turned to leave. It was as Rob was at the door that Mackie, changing tack, said, 'It's twenty-six years today.'

Rob turned to him and frowned. 'What is?'

'You probably don't remember.'

Rob stood by the door. 'Remember what?'

'The day the Gunn's lassie went missing. A freak wave off

Whaligoe, either that or she was packed off in shame, or she ran off with some waiter from the hotel. We never did get to the bottom of what happened and Lachie's not saying. Word was drugs were involved, the ruin of youth. Doubtless you know all about that, Sinclair. But that Beth, by God, she was a wild one. Who would have thought simple old Mary Gunn could birth a wild one like that.'

'Lachie's at the hotel.'

'Aye, no doubt. He makes a vigil. Every year on this date he's there. That's where his lassie worked. A few shifts till they sacked her.' Mackie came round from his counter. 'Mind the shop for me, Rob. I'll go to him. He never saw eye to eye with your father. I'll go. It's grief, or regret, it can cut a man up.' With that Mackie hurried down the narrow aisle of his shop, snatching up a box of Celebration Roses chocolates. Rob saw him hesitate, then put them back and reach for something less happy. Black Magic. Rob hung about by the counter, hoping no-one would come in. And hoping Sophia was still asleep.

He read the headlines from the newspaper rack. *A fire in the Indian restaurant in Wick. Triplets born in John O' Groats.* Rob leant on the counter and flicked through the local paper. It was there, tucked away near the back, about the missing girl. *On this date, 21st February, in 1999, Elizabeth Gunn, daughter and sole child of Lachlan and Mary, was last seen. Police were pursuing a possible involvement with a drug trafficking operation but her father, Mr Lachlan Gunn, insists she travelled south on that evening for work. Two sightings, one in Carlisle and the other in South London, were reported but leads proved unfruitful. The police have declared the case closed.*

The bell above the shop door tinkled and Mackie came back in. He was shaking his head. Rob put the paper back in the rack. He vaguely recalled Beth Gunn being missing, and had some hazy recollection now of Jake saying she had lost him and his brother a fucking fortune. Most things from that time existed in a haze.

'Poor man,' Mackie muttered, making his way to his usual post behind the counter. 'And here's me with our Cath down the road in Inverness, Sanders in Dounreay, and young Donald over on the farm at Bower. Plus we've a string of grandbairns. It's not fair is it, Rob? They've got no-one. Even the beautiful stranger left them,' he raised an eyebrow, 'for you. Gunns are not keen on Sinclairs at the best of times. This'll just stoke his fire, Rob. I'm not one for doling out advice, but you and that lassie should probably keep out his way.'

Rob turned to leave. 'I mean,' Mackie called after him, 'it's not as if I like the man. I don't. But doesn't mean I don't feel sorry for him.'

Before reaching the door Rob called back; 'Got any real coffee?'

'What's that, Rob?'

Rob knew he had said the wrong thing.

'Nescafe not good enough for you and her, eh? It's fine for everybody else. You got yourself a highflyer there, Rob, and suddenly we're not good enough.'

'It's fine,' Rob said, leaving and walking back past the hotel. Lachie's jeep had gone.

27

ROB KNEW ENOUGH about preening, strutting, puffing and all the rest of a male seabird's bold attempts to woo. So, he combed his hair. Scrubbed up. Shaved. Found a clean t-shirt and denim jacket at the back of the cupboard then sauntered down to the beach.

Sophia was there. These days she was rarely anywhere else. He pulled his shoulders back, coaching himself to look confident, strut. She was bent over a rock, tugging mussels then placing them into a small bucket. She was wearing her long green dress and, over it, Rob's gansey. The fur coat for once was off her back. The day was fine, with warmth in the early March sun. An oyster catcher piped and flew off. A good-looking bird, but he wasn't too bad himself. He wasn't past it.

'Lass,' he called and waved when she glanced up.

She stared at him, impressed, he thought, the way she took him in. 'Fine clutch you've found there,' he said, smiling now.

She dropped a mussel into the bucket, then, eyeing him, smiled back, as if noticing his good looks, the effort he had made.

'Oi, Robbie.'

Rob turned to see his cousin Doug stumbling towards him over the stones. Doug was grinning at him, and didn't seem to notice the woman, who had quickly shifted further along the shore. Rob saw how fast she could move, and how she now hunkered down by some rocks, and seemed to merge into the beach, like the eggs of an oyster catcher did. 'Sharp, Robbie man, looking sharp.' Doug whistled. 'I was passing, man, thought I'd pop in, Happy New Year and all that.'

'Bit late for that.'

'Never too late for a bit happiness, eh, Robbie?' Still grinning he slapped his cousin on the back. 'Like I said, man, I wis jist passing.'

Only Orkney-bound tourists who had taken a wrong turn passed Ronester. 'Got a bit short over the festivities.' Doug laughed. 'Wondering if you could slip me a twenty Robbie. Or thirty. Just for a couple o' weeks. Eh? Tae tide me over. You know me, always pay it back. You flush, Robbie?'

Rob watched Sophia bend to pick mussels. 'Hey, nice hairdo by ee' way, Robbie.' Doug steered him up the beach to the cottage, and he still hadn't noticed, or mentioned, the woman.

Maybe, Rob thought, glancing back, he had dreamed her. And maybe he had because she wasn't there.

'You got yourself a bird, is that it, Robbie, eh?'

'Fuck off, Doug,' Rob said, but not unkindly. He shoved two twenty-pound notes into his cousin's hand.

'Life saver, Robbie. I knew you wouldn't let us down. Hey, cuppa, Rob? Or something stronger. Tae toast the new year.' Doug laughed.

'Instant coffee,' Rob said, putting on the kettle. He glanced out the window and saw her heading back, carrying a pail of mussels. Doug was helping himself to biscuits. 'By the way, she's a lodger,' Rob said hurriedly, as the back door opened. He set three cups on the table.

'I knew it.' Doug whistled. 'One look at you, Robbie, and I knew it. Lodger eh?' He laughed and winked. 'But no for long, is that it, Robbie? Eh?'

Then she was there, standing in the kitchen, staring at Doug, and bringing in the whiff of fish. She set the bucket down by the door. 'Sophia,' Rob said, 'this is my cousin, Doug. Doug, Sophia.'

Rob waited for the usual question. For once it wouldn't be him wanting to know – where are you from? But Doug, too astounded-looking to even speak, just stared at her. In her long, green dress, shell necklace, Rob's baggy jumper, fishy smell and round, elfin looking face, she resembled some nymph of the sea. 'Hi,' was all he finally managed.

'Hello.'

Rob saw the flash of fear in her eyes. Saw how she glanced from him to Doug. 'Coffee?' Rob said, smiling at her.

Doug found his tongue. 'What are you doing slumming it wi' Robbie?' He laughed nervously and slapped his cousin on the back. 'Hey, not saying I blame you, Sophie. He's handsome. We got good genes, eh, Robbie? okay, you got better genes than me, but I'm not too bad, eh?'

'She's my lodger,' Rob said again. He eyed her over his cup. 'That right, Sophia?'

She nodded and cradled her hands around the coffee cup. Rob expected her to hurry off to her room, or back outside, but she stayed there, sipping coffee, not speaking. She and Rob looked at each other.

'Right then, Robbie, I better be heading off.' Doug looked uncomfortable, set his half-drunk coffee on the table. 'Thanks, eh. Thanks again, mate. Yea've saved my bacon.'

'No worries, Doug,' Rob said, suddenly feeling sorry for his cousin, the eternal single man who grew awkward around women. Especially beautiful ones.

Rob smiled at his cousin, a small gesture that seemed to loosen Doug's tongue, and change his mind about leaving. He grinned back. 'Maybe she's got an eye for us Highland lads, eh? Tall, dark and depressed.' He laughed at his own joke. And perhaps because Rob laughed too Doug kept going. 'Aye, that's us, eh? Charming, hard-working and...' he was fumbling for the word, his fingers tapping on the table, 'lovers of tinned custard.'

Sophia smiled. 'Very funny,' she said.

'Don't get him started,' said Rob, but enjoying his cousin, lightening the atmosphere.

Doug laughed. 'Aye, I might go on and on, like *Eastenders*. Sophie, did you hear the one about the lobster that goes into a bar and wants a pint but the barman said – out you. I'm not serving you, and the lobster's all upset and says, why, what's the problem and the barman said, you were in here last night,' Doug lifted a hand and started snapping his fingers up and down, 'giving it that! Giving it that!'

Rob laughed. Doug roared with laughter and continued snapping his fingers and repeating his punch line, 'giving it that! Giving it that!' Sophia smiled.

'I lift lobsters, and I never heard that one,' Rob said. He did the same finger snapping movement. 'Giving it that!' He laughed.

Doug looked pleased, sitting up in his chair and beaming at them both. 'Oh, I've got more Robbie. I could tell you jokes all night, then I might be moving in, then I might be...' whatever he was going to say, he stopped. 'Aye, well, you'll not be wanting me playing the wallflower. You probably want a cosy night in.'

'Doug, man, yer a'right,' Rob said.

But Doug got up anyway. 'That's me off,' he muttered, sniffing his armpit and pulling a face. He laughed again then headed for the back door, 'Tattie bye.' He waved then did a wee bow, looking like some master of ceremonies from the old music hall days.

When Doug had gone, Rob, emboldened by his cousin's brief visit, and the laughter like a fresh wind, sat opposite her.

He wanted to keep the light mood. He wracked his brains for a joke, but couldn't think of one. 'Aye, well, giving it that, eh?'

'You have family,' she said, staring at him. 'Somehow, I thought you had no family.'

'Aye, Doug's about the extent of it. Not exactly a dynasty.'

'No.' Then she smiled. 'But funny.'

Rob shrugged, wondering what had happened to his own funny. 'Aye, he's a'right is my cousin, Doug.' The question of families seemed to hang in the air between them. But Rob held his tongue. If she wanted to come clean about her family, or lack of one, she didn't need him to push and pry.

Giving up on humour, he took a different tack. 'Was it war?'

'What?'

'In your country. That happens. War, then people leave to find a better life. Scots did it. Got cleared off the land and were shipped to Canada, America. God knows where else. So it happens, shifting around. Looking for home.'

'A kind of war.' But she looked distracted and gulped the coffee.

'Yeah, and, as well as the clearances we've had a few clan battles. The Gunns fought the Sinclairs a few hundred years ago.' Doug's visit had triggered something in Rob. It was the way his cousin had shrunk, turned awkward, that touched him, and hurt him. The way women can do that to men. And all they want is love. Why is that so hard to win? He felt an anger towards her, on behalf of his cousin, and for himself. For weeks he'd been trying to get it right. Playing it the way she wanted.

She pushed the coffee cup away. 'The coffee is shit.'

'Yeah, well, traveller to the far north, that's what you get here. Shit coffee. Shit lovers. Shit weather. Sorry.'

She glanced at him, blinked and saw, or thought she saw, her mother loom behind him. She blinked again, trying to rid herself of the vision. 'Get away,' she muttered.

'Fuck it!' he snapped. 'I ask a civil question, and you, not once, not fucking once, give a civil answer.' His eyes were blazing.

She was staring into space like he wasn't there.

'I'm not a damn machine, in case you haven't noticed. I've a right to know. To know where you came from.'

Now she looked at him directly. 'A right? Really?'

Her coolness knocked some of the fight out of him. 'To know who you are,' he went on. 'Or, just something. Christ, Sophia, give a man a crumb, at least.'

She touched his arm, as if somehow he'd protect her from visions. 'I have no cousins,' she told him, grasping for anything to say.

'Aye, well I do, and he's alright is Doug. And can't get it together with women. Why is it so hard, Sophia? Why?'

She shrugged. 'You are not shit lover,' she said, then got up, lifted her bucket of mussels and went outside.

Rob followed her. He caught up with her on the grass track that led to the beach, took her arm and pulled her to him. 'So, how about I try and be a better lover?'

She didn't resist. She dropped her pail, mussels spilling onto the grass. He carried her back inside, like he was lifting his bride over the threshold. She clung to him, and when he laid her down on his bed she smiled at him.

And this time he went slow. He kissed her breasts then down, tasting the salt on her skin. Tasting the salt between her legs he kissed her there, his tongue finding her, going inside, his wet mixing with her wet. She was moaning now, pulling him to her. 'Please,' she cried, 'yes.' And he slipped inside, her fingers guiding him until her hips arched, her nails dug into his back, and she was the one crying out.

Then laughing. Kissing his scar, and his shoulder that still bore the whiff of seaweed.

'Not a shit lover at all, fisherman,' she murmured.

Then later, when he lay back and she nestled into the crook of his armpit she suddenly said, 'Take me out in your boat, fisherman.'

'Aye, aye, selkie.'

'Hop in. Good thing the rain's stopped.' Like a tourist boat collecting a passenger, he helped her in, then started the engine and headed for the open sea. Sophia was grinning at him, standing up, almost toppling over. 'You better sit down,' Rob shouted, but kindly, nodding to the bench-seat.

'Aye, aye, sailor man,' she said, saluting him.

'Sailor man at your command,' he said, saluting back.

Though the rain had stopped the wind was up, cresting waves throwing spray over the prow where Sophia was sitting, her face wedged between the rails. Rob worked the rudder, steering the *Stella* close to the coast towards Duncansby Head – keeping the cliffs and stacks in view. He wanted to show her the grandness of his county. Soon the mighty conical shaped rocks loomed into view. 'Wow,' Sophia shouted, 'like giants in the sea.' Rob felt proud of his dramatic coast and seascape, and how he could navigate it. He watched her, face to the salt sea, whooping and shrieking.

'Aye, well, you can't travel the north and just stay in Ronester,' he said, sounding upbeat.

'It is fantastic!' she shouted.

It was. Freedom, a pale sun, just the two of them. They spotted the dorsal fin of a dolphin and Sophia yelled with excitement.

'You want a cup of tea?' Rob shouted, lifting the flask he

had made. But she shook her head and turned back, to watch for whales, she said. But after some minutes she lurched up and grasped the rail. Her fur coat fell from her shoulders. 'I want to swim,' she yelled, pulling off her jumper. Rob cut the motor. If she dived in, he would have to drop the anchor. These were dangerous seas, the cape where the cold North Sea flowed into the churning Pentland Firth. He wanted to ask her to stay where she was, but he didn't want to spoil things. He'd never seen her so happy. Love making was good for her. Good for him too.

Without waiting for any anchor to plummet she pulled her dress over her head, tugged off her wellington boots, and dived in.

It wasn't the anchor plummeting now. It was Rob's mood, cursing himself for ever thinking this young, exotic, mysterious woman could love a dour, boring fisherman like him who'd never been anywhere except the flaming terror place on repeat inside his head, and Aberdeen. He watched her swim away, feeling the emptiness suck him down. Dutifully he dropped the anchor then slumped in his bench-seat by the rudder. Water slapped against the hull.

In minutes she was back, calling for him to help her up. And he jumped to it, leaning over the side of the boat, extending a hand to his selkie in the sea. He felt her slippery in his arms and held her close, smelling the salt off her as he lifted her, and kissed her. On deck she laughed, shaking off water, and her eyes shining. 'Amazing, so amazing,' she cried, smiling right into his face. 'Thank you, sailor man.' She laughed. 'Perhaps I really am selkie.'

Perhaps she really was. He found himself glancing at her toes for signs, but hurriedly she slipped her boots on. Then she shifted towards him and again kissed him on the cheek. He felt the salty tang of the sea on his skin and the cold softness of her lips.

Rob fumbled with the rudder, starting the engine, wanting her to kiss him again. But she had flounced off to her lookout spot at the prow, wrapping her fur coat around her. If she really was a selkie, surely her coat would be of seal skin. He studied it. Maybe it was? Rob shook his head, telling himself to get a grip.

As he brought the boat back to Ronester, and into the bay, he tried to shake off his dad's notions of sea-spirits. It was important for his recovery to grasp reality. To know with certainty what was what. She was a woman down on her luck. And he was helping her. Rob felt a swell lift the *Stella* and nearly crash her into Jake Henderson's boat. 'Sorry,' he called out, aware he was making a habit of apologising.

But she grinned as they made their way back to Seaview cottage, her running ahead like a child. 'We can do that again,' she sang, skipping back to walk by his side. 'Can we?'

'Aye.' He reached for her hand, and she didn't pull away. 'We can do that again. And you can kiss me again. I can come to your bed again.'

She laughed. 'It is your bed.' She kissed him on the cheek. She kissed him by the back door. They undressed each other urgently and dropped to the living room floor. This love making was quick. He pulled her to him. She opened to him, and he entered her. It was already feeling familiar. He was learning her body. She was learning his. He sniffed the nape of her neck, breathing in the salty whiff of the sea, and she pulled him in deeper, moaning and rocking, like the sheepskin rug under her was the rolling sea.

Early next morning she slipped out of bed. She stood in the rosy dawn light and studied him, one part of her longing to crawl back in and hold him tight, the other wrestling to silence the voice rustling like dry leaves.

Push him down Whaligoe, daughter!

Later, when he reached to put his arms around her as she sat in the kitchen, she kept her gaze trained on her coffee cup. The voice was back with a vengeance. *A promise is a promise...*

He mentioned another trip out in the boat, but she shook her head and said nothing. He recalled his father, after his mother had left. Women are a mystery, he would say, defeated. They're like the moon. Always changing.

28

ROB WATCHED HER. Always. Like a portrait painter, wanting to know every crease and fold, every slope of soft skin. When she went to the beach, he found some excuse to go to his outhouse, and from there watched her, collecting shells, seaglass, flotsam and jetsam the tide brought in, rubbish most of it, but sometimes she brought back an old coin, or an unusual stone, or a spar of wood for the fire, presenting her finds as if she was making a contribution to the household.

She looked like a mermaid this morning as she came into the kitchen. Her shell necklace had grown, with more periwinkles strung with twine. The shells clattered softly at her throat.

He pulled a pale blue periwinkle from his pocket, wishing it was a silver ring. 'For you, lass,' he handed it to her, 'for luck.'

She smiled sadly as she twirled the shell in her fingers. 'I hope so.'

'You're good for me, Sophia.' He leant forward to kiss her.

She stepped back. 'No, I am not.' She looked at him, her face a picture of sadness. 'You don't know me.'

'Not for want of asking. I want to know you. All of you.'

'I should go,' she said, shaking her head, 'away, while it is okay. But... I don't know where...' She brushed her sleeve to wipe her eyes. 'Oh, Rob.'

'The story my dad told me,' Rob touched her arm, heartened when she didn't pull away. 'Was how the selkie loses her seal skin because the fisherman took it. So she marries the fisherman.' The words were flowing now. He hardly knew what possessed him, but he wanted this more than anything. The kettle was whistling. He ignored it. 'Will you?'

'What?' Her eyes flashed.

'Marry me.'

'Oh, Rob.' Tears were rolling down her cheeks now. Her earlier resolve to tell Sinclair the sailor man the truth had left her. Twice she had tried but the words died on her lips. The ghost of her mother wasn't interested in talking. Deeds, that's what she hankered after. She let him wrap his arms about her.

'Please, Sophia, we can do this, you and me. Please,' he blurted the words, over the screeching kettle, 'when I first saw you, I felt alive like I haven't felt in a long time. It felt like, in a way, you had come for me. To save me. I know it sounds weird, but to me it makes sense. I was practically a dead man, and you brought me to life. Maybe I can help you. Please, Sophia…' He drew back a little to look into her face, wet with tears.

'What?'

'Marry me… why not?'

Mairi stared at him, as if considering that possibility, the two of them, starting over. More than anything she wanted that, but the voice in her head wanted revenge. Another tear splatted on the kitchen floor. 'Your dad was a good storyteller.' Then she took her pail and went outside. Rob could hardly credit it. He, like a love-sick fool, had asked her to marry him. She hadn't, he consoled himself, said no.

Or yes.

He lifted the kettle off the gas ring.

His dad would say he had summoned her at New Year with the spirit sprinkling. Maybe he had.

Rob had a distant memory of his mother, shouting at his

father when he dared mention the selkie. 'You're away with the fairies,' she had yelled, 'you're off your salty head. That's what happens when you're so much alone, you imagine things.'

So Rob tried to reign himself and his longing in. Put daft notions away, for why would a young and beautiful woman like her want to marry an old, broken man like him? Though, she wasn't that young, he consoled himself, and he wasn't that old.

After his 'marry me' speech she seemed sadder, more confused. Sometimes she brought a pailful of mussels in. Helping out, she called it and Rob laughed, but stopped when he saw her face. Thank you, he learnt to say, to whatever she brought; mussels, shells, stones, an old penny found in the sand. There was no more talk of marriage, or selkies. Sometimes, when she walked down to the beach, he bolted upstairs to his bedroom, which was now hers, occasionally theirs.

Her tide was out, her tide was in. Like those dandelion clocks kids blow. She loves me. She loves me not.

'We men are more like the sun,' he recalled his dad saying. 'More predictable. It's the women are the moon. Us fishermen come to know the moon through the tides. So,' he argued, 'by rights, us fishermen should have more luck with women than most men.' He had sighed long, Rob recalled. 'Maybe you will, son.'

From the window Rob, through his binoculars, watched her drift along the shore. He had found a green chunky sweater in the charity shop in Wick and given it to her. In it she was not as intriguing as when she drifted along the shore in her red or green dress, but still managed to look exotic. The way she bent low to examine finds on the beach, the straight way she carried her spine, the sway in her walk. Rob lowered the lenses and watched the curved shape of her.

She wasn't fat, but round, soft. Like the MacCodrums; a family Rob had read about, said to hail from the seal people, and known for their plumpness. She was standing gazing out to sea, then suddenly turned and faced the cottage.

She might sound like the spy, Rob thought, quickly stepping aside from the window, but he acted like one.

The next day, as he dressed in the bathroom, he could hear his sad selkie down in the kitchen. Was she snooping around, trying to get the measure of Rob Sinclair? All she had to do was ask. He wasn't hiding. He wasn't making a huge secret of himself, like she was.

As he pulled his thick shirt on, Rob stared at himself in the mirror. Was he real? Sophia, padding about in the kitchen, was she? Since the rig fire Rob had seen things that weren't there. Seen burning bodies as he walked down a street in Aberdeen. But they weren't there. They were one hundred and thirty miles offshore, stuck on a hideous replay from that fateful day in July 2015, but he could still see them, in shops, crossing roads, in rearing waves, at the frothy bottom of a pint of beer, in smoke, in the coal fire. He could still hear their blood curdling cries. Still see that halo of fire and the eyes he could not meet. It is triggered memory, playing cruel tricks, he was told. It will take time. Was the possibility of love with this strange woman who had waded out of the winter sea another thing his triggered memory had dreamed up?

But, since she had moved in and was sleeping under the same roof, the nightmares came less often. It was her presence; he was sure of that. Because that was part of the agony of those nightmares, that he felt so alone, like the man on fire was alone and wanted desperately in his last minute not to be.

'Talk about it, Rob,' he remembered the doctor saying.

When he felt he might get round to it the time was up. The time was always up. So, he never did, not really.

He would be that doctor and coax her to talk. But he would give her all the time she needed. Who was she, really? If he had made her up, he needed to know that. Talk sorted things. Talk, the wonder cure that the doctors had kept going on about. Talk, that his dad had been so scarce on and his mum hungry for. Talk about anything, a few well-meaning friends advised; the weather, a film you've seen, anything.

The urge to talk fuelled him as he lurched downstairs. He could ask her about sea swimming, and seabirds. He could talk about the Gunns up at Heatherlee, and about their lassie that went missing. How he'd read it in the paper. Of course, it wasn't the Gunn lassie he wanted to know about, but it might open a door. He burst into the living room, and through to the kitchen, running his fingers through his hair, pulling a strand to cover his scar. 'How are you doing today?' he blurted, heading for the kettle.

She was sitting at the table and as he burst in she looked up at him. He couldn't fathom the expression on her face. As if her eyes were seeing something he couldn't.

'What?'

'How's the wild swimming going? Bitty warmer, is it?'

She bit into a slice of bread. 'I like cold.'

He clattered about making tea. 'Like you said, you didn't know me.' She seemed intent on her bread. He carried on, steering his boat against her tide of disinterest. 'Thought you... might like to know. Um... you probably never heard of Blackrose.' He waited, for something, he wasn't sure what, but she showed no reaction. 'Oil rig – went on fire. And I was sent to try and put out the fire. I mean, not just me, obviously. And, anyway, it was, pretty horrendous. Men died. And... one...'

Now she did look up, pity softening her features. 'I'm no hero,' he blurted.

She continued to stare at him. 'How terrible, Rob.'

Rob felt his words dry up. 'Yeah… it gets to me…' he trailed off, batting away the images. 'So, how are the old Gunns doing? They're getting on, eh? What about the lassie? Bethie. Did they mention her much?'

The bread stuck in her throat. She tried to swallow. It felt like a wad of tissue in her gullet.

'Oh, come on, lass. I'm not asking about you, that was the deal, eh? No prying, so I'm asking about them. I just wondered, are they still hurting? Lachie and Mary, I mean. They must have said something.' So rarely had he spoken about Blackrose, he felt himself reeling, needing to change the subject. 'They probably want to talk about her.'

Mairi coughed out the bread. She stared at the white mash of it. 'They are hurting,' she said, willing him to go on, to say more, tell more. Now it was her desperate to break her own rule. What was Izzy like? Before she left here, was she happy? 'Bethie?' she whispered. *I loved it there,* the voice whispered in her head. *Fucking loved it.*

'The Gunns' girl,' Rob explained, now cutting a thick slice off Betsy's loaf. He took his time, looking for the jam, peering into the half empty cupboard, aware that, whatever he had said, he had her hooked. 'Yeah, small place, you know everyone. We went to the same school. She was older.' He laughed, though forcing it, 'She was hardly there. I knew her. I mean, not much, she was pretty wild and I was… shy.'

She used to hang round Seaview cottage, tapping on the window, till his dad sent her packing. Once, Rob remembered, his dad had set the dog on her. A right bad influence, his dad had said of Bethie Gunn. Rob thought of that now as he spread jam on his bread. 'It was in the paper a couple of weeks back,' he told her. 'Twenty six years ago it was, since she went missing. I mean, that's why I thought about her.'

Mairi felt a hunger growl inside her. She wanted to know everything about Izzy. The good bits. The happy mother. Rob was now at the table tucking into his jam piece. Her heart churned. She wanted to know about him too, and the cause of his nightmares. She wanted to soothe him. But first, she needed to soothe herself.

'They did not speak much,' she forced herself to say, keeping her voice steady. 'Lachie and Mary. No, not much.'

'Yeah, that's the problem round here. Folks keep the real things locked inside, and blab on about films, the price of coal, who kissed who...'

'She was very beautiful?' *I told you I was. Too bright for them, too wild.*

Rob stopped chewing and stared at her. 'Who? Bethie?' He shrugged. He felt her like a fish on his line. 'Aye. Well, what some might call. She had long blonde hair out of a bottle, and wore lipstick before anybody else did.' He found it was no effort to remember. The Aberdeen years might be a blur but Rob could remember his young life in Ronester before heading to Aberdeen. And he could remember Bethie Gunn, how she was always hanging about outside the doors of the hotel asking for a light, or snogging Jake Henderson in the pub when he was fourteen, or how she used to creep around Seaview cottage, wanting to cadge tobacco from Rob's dad and him sending her packing. If there was one person not under her spell it was Rob's dad. 'She's a little witch, that one,' he used to say. Of course, she was a Gunn, and that, as far as Rob's dad was concerned, was the real trouble.

'What was she like?' Mairi asked, still looking down,

fiddling with the half-chewed bread in her hands.

This talk, though not what he wanted, was better than silence. Rob guessed Sophia had grown fond of old Mary and felt sorry for her. 'She acted like she was grown up,' he said, 'she was always getting kids to buy fags for her, and drink, running wee errands. She thought the Gunns were better than anybody else. She was never just Bethie, aye, she was always Bethie Gunn. At Wick High School she went pretty wild. Lachie was that strict on Bethie it was no wonder. If anybody had a party Bethie was at it. Bethie liked the boys. That's what folks said. Lachie would hunt her down, drag her out. If anybody had Vodka, Bethie drank it. But, maybe she just wanted to have a good time. She just... didn't know when to stop... or who to trust... she just kept going when everybody else had stopped...'

He stopped then, thinking people had said exactly the same of him.

'A good time?' Mairi asked, trying, failing, to keep her voice calm. *I was too much for them. Too much for the north. But I loved the wind. The wild.*

Rob stared at her, then nodded. 'Aye, a good time girl. But she could be a laugh too, and loved the sea. Running into the waves for a dare, yelling her head off, or hanging over the edge of the cliffs or going down to the beach at night. Ronester was too small for somebody like her.'

He saw her in his mind's eye, saying she had nicked fifty quid, so they could all go to Aberdeen for the weekend, clubbing, drinking, partying, popping pills. Were they up for it? Jake said he was up for it, and had some pills, and Jake's big brother was up for it, and he was the only one who had a car. Rob said he was up for it so the four of them sped to Aberdeen in Donnie Henderson's Vauxhall, Bethie boasting how she had a lover who was wild about her. How they met up in the tinkler's cave. She did some shifts in the hotel, washing dishes, he remembered. The fifty quid might have come from their till.

Rob glanced up. Sophia was still there, waiting. 'It was just me and the old man then,' he said. 'I was still going to school. I was kind of shy, like my dad,' he laughed quietly, wanting her to ask about him, and his dad, but she didn't.

'What happened,' she said, her voice dry, her fingers twisting together, 'to Bethie?'

Rob shrugged. 'I don't know. She was around then she was gone. It happens up here, people shift south. I heard the old mother took it bad, her only kid going away. Old Mary took to her bed for months, poor thing, and that Lachie clammed up like a shell and never mentioned her again.'

Maybe it was talking about Bethie and remembering the way she could influence folk, but Rob felt he had gained some power over Sophia. Maybe this was how it would be now, they would talk about stuff, listen, open up. It wasn't Bethie he wanted to talk about, but them, Rob and Sophia. And his own burden of a story. But the Gunn girl seemed to interest her more than he did. He saw the way she was alert, wanting him to go on. Him teasing this new-found power, leaving gaps of silence, buttering another slice of Betsy's loaf.

'Was she pregnant?' *Handsome, black eyes like the night sea.*

'No embargo on questions now, eh?'

He saw the way she shot him a glance, confused, or angry, he couldn't tell which. He had no idea if the Gunn lassie had been pregnant. She was young. Liked the boys. Boasted about lovers. He shrugged. 'It happens. Probably she ran away. Folk do. The quiet gets too much and they jump on the first bus south.' What about you, he wanted to ask. Who are you running away from? He tried to catch her eye, but she was staring at the bread. Rob pressed on, feeling her retreat. 'Some people who are running away end up here, because they run out of road.' Is that you, he wanted to ask.

Because it's me, he wanted to say, not gossip about some wild-child Gunn lassie.

'Poor Mary,' Mairi murmured.

'Aye, poor old Mary,' Rob did what he always did, folded his own pain away. He looked across at Sophia, who seemed to be clutching the edge of the table like it was a boat-rail in a storm. He wanted to put an arm around her. But some force field around her stopped him. 'Anyway, it's not our business.' It came out snappier than he intended. 'I couldn't give a fuck about Lachlan Gunn. Thinks he's some big cheese. Thinks Gunns are some mighty clan. It's all shit. Who gives a fuck about clans? We're a' Jock Tamsin's bairns.'

'Poor Bethie,' she muttered. *Men ruined my life. Get even, lassie. Do it for your mother.*

'Who gives a fuck about her?' Rob snapped.

'Men don't understand.'

Some dam burst in him then. 'Christ, I understand some things. I'm more than a bloody Sinclair. I know that. I understand how the past can drag you down. Fuck! What does it even matter? Who your people are? Who my people are, or were?' It flashed in Rob's mind that it did matter. He couldn't rest, not knowing who she was. 'But it mattered to my dad, God, it really meant something, him being a Sinclair, and there's old Gunn struggling with that bit farm thinking the same fucking thing, thinking he's still at war, been wrong done by. Like, while all these clans were warring the big guns come strutting up from Surrey and buy up the land. There's no fucking Clan Ryder, that's for sure.'

He paused, his heart racing. He stared at Sophia. She seemed to hardly hear him, like she was still wrapped up in her poor old

Gunns and their missing daughter, who probably thumbed it to India, or Benidorm. He grabbed his pouch of tobacco from his shirt pocket and started rolling a cigarette, his hands trembling.

'Poor Beth,' Mairi said again, then slowly lifted her head and stared at Rob, her eyes cold. 'She just wanted to be free.'

Who was it alerted Lachlan Gunn? Who ruined Izzy's life? Who was it out that dark night on the boat? She pictured the fisherman young, before some haunted look had set over his face. She pictured him fuming with anger at his torn nets, and him lifting his gun with the silencer, aiming at the seal's head. She pictured him, like the other gossips in the village, alert for anything new. She pictured him seeing the young Beth Gunn on the steps at Whaligoe, the girl who was way wilder than him, who loved a handsome stranger and not a local like him. She pictured this spurned local lad telling tales into his radio – want to catch a big fish, he might have said, gloating, to the sergeant major. She pictured him, this surly man, ruining her mother's life. And her own, for Izzy was pregnant, as she was hauled up the year of steps then taken south.

But all Mairi could do was stare at him, her lips clamped shut. She wanted to cry at the top of her voice – that was my mother! And she was just a child! She loved it here. She felt free, and you betrayed her! You killed my father, and you banished me!

But she couldn't. Like the bread, the words stuck in her throat.

Rob felt her accusing look, as if all her anger wrapped itself around one despicable word; Men! 'Look at me, for God's sake,' he said. But she didn't. She kept her eyes on the stone floor of the kitchen. 'It's like you're hiding something. I'm not God's gift. I know that. I'm no hero. Not one of your old Hollywood stars, but for fuck's sake, I'm here and they're not;

Bogart, Brando, James Dean, whoever. They're all dead. They're not real.'

'Leave me alone,' she said, but she didn't snap like she sometimes did.

Rob, too wound-up to sit, stood by the kitchen door. 'What's up, Sophia. Tell me what's wrong?'

She looked at him through the blur of her tears, but said nothing.

Rob rammed his cigarette into his mouth and stomped out into the morning, and like the clansman he swore he wasn't, shook his fist and shouted into the howling wind. 'Women! Gunns and fucking Sinclairs!' He ran down to the shore, kicking up stones and yelling. The crashing waves and screeching gulls bounced his cries back so his yells became part of the big music of wind and sea.

Pibroch.

He stumbled over the stones, the gale tearing at his oilskin jacket. He couldn't take it anymore, her secrecy. Her blowing hot and cold. Her loving then rejecting him. Who the fuck was she, and whose was she? Not his. He didn't know anything about her.

He ran to the harbour and took the *Stella* out. The sea would give him solace. The gulls would follow him. His pet gull would come. You knew where you were with birds. And there were surely mackerel to catch. Out at sea he flung out lines. This was good, this swell of the sea, this force of nature under and around him. If he'd summoned any sea-spirits he called on them now. 'You hear me,' he yelled, 'make it alright.' He heard a cry and for a wild moment thought it was the sea-spirit, answering. Rob looked up to see his pet gull swoop down and land on the rail.

When Rob brought in the few fish and had given them to

Archie who begged to gut them, the raging fire in him was out. The fish were for bait. There was no need for gutting but Archie like the job. 'Take a couple for yer tea,' Rob said, then left him to it, and took a pint in the pub, for there were still embers in him.

Birds, Rob felt, finishing his second pint, were easier to fathom than humans. His pet gull cared, even if Sophia didn't. Or whatever she was called. He left the pub and made his way home. She was sitting by the fire, smiling up at him as he came in. Warily he watched her.

She loves me, she loves me not.

Right now, she seemed to like him a little. Like the love-sick fool he felt, he smiled back at her. Then it was she who put more coal on the fire and made him tea. By the side of the cup, she placed a chocolate biscuit, and on his head a gentle kiss. 'You are good and kind man,' she murmured. 'Sometimes, I am not well. I am so sorry.'

Her eyes filled up with tears.

29

SHE SEEMED TO have softened towards him, making him coffee, cutting him a slice of bread, brushing her hand against his, lingering there, skin on skin. She brought up stones and shells from the beach and arranged them on the shelf in the living room. Her shell jewellery, he noticed, was improving. She had several necklaces now strung with washed-up blue twine. 'Nice work,' he said, nodding to the one she wore around her neck. 'Maybe Mackie could sell your shell necklaces in his shop.'

She ran a finger over the shells. 'People will buy?' She seemed pleased.

'Aye, why not. Call it selkie jewellery.' He smiled. 'Then they go home with a bit o' wild magic about their throats.'

She shrugged, but he could see the brightening in her. 'Good magic?'

'Aye, good magic.'

Rob tried to fathom the change, thinking perhaps his outburst, his attempt at 'talking' had set something free. Maybe it had taken the chat about the Gunn girl to loosen her, and maybe some opening up of his own tale of woe, plus his rant on the clans to clear the air. And maybe because she had seen him in his wildness, down by the shore. Or maybe because she had admitted that, sometimes, she was not well. Whatever it was, something had shifted.

Making her an instant coffee he saw the way she winced at the taste. 'I'll get you that real stuff,' he said.

She shrugged and half smiled. 'Thanks, real coffee would be good.'

'I'll find it,' he promised. He would go to Inverness for real coffee, if he had to.

It took some hunting but finally, after delivering lobsters to the hotel in Wick, Rob found a cafetiere and a packet of real coffee. The man in the gift shop told him they were in high demand nowadays. 'It's French this and French that,' said the man, admitting he was a pot of tea man himself.

'Me too,' said Rob.

The man paused. 'Aye, cappuccinos, lattes and skinny what-nots. I can't keep up.' He resumed his slow wrapping. 'You should pick her up a crescent, to go along with the fancy coffee.'

'A what?'

The man looked embarrassed. 'A wee flaky bun thing. You'll get it in the baker's shop.'

Rob waited till he was out on the street till he burst out laughing. And God, when was the last time he did that? This woman was good for him. Even if she was forever taking off and wandering the shore like a beachcomber. She had her moments, when her sun came out from behind the clouds. And she was still in his bed, even if he wasn't always in it with her.

He went to the baker's shop and bought four croissants. Might as well go the whole hog, Rob Sinclair, he said to himself, seeing daffodils growing in the small patch of ground in front of the bank. He pulled up a few then bundled his offerings into the van and drove up the winding coastal road. The sun was up, the sea flat and shimmering.

By the back door he stopped, arrested by the booming, plonky noises coming from inside. His first thought was she was breaking things. But then he recognised the old piano.

Inside, he stood staring at her back, astounded at the jarring racket. She was crashing the keys like some eccentric musician, her hands lifting then banging down, over and over. 'Sophia,' he called. He put a hand on her shoulder and immediately she stopped. The noise echoed through the cottage, disturbing the old ghosts. The dark cloud, he could tell, was back. *Do serious damage to a bastard called Sinclair the sailor man.*

'Wow! Sounds like you were composing a storm piece. You play?'

Her fingers slumped on the keys, producing a final dissonant wail. 'Obviously not.'

'You could learn. High time somebody played it.' Rob set the wrapped box on the table, the packet of coffee next to it. Mairi turned and watched the things arrive, trying to ignore the vengeful voice that seemed to shout from the ceiling, then howl down the fireplace, searing her scalp.

'Real coffee!' he announced, gesturing to his offerings.

She took the flowers and only then did he see how her fingers were trembling. 'Hope you like it.'

She buried her face in the yellow flowers and sniffed them. Then she took up the packet of coffee and sniffed that.

'Hey, Sophia. Um... that marry me stuff, I was getting way ahead of myself.' He laughed. 'I got it the wrong way round! Like I said, I'm out of practise. So, how about a date? You know, a wee walk? You and me? Or up the pub?'

'Maybe, Rob. But you ask me no questions, please.'

'That again?'

She nodded, staring down at the daffodils. 'I don't ask you things. How you cry out in the night. I can hear, and I don't poke.'

'I wish you would. Because I would tell you. I'm not hiding stuff.' Maggie flashed into his mind. Aye, well, maybe he was.

'But I am.'

'Well, just give me a clue. Are you in hiding? Are the police going to come looking for you? Is some jilted husband going to come and beat me up? Did you nick that fur coat? Just tell me what's what, then I'll shut up. Then I'll do it your way. No questions.'

'No. To your questions all answers is no.'

'And you can drop the phoney accent. This isn't some theatre where you swan in, pretend you're Marilyn Monroe or whoever. Can you not just be yourself.' His face was flushed now, his eyes bright. 'Is that too much to ask?'

Do damage to Sinclair the sailor man. She imagined Izzy pummelling the window. *Serious damage.* She glanced up, her eyes quick with fear.

'Just the wind,' Rob said, 'it's picking up.'

'Myself...' her voice trailed off. If only. The thought flashed through her that there was no voice, no ghost of Izzy. This mad voice thing was her fear, or guilt, and the wind. She'd been so groomed with Izzy's Ronester ghost stories she was gullible to them. Another word Izzy threw at her.

'See you, you're too gullible. Not even human, that's your problem. You haven't a fucking clue what's what.'

Whatever the thing was, it moaned on, slicing like a blade through her brain; *Then I'll rest. He ruined my life.* Mairi snapped her eyes shut but the whining voice went on. *Set me free.* She started humming, batted her eyes open and reached for a croissant. She cut open the packet of real coffee. 'Oo la la!' she sang.

'What is it with women? Are they all so... secretive?'

'Men,' she said, wagging her finger. *A quick nudge down the steps at Whaligoe.* She bit into a croissant then started unwrapping the box. 'Thank you, mister fisherman.' *That fucking sailor man ruined our lives.* She busied herself, making real coffee, arranging the daffodils in a jar of water and heating the croissants under the grill.

Rob watched, envious of her ability to shut whatever was in her past, like a book. That was her motto; live for today. What's gone is gone. What's done is done. We only have now. When he did poke and pry that's what she said. She said it now, as she carried the heated croissants to the table. 'Eat for today. Live for today.'

'But you know that's not true,' he said. 'We've got yesterday, loads of yesterdays, last year, all the things we've done, seen. They're in us. We drag them all around.'

'Better to let it go. Live for the moment.'

'But... that's not human. And maybe there's stuff I want to remember. If I just lived for the moment I'd forget my dad.' He stopped then, looking away, as if hearing his music.

'Then you don't smell this coffee,' she said, glancing up from pouring boiling water into the coffee grounds at the bottom of the shining new cafetiere. 'You smell ten-year-old tea.'

Aye, Robbie, he thought, what's done is done. Live for today, and tomorrow. 'Maybe you're right.' He smiled at her and she smiled back. He was in love with this beautiful, mysterious, troubled woman who had turned up in his life, made necklaces from shells and kept film stars' pictures. Who, when she seemed at ease in herself, was tender with him, and gentle. Who often sang in the house and had turned it from a lonely, empty hovel into a place that had colour, song, dance, love and mystery. Whoever she was, he loved her, even if she did appear to carry the weight of the world on her shoulders some days. 'So, for our wee date, is that a yes, then?'

'A small walk, yes,' she said, seeming brighter for the array of breakfast things on the table, the smell of strong real coffee. She sat down and slowly plunged the cafetiere, then leant over and kissed him on his scar. 'You are kind, mister fisherman, thank you.'

'When did selkies get a taste for coffee?' he murmured, kissing her neck.

'Oh, we often come ashore,' she murmured back.

When they did finally set out, she slipped her hand into his. Gulls glided overhead as if escorting them. 'What is that one?' she asked, pointing to the bird swooping ahead of them.

'Herring gull,' Rob said, 'two years old. It's still got speckled brownish bits. That's how you can tell.'

'Wow. You are bird man. Bird man, and fish man, and lobster man, and crab man!'

'I'd rather be your man.' He slipped an arm around her waist.

She leant into him, whispering, 'there are ghosts here. Mary said.'

'Aye. Shame they don't eat lobster, or fish, or drink beer in the pub, or buy stuff in the shop. They don't contribute to the local economy.' He laughed. 'They're company, of sorts.' He squeezed her waist. 'But I'm real, Sophia.'

'Bird man,' she said, laughing and breaking away from his touch.

'I can't fly,' he called after her.

'Maybe I can!' With aeroplane arms she turned in circles, her face lifted to the racing clouds.

Watching her antics, he felt nervous. Why had he suggested this windblown height for a walk? He had imagined them hand in hand, sauntering while he pointed sights out to her; the cave, the broch, the stunted Hawthorn trees. A red throated diver. A black-backed gull. Not her jumping up and down near the cliff edge like a child. 'I love wind,' she yelled.

Next to her Rob felt old. That was something else he was in the dark about. Seeing her skip along in that green dress, arms spread wide, she looked about eighteen. This love story he was living in his head was madness on many levels, age being one. In three years he'd be forty. Looking back down the corridor of years his life seemed dark, flat, with hazy gaps. Where had his thirties gone? Or his twenties for that matter?

'Hey! Wait!' he shouted, running after her.

'I love wind so much,' she cried, spinning around like a dancer. Rob found himself worried others would see. Then his beautiful stranger would be the talk of the local shop, if she wasn't already. Gladys would probably, at this very moment, be peering at them through her binoculars. Well, fuck them all. Rob tried to run like her, to put his arms out to the sides, be young and free, but couldn't. And maybe Mairi noticed for she slowed down. 'Thank you for this walk,' she said, but soon took off again.

'Yeah, but that wasn't what I meant,' he called, but the wind whipped his voice.

He wanted a beer. He wanted to go out on his boat. 'Let's head back,' he shouted, but she shook her head.

'I love it up here, it's like I can breathe. So much space.' And the grating voice had stilled, as if here Izzy couldn't find her.

Rob thrust his hands into the pockets of his jacket and headed back along the breezy cliff path. He might be nearing forty, but the mood creeping over him felt like a four-year-old's huff. Two beers he would take, or three. A fag, and a cup of tea. He glanced back, hoping she would follow, but she was still out there, her arms stretched like wings.

Three beers he took, and still she wasn't back. He couldn't help it. The pull to know her, watch her, was stronger than his common sense and the beer waylaid that.

He went up to the bedroom, to his lookout spot by the window. The binoculars were in their place, hanging from a nail. Did she follow the flights of fulmars and oyster catchers like he did? Did she ever bother to look at him, follow him on the *Stella*? His eyes fell on little trinkets she had set out on the windowsill. More shell jewellery lay on the shelf. It touched him, her little home-making gestures. She had a postcard of some sultry film star, Greta Garbo maybe, propped against the wall. Hurriedly he looked at the back of the card, for some clue. But there was nothing. He looked under the bed. Nothing. In the drawer was one red dress and one green jumper. She owned even less than he did.

He took the binoculars, training the lenses on the far cliff. Was she still up there, skipping like a child? The window was smeared with salt and vision was blurred. He forced the window open. As he scanned the coast he heard the click of the back door, and her bright, windblown voice echoed through the cottage, 'wow! That was fantastic!'

In seconds he was in the bathroom, where there were still a few strands of her long blonde hair, fanned out. He looked at himself in the mirror. The well of need that looked back shocked him. He shut his eyes and breathed. Two. Three. Four.

30

SINCE THE WALK up on the cliffs, going for a walk turned into her daily activity. The voice of Izzy lessened up there, perhaps because the wind was louder. Mairi cried to the buffeting, battering wind. Hurled stones over the cliff, all in an effort to rid herself of the dead that wouldn't die. The wilder the wind the better. 'Don't go near the edge, please,' Rob said, when she came in from these walks, her cheeks red and her eyes bright, 'it's dangerous.'

'But perhaps I would fly,' she said. 'Like your seabirds.'

'I wouldn't recommend it.'

She shot him a glance. 'You can't tame the wind, no?'

He had come to notice that look, that hardening in her eyes, that coldness that came over her. 'I'll see if I can catch us fish for dinner,' Rob said, stepping into his boots, pulling on his jacket, knowing by now to give her space.

He brought back three sea bass. She drank more wine than usual and seemed ill at ease. When he leant over to kiss her she pulled back her chair and hurried up to the bedroom. Rob watched her go. He wasn't invited. So then it was two, three hours of drinking beer, and staring into the dying embers of the coal fire before tiredness swept over him and he crawled into his sleeping bag.

Two hours after that, Mairi got out of bed while still sleeping, walked down the stairs, asleep, took the poker from the fireplace and stood over him.

A clatter of wind against the window woke her. She gasped, the embers in the fire enough to see where she was, what she held in her hand and him beneath her, asleep in his tattered sleeping bag. She replaced the poker and hurried back to bed where she lay, eyes wide open, watching for the dawn.

Rob woke none the wiser. He had seen the way she made coffee in the cafetiere and made some now. When she came downstairs he offered her a cup. 'It's real,' he announced, smiling.

'Like me.' She met his gaze, letting the salt blue eyes of him fall into her.

'Thank you, Rob.'

'A bitty strong, maybe,' he said, sipping the coffee and wincing. 'I'll learn. I'll get better.'

All she could do was nod, because she had a job to do and a voice she needed to silence. She stared into the black coffee like she was staring down a bottomless pit.

'I... I often wondered.' Mairi looked at her mother who was pouring herself a glass of wine.

'Big disappointment, eh?' Izzy lifted the glass. 'Here's tae us.'

'I mean... about him, I wondered... about my dad?'

'Don't waste your brain wondering about him. Bloody sure I don't.'

A lie. Two glasses of Riesling and the lover who met her on the beach got plenty air time; the strength of his arms, the silkiness of his hair, his sexy accent.

Izzy finished her drink. 'Just you and me now.' She sneered. 'Gone the grey selkie. Gone the fucking sergeant major, gone the weakling of a mother.' She waved an arm through the air like some dejected fairy godmother then upturned the wine glass and a last drop fell to the floor. 'Poof! All gone!' Then she narrowed her eyes and stared at Mairi, as if challenging her to go the way of everybody else.

'I… I won't leave.' Mairi said, 'I promise.'

'Good,' Izzy said, 'coz I'm not well.' She started to cough, as if demonstrating. Not that she needed to, with her grey pallor. When she had recovered, she said, her voice weak now, breathy, 'make a ghost a promise, that's a bond.'

'What?'

'In that old book,' she nodded in the direction of the shelf, 'it says bonded in blood.'

Rob finished his coffee, wanted to kiss her but could read the distant mood on her, so put on his oilskins and walked away, cigarette smoke batting into the wind. Mairi went to the back window and watched him trudge away, his shoulders slumped.

She etched this Robert Sinclair into her heart, the way he twice turned round, the way he grew smaller walking away. The way he lingered over the bridge, as if he might find something in the river. He was always searching. The fisherman. The sailor man. The hunter. She loved him, though hardly knew what that meant, but the ache of it threatened to undo her and kill him.

When he was out of sight, she wanted to run to him. Under the worry, the smoke lines, the stubble, the scar, he was handsome in a rugged, weathered kind of way. And more than handsome. He was good. Loving. Kind. He loved her. She felt a pull under her ribs. If she had any inkling of what love was, she loved him. It didn't matter he was so much older.

A shudder ran through her. She had come so close to doing damage to him.

One quick nudge down Whaligoe Steps. Then I'll rest.

A SWELL IN the bay. The lift and drop that turns most folks' stomachs, but not Rob's. His sea legs stood strong, his body moving with the shifting mounds of briny water, his lungs pulling in the fresh south westerly. It felt good. His creels were set, a line of orange buoys marking his hunting beds. Strange phrase; hunting beds. He thought of Sophia, in his bed, and him, the hungry hunter. He rolled a cigarette, wanting her. He had laced his coffee with whisky.

His dad had said it was no coincidence them having the same name; spirit. Rob drank his tea and sniffed the lingering spirit. Drink-fuelled, crazy acts of the past flicked through his mind; jumping out a third-floor window, fighting a bouncer in a nightclub, ramming a car into a hedge. Here, out on the *Stella* in the early morning, the old craziness beckoned, though it felt different now. Fuck it! He pulled off his oilskins and fleece shirt, trousers and t-shirt, then stood naked, his whole body thrilling at the salt spray and the feeling for once of being untrammelled, potent, essential. A non-swimmer, he wasn't about to dive in. He wasn't that crazy. But he would get himself in and hold the rope, just to feel what she felt. He'd smell like her, briny. He clambered over the rail and held onto the rope attached to a fender. He pulled it hard to check. 'Right, Robbie lad,' he said, nothing muted about his voice now, 'get yourself into that bloody sea!'

He lowered himself, shouting out as the cold water slapped his legs, yelling as it reached his shrinking cock. He kept going. Cold water lapped around his torso, snaked under his armpits. He yelled. He couldn't believe she did this. When the cold sea reached his neck the shock of head freeze slapped him hard and he let go the rope. Immediately he sunk, then he was back up, spluttering, gasping, trying to reach the rope, but the swell pulled him away from the boat. Again he went under, water green, swirling, bubbling, heavy. He thrust an arm up and managed to claw back up to the surface, everything in him thrashing forward but the boat out of reach. Under again, like an unstoppable force sucking him down. Then the almighty effort to push up. Choking, retching. This was it, he thought, picturing the *Stella* smashed on some rocks, Sophia standing at the back door crying his name into the darkness.

He heard an old tune of his dad's on the wind. And the *Stella* was right there. He reached for the rope as if something was helping him. And Rob's hands, tingling with cold, wrapped around the rope, and a swell of water lifted him. His whole body shaking, he hoisted himself over the rail.

He lay on the deck, gasping, spluttering, his body tingling, trembling, then he started laughing.

There was magic in the sea, he knew it now.

He pulled on his clothes and drank the last of the hot coffee fortified with Old Poultney. As he lifted the anchor he looked for her; the spirit of the sea. White horses broke on the crinkled waves. 'Aye, Robbie lad,' he shouted, 'that was close. Bloody close. Bloody freezing. And bloody great.'

He had a spring in his step, heading back across the bridge. He wanted to tell her what he had done. And how he had been saved by a selkie. 'Sophia?' his voice echoed in the empty cottage.

'Sophia?' She wasn't there. Probably on one of her long clifftop walks. Again.

His pouch of tobacco was empty.

So he headed back out, bending into the wind, turning the collar of his jacket up and his head down, trudging over the mud-rutted track. He didn't see the four-by-four until he was practically upon it. There was only one person gallus enough to leave their vehicle blocking his path: his landlord. Sure enough, there he was, leaning against the other side of the massive car, fiddling with camera equipment. Rob took in the predictable uniform of Barbour jacket, Hunter's wellington boots, deer stalker, tweed trousers. All dull green. Even the car. What a pratt. Though if camouflage was the intention, it had worked.

Ryder looked up as Rob approached but didn't say good morning. Neither did Rob, who kept his eyes lowered. When Rob had passed Ryder spoke up. 'Been swimming, Sinclair.'

Rob ran his hand through his damp hair and kept walking.

'I see you've taken a lodger.'

Rob felt his pulse quicken. 'And?' He slowed down but didn't look back.

'It's not in the lease.'

Then Rob did turn to look at the big man, symbol of entitlement and power over Rob, like Ryder's father had had power over Rob's own parents. 'I can have visitors,' he said, his lips tight.

'No harm in a visitor, but word is, Sinclair, you're hitched. Word is, she's there all the time.' Ryder continued sorting his lens, as if the camera was far more interesting than the petty love-life of one of his shabby tenants.

Rob turned away from him and flexed his knuckles. He despised the landlord and his mansion which sat a mile down the coast, with acres of land and a helicopter landing pad. He loathed his Land Cruiser on his path, his accent, his clothes and the power he had over him, and the power the Ryders had had over his parents.

'She can stay,' Ryder said, then the camera clicked. Rob swung round. Ryder had the camera trained on him. 'Just put it in writing to the estate office. Make it official, Sinclair. She'll need to be on the voting register. More council tax too, as you're no longer single occupancy.'

Rob wanted to grab the expensive kit and hurl it into the mud. Ryder lowered his camera. 'I'm not making this up,' he said. 'It's the law.'

Rob's fists were in his pockets, fingers cutting into his palms. Gasping for a cigarette didn't help. 'She's not staying long,' he blurted, his mind racing. No way would she want to be on some voting register. But his mind raced further. They could trace records, visas. Birth certificates. Then he would know who she was. Ryder brought the camera up again, training it on his tenant like a gun.

'Put that down,' Rob said.

'I don't want any trouble. I am actually trying to be helpful here, Sinclair.'

The two stared at each other, Ryder through the lens, Rob through slit eyes. 'Fine.' Rob took a step back.

Ryder lowered the camera. 'As I say, no harm in having visitors. But if she's living in Seaview, they need to know.' His landlord walked away then, down the track, towards the cottage, head held high.

'Where are you going?' Rob shouted.

Ryder didn't do him the favour of turning round. 'Off to photograph the beach.' My beach, he didn't add, but it was clear it all belonged to him.

Rob ran the rest of the way up to the shop. Old Mina was in, nattering. And Mackie prided himself on old-fashioned values and never hurried anyone. Rob cursed them under his breath. Mina hushed and stared at him. 'Talk of the devil,' she muttered.

The devil kept silent.

When finally the old natterer left, Rob, who had only meant to buy tobacco, bought six cans of lager too.

'See the hotel's finally open,' Mackie said, slowly counting Rob's change.' Rob stared as pound coins were methodically placed into his outstretched palm. 'Aye, well, that lass who turned up was wanting a job there. Mina was saying they're taking on staff for the season. You might let her know.' Still Rob didn't answer. Nosy old git. He wasn't giving Mackie as much as a crumb and was out that shop double-quick.

And as if he'd been waiting for him, there was Jake, leaning against the shop front, like he was posing for a band photo.

'They're saying she's drug running,' he said, his voice low, looking not at Rob but out to the far sea. 'I owe you one, man, so just saying. Don't want to see you getting banged up.'

'Aye, Jake, you'd know all about drug running.'

'Water under the bridge, Robbie, water under the bridge. I'm just saying what they're saying and don't want to see you hurt.'

'Bit late for that, is it no?'

'Fuck sake, man, I said sorry. What else do you want me to do? Kiss your fucking feet?'

'Would be a start. And who's they?' he hissed.

'The locals,' Jake muttered.

'Oh,' Rob sneered, 'those great founts of knowledge.' But all the same, of all the thoughts that had crossed his mind, some kind of drug involvement was a new one. He felt a fool. He'd been veering down some supernatural track, influenced by notions of his dad, and his own growing tendency to doubt reality. What an idiot. Of course, her shifting moods, her ups and downs, her fur coat, her secrecy and shady past. But Rob didn't want to give Jake one ounce of satisfaction. Jake mentioned Whaligoe Steps, and how they did handovers in the dead of night.

'Nothing changed there then?' Rob said, wryly.

'Aye, it's still a fucking creepy place.'

Jake was going to say more but Rob turned and walked off.

'See you, man,' Jake called, but Rob ignored him.

The more he thought about it, the more he thought Jake was right. Rob was more of an alcohol man these days, but he remembered the highs and lows of pills, mostly given to him by Jake, via his brother, the elations and the paranoia.

He felt a prize eejit. Her ups and downs. Her turning up here in winter and making out like she was some foreign actress down on her luck. Between jobs, she'd said.

Right enough, between jobs.

Probably lover boy was some big dealer and she was a pawn in his game. A drug mule. Probably she was getting ready to go to Whaligoe Steps, fetch a parcel, or board some boat for Aberdeen, or Orkney. A plane to Mexico for all he knew! Rob smacked his forehead. It had been staring him in the face and he had been too lovesick to notice it. Too swept up in selkie stories. What a fool.

They hand over at night, Jake had told him. Usually the dead hour. Three am. Easy for her to sneak out in the middle of the night. Sometimes she did for a mad swim.

Rob would go after her. He'd get to the steps and confront her, smash her little game, like his own father had done with wild Bethie Gunn.

Like father, like son.

32

LATER THAT AFTERNOON Rob went out in the boat, not to plunge into the ice-cold sea this time, but to lift a few creels. It was a long wait until 3 am. And Sophia still hadn't come back. Her cliff walks, he had noticed, were getting longer.

'You got a girlfriend?' Archie blurted out. 'Have you, Rob? A girlfriend, eh?'

'It's a secret,' Rob said, winking at Archie.

Rob was not long off the boat, oilskinned from neck to toe and making his way, plodding in his big yellow wellington boots, along the quayside. The small catch, ten lobsters, was packed in the cold store, draped in kelp strands to keep them moist, and alive. Rob slumped on the harbour bench and Archie sat next to him. Though spring, the wind was bitter and Rob pulled the stiff collar of his oilskin jacket past his ears. He stretched his legs, also stiff in the dark green oilskin trousers, and saw how Archie tried to imitate him. Rob stared at his yellow boots.

'You're lucky,' Archie boomed, grinning.

If you just knew, Rob thought. Quickly he rolled a cigarette then lit it, pulling in the tobacco. But it was her he needed, her he wanted, drugs or no drugs. He was hardly a saint. He could help her get out of it. 'Aye, right lucky,' he said. Then he nudged Archie. 'You're getting married soon, don't forget.'

'Got to find a girlfriend first,' he said, grinning.

Archie winked then raised his thumbs, and already Rob was taking off, not stopping to wave back to Archie. Just thinking of her he felt hungry, heart hungry, body hungry. He wanted her, whatever she was mixed up in. He wanted to take her in his arms and hold her tight. He'd messed up, and his dad had been there for him. He would be there for her.

He burst into the house, and again called her name. No-one answered. He ran upstairs but she wasn't there. All trace of her was gone. Her clothes were gone. Her little bag was gone. Her postcards, shells and toothbrush, gone.

Maybe the boat she had been waiting for had already come. She might be thumbing it south with notes bulging from the pocket of her fur coat. He grabbed the binoculars and peered through them, his trembling fingers training his view on the sea. A seal lifted its head from the water and seemed to look straight at him. A gull swept low then landed on the shore, jabbing into a razor shell. He dropped the binoculars.

Where was she? He ran through to the bathroom. Even the last remining wisps of blonde hair were gone. Rob sunk to his knees, struggling to breathe. A terrible empty feeling slammed into him. The haunting images were back with a vengeance, men jumping from the burning rig, voices screaming in a way that ripped beyond human. The sea on fire. Smoke and midnight and flames. Gasping, Rob pressed his hands over his racing heart and tried to catch his breath, to reign in these bolting horses. He pulled in the soothing murmur of doctors who had tended him; breathe, count, this too will pass.

But it was ten years now, and it hadn't. A cry ripped from his throat.

A cry that his neighbour, Betsy Manson, heard as she bent to pick rhubarb from her front garden.

A cry that Mairi heard as she sat, huddled in the cave at the far end of the next beach, a small fire in front of her. She wondered if the distant cry was a gull, a seal, or a ghost. *The* ghost. A shiver ran through her. The orange flames flickered.

She didn't want to hurt Rob. If she had any inkling what love might be, she loved that man. She had fled to keep him safe, not trusting what the bitter ghost of her mother might do.

The awful faint cry sounded again, carried by the wind. Mairi glanced around fearfully. She threw another piece of bleached driftwood onto the fire. 'Stop it,' she pleaded, 'leave me alone.'

Betsy knew that agonised cry, and with trembling fingers set down her rhubarb and picked a few daffodils. She would take them to him, later. When the torment had passed. And she would take ginger cake. Perhaps she would invite both of them round for dinner, a spaghetti carbonara, then rhubarb crumble. She'd get out the penny whistle and give them a tune. 'Ae Fond Kiss'. Or something merrier; 'Step We Gaily'. A shudder passed through her as another pained roar came from Seaview cottage. The daffodils fell from her grasp.

It was late April and the wind howled. Hardly the weather to live in a cave, but Mairi could see others had. There was a rough stone seat, even a table of sorts. The fire she was now warming herself by, in its circle of stones, had been made by someone. A selkie man perhaps, sliding off his animal skin and warming his human skin by the fire. Waiting for his land-girl, perhaps, his night of love. A few tin cans and empty wine bottles littered the back of the cave. Also some bones, seal or deer. There were stubs of candles. Mairi was sure she could manage a few days there, time to clear her mind and work out what to do next.

The last thing she wanted was to do damage to Robert Sinclair.

For now, she had shelter, a fur coat and fresh water that dripped from the hill near the cave. Before leaving the cottage she had taken biscuits, bananas, chocolate. And she could gather mussels and cook them over the fire in a tin filled with salt water. There was something freeing about being so close to the sea, with the briny whiff of seaweed, the moaning call of seals, the constant blowing of wind.

And maybe the spirit of her father would look over her.

And maybe she could peel the ghost of her mother from her. Maybe the young Robert, out on his boat that night, had just wanted to help. He wasn't to know his call to Lachie would result in wild Bethie's banishment, bitterness and now restless death.

She couldn't imagine anywhere further from that dismal flat in Tooting. If this Rob Sinclair really was the one she was to 'do damage to' she couldn't stay under the same roof. Afraid Izzy was slithering like a viper inside her, afraid she might sleepwalk in the night and kill him. Mairi had heard about such things. Possessions were described in the book, driving the possessed mad.

Slowly, the rhythm of the waves washing up the stony beach worked on her breathing, easing her jangled nerves.

Set me free…

It seemed to work like that, when she relaxed, when she thought she was free of this haunting, the voice rose up, a whisper then a moan – *set me free…*

What if the voice never stopped, pushing her to the edge of madness? What then?

Then she'd fling herself off Whaligoe Steps.

It was growing dark. She gazed into the flickering flames. Remembering the spells from her folklore book, she sprinkled sand into the small fire; 'spirit of sea,' she murmured, 'take the restless soul of my mother and set her free. The ring is returned, her ashes are scattered. Let her have peace now. Let her leave Rob, and me, in peace. He meant no harm, let him be happy.'

To eke out the fire and push back the night she burnt Elizabeth Taylor, Judy Garland, Bette Davis, Katharine Hepburn, Marilyn Monroe, Audrey Hepburn, Demi Moore, Joan Crawford, Judy Garland, Grace Kelly, Sophia Loren, Lauren Bacall, Natalie Wood. And finally, the photograph of her mother in a blue jumper.

Betsy waited until the sun went down and dusk blurred the edges of everything. Then she wrapped her ginger cake in a clean white towel, bound the daffodils with a green ribbon and made her way to her neighbour's cottage. All had been quiet there for hours. Rob didn't lock the door. Only incomers did. She knocked gently on the back door. Hearing no sound from inside, she let herself in. 'Rob?' she murmured. 'Sophia?' Nothing. Normally she would leave her gifts and go, but this evening she felt compelled to stay, make sure he was alright. And Sophia? How would she have coped with that wild outpouring? The woman looked fragile herself, and hearing a man howl like that could terrify. 'Rob?' she called again, louder this time. She went into the kitchen and from there into the gloomy living room. No fire was burning in the grate. She called up the dark stairway. 'Sophia?'

She wondered whether to go on upstairs, struck by a sudden image of Rob hanging from the rafters. She'd read what trauma can do to a man, and prayed it would never do that to Rob Sinclair. 'Rob?' she called, louder now. 'Rob? Are you alright?'

No sound. Even the ceaseless wind had died. Betsy grasped the banister. Her heavy tread creaked on the stairs. Ginger cake seemed wrong next to the awful possibility of suicide. 'Rob?'

She paused on the stair, steeling herself for what she might find, the sight she had feared for three years.

He woke from a deep sleep, stiff on the bathroom floor. A noise. Someone in the house. 'Sophia!' he cried, jumping up, hitting the side of the bath, fumbling for the light switch. Then he lurched for the door and pulled it open.

A shaft of light from the bathroom spilled down the stairway, landing on the stricken face of his neighbour, Betsy Manson. 'Oh, thank God,' she cried, 'oh… I… worried… sorry, I did knock, Rob. Here, I… I brought you some cake.' She gazed up at him, her face opening into a smile. 'For you and Sophia. Ginger…'

'She's gone,' he said.

'I'm sorry, Rob. I am so sorry. I really thought, this was it, a good change, a new wind.' She talked on hurriedly, as he made his way groggily down the stairs. 'You deserve better, Rob, you really do, after all you've been through.'

'Aye, well,' he said, passing her and going into the living room where he flicked on the bright overhead light then slumped onto the sofa, 'probably so does she. She's young, and I got way ahead of myself.' You too, he didn't say but she nodded, knowing what he meant.

'It's called hope,' she said, setting the cake on the table, then busying herself finding a milk jug, filling it with water and arranging the flowers. 'Better hope than despair, eh?'

'He wanted me to see him,' Rob blurted, 'and I couldn't. I couldn't keep looking. So, he jumped, on fire, and I wasn't man enough to witness him.'

'You were braver than many people I know, Rob. And I'll bet you've been seeing him these past, what is it, eight years?'

'Ten come July.'

'Let him go, Rob.'

'Easy said.'

'Well, when he comes, Rob, tell him you see him, then imagine a bird flying away.' She laughed, half in embarrassment. 'You could try it. It might help.'

Rob looked at her and nodded. 'I will.' He made them tea and they sat at the table in silence, chewing the ginger cake.

It was Betsy who broke the silence. 'Mary was here.'

'Mary Gunn? I doubt she's stepped over the boundary of Heatherlee in years.'

'Aye, but she was here yesterday, fretting and wanting to see the lass. She'd knitted blue woollen gloves, bless her.'

'What did you tell her?'

'To come back later.'

Rob glanced over his shoulder, as if old Mary Gunn might be standing by the kitchen door.

'Now, old Mary is a great one for making fruit scones.' Betsy laughed. 'Not like my Sharon. She tries, bless her, but they come out like rocks.'

'Who's Sharon?'

'She's my girlfriend, Rob. The villagers don't need to know. That thing about the bird flying away, that's Sharon, she likes these things. Rituals, she calls them. But,' she laughed again, 'she's not so hot on baking!'

Rob smiled at her. 'Maybe Mary Gunn could teach Sharon to bake scones. I heard she's an expert.'

They laughed then and their laughter drifted out into the spring sunshine, reaching the lapping waves and the nesting fulmars on the cliffs and the crying gulls in the blue air, reaching the bleating lambs up at Heatherlee farm, where the gorse brought a scent of coconut to the county, reaching old Mary Gunn who sat by a new-mended wall in the spring sunshine, twisting a heavy golden ring round her bony finger.

33

WITH DUSK, SHADOWS filled the cave. The small fire glowed faintly, but there was little wood left, and it was too dark to look for more. Mairi made sighing noises, just to hear her voice. Then murmured her name into the darkening cave;

'Mairi.'

It had been months now since anyone had called her by her name.

Mairi who?

An orphan in search of a family. A selkie with no seal skin. A woman in a cave who might be dead by morning. A daughter in love with the man who had ruined her mother's life. Too wound up, and afraid, to sleep, she unpeeled a banana and held it over the fire.

Mairi bit into the charred banana, trying to batten memories down in a box marked Past. That was another box needing scattered. Desperately, she tried to stay in the moment, tasting the sweet, slightly burnt banana, feeling the warmth on her cheek from the dwindling fire, feeling the thick fur swaddled around her. The now was where she wanted to live. Not always this...

'I was screwed up,' Izzy said, 'wild and sixteen. So not ready for... you.'

'I understand.'

'Aye, well, I doubt you do. I was waiting for him down by the beach and in washes a dead seal. Like some sick joke. Then a few weeks later I was banished from clan and county like some medieval princess. Fuck them.'

Izzy leant forward and stared into Mairi's eyes. 'You want to see where it all started. Go home, you might say. You want that, eh?'

'Home?' She tried to keep hope from her voice.

'Where me and the selkie man made you. In fact,' Izzy coughed, a hacking cough that went on for ages. Mairi fumbled in her bag for tissues, but Izzy waved her off. 'Fuck! Right, where was I? Oh yeah, the hotel. The Aurora. It's on the cliff above the beach. Get a job there. I'll set it up, then you can get out this shit hole, and do these wee jobs. Scatter the ashes on the sea when the tide's coming in. Return the ring to Heatherlee and do damage to a bastard called Sinclair the sailor man.'

Izzy coughed that hacking cough again, then stared at her daughter. 'Aye, duck, forty bloody years old and it's curtains. I'm bowing out so I can haunt the bastards that banished me.'

Izzy had been dying for years. Every time Mairi had suggested getting her own flat, Izzy had a relapse. 'You can't leave now. I'm dying.' Everyone else her age flew the nest. Not Mairi. Twenty-four years old and still at home, caring for her mother. She could be thirty-five, forty, and Izzy would still be dying. But never actually die.

Until now.

Curtains!

Mairi lay down and wrapped the fur coat around her. The wind howled. By the mouth of the cave waves thudded on the rocks, rolling in, sucking back. 'I did it,' Mairi murmured, 'I scattered your ashes. I returned the ring. So let me go.'

Finally sleep took her from the chill of the dark cave into the sailor man's warmth, where she was stroking his scar, and pleading with him to hold her and never let her go.

34

THE COTTAGE FELT emptier than ever. Rob watched the last red coals die but didn't stir to bank up the fire.

It was like the days and weeks after his mother left. When the place felt empty. When the home feeling had gone. Empty, his dad kept saying, it feels so empty. How things repeat. First his mother, now his lover.

For a long while he sat there, slumped, numb, until the clock struck 2am. Time to go to Whaligoe Steps and bring his woman home.

Rob knew a little about drug running. Knew, because Jake told him, 3am was the dead hour when all the upright citizens are tucked up in their beds. If it's a new moon, and high tide, even better.

So, under a sky of stars and a sliver of moon, tide coming in and the dead hour approaching, Rob drove to Whaligoe Steps.

The only car on the road, Rob rehearsed what he would say if he found her. It's alright. Lass, it's alright. And he'd speak softly. Let her know she didn't have to hide anymore. He would help her get out of whatever she was in. He'd had some practise. He'd had a life. And fuck it, they could both start again. He loved her.

Maybe he'd start there. I love you, and it's alright.

He pulled off the main road, left the van up on the verge,

then took the rough track to the small car park. He crept past the three small cottages there. No sign of life in any of them. He made his way to the cliff, with just enough sickle moon, and his good night vision, to distinguish outlines and the cliff edge. He reached the steps and began going down, holding to the cliff side and feeling forward with his feet.

He didn't want to give her a shock. Whaligoe Steps were lethal and a slip could mean death. A few tentative steps down and he was struck by the roar and boom of waves far below. He pictured her, down there, her fur coat hugged against the elements, waiting for the boat. He looked out into the vast black of ocean. No sign of one. But there wouldn't be, would there? Sonar and lightless, these boats were like subs. Down he went, into the night, the tunnelling wind, the crash of waves. He counted as he descended; thirty-two... thirty-three... thirty-four...

Already a month of steps.

A winter of them.

Now he could hear the moaning of seals. He pictured her at the small landing bay, deafened with the roar of the crashing waves, ready to collect the stash brought in by a boat. Maybe she'd been told where to hide it. Or maybe she was the runner, and was to pass it on to someone, in a café in Thurso, for instance. Or in some car park in Wick. Or maybe this was her drug baron boyfriend, come to fetch her. Take her to Mayfair, or Columbia.

Ninety-seven... ninety-eight... He didn't notice the cold. Hardly noticed the battering of his own heart. At two hundred he cupped his hands about his mouth and hooted like an owl. That was the sign, Jake had said. Rob stood still and waited. No owl called back.

Three hundred and forty...

The waves echoed around the geo of cliffs.

Three hundred and sixty-two…

Three hundred and sixty-four.

A whole year of steps and she wasn't there. He stood at the foot of Whaligoe Steps and yelled her name to the wailing sea. 'Sophia! Sophia! Lass!'

The seals moaned. There was only one person on Whaligoe Steps, and that was him.

Jake had a history of getting things wrong.

It was 4.30am when Rob got back to Ronester.

35

A RAT GNAWING on a pack of biscuits woke her at dawn, grey light a relief after the long night. She wasn't as freaked as she thought she would be. She watched the rat drag the pack of biscuits to the mouth of the cave, not wanting to relinquish his find, but putting distance between them. 'It's okay,' she said, more relieved to have survived the night and to have slept, as far as she was aware, well, a warmth flooding her. She looked around, half expecting to see more animals. A seal perhaps? An otter? Rob had told her about otters he had come upon, and seals.

She could go home soon. And it *was* that. To him.

A night alone in a cave had silenced the ghost. For the first time in a long time, Mairi felt the possibility of freedom. She was no-one's puppet.

She stretched then went to the mouth of the cave. A pink glow lay along the eastern horizon. With dawn came hunger. But the chocolate, she discovered, hadn't survived. The thought of the animals' midnight feast going on while she slept made her smile. But she was hungry. Her earlier notion of scraping mussels then cooking them now seemed overwhelming. How would she even start? She wandered round to the trickle of waterfall, letting icy water splash into her palms. Noisily she drank, then set about combing the beach for driftwood.

The sun came up and for a few hours Mairi lived the simple

life. She made a fire, drank more water, then took off her coat, her dress and swam. After the swim she warmed herself with fire and fur, wishing it could be like this all the time. This simple.

Most of her knowing it couldn't be. She wasn't an otter, or seal. And it was highly unlikely she was half a selkie either. She was a woman, trying to break free of her mother's twisted stories and be herself, whoever that was.

Standing at the water's edge that spring morning she felt finally released from a mother who could never let go of the past. Who had grown sick with it. Maybe her spell had worked. Mairi breathed in great gulps of air. This was what she wanted, this sun over the water, this wind blowing and these gulls soaring. This air in her lungs. And a good man by the shore, waiting for her.

It struck her, the wild wind, the open sea, the freedom of gulls and love, was what Izzy wanted too. *I fucking loved it there.*

Mairi turned, hearing a boat puttering along the shore. Her heart fluttered seeing the *Stella*. She lifted a hand and waved.

At first he thought it was a lingering patch of haar, then saw it was smoke. Through his binoculars he saw her, standing at the mouth of the cave. Not Whaligoe Steps then. His mind raced, thinking some drugs handover had happened here – in the tinkler's cave! He was surprised when she waved. He could see she was smiling. He took that as a sign to approach, but cautiously. The tide was in enough that he could take the *Stella* close, but not so close he might beach the boat.

'Good afternoon,' she called out, 'it's lovely here.' He was close enough now to see the fire she had going in the cave, and the dampness of her hair. He knew that cave. More than once he had spent the night there. 'I just needed to get outside, breathe,' she was explaining, her wavering and ever-changing accent, Rob noticed, dropped into something simpler. She seemed friendly and relaxed.

'Was that all?' He hadn't meant to sound accusing.

'Just needed space,' she shouted, 'but I'm better now.' She beamed at him. 'Like a new person.'

'I've got mackerel.' He cut the engine some thirty metres from the shore. 'It'll taste fine over that fire.' He'd lost the habit of shouting, unless in stricken dreams where every shout ever buried burst from him. But the breeze carried his low voice to her.

She laughed. 'That's great, coz I'm starving. I took your biscuits, sorry, then a rat got them.' She seemed young and at ease. English, he could hear that plainly now in her vowels. She looked the picture of innocence, standing there, smiling. He batted away Jake and his drug story.

'No worries,' he said, 'they're not good for me anyway.' Something told him to throw her the fish then continue on his way, keep any pride he had left intact. 'I'll gut them for you,' he shouted, whipping out a knife and gutting the fish, throwing the innards over the side then lifting the glinting mackerel into the air like trophies. 'Lunch,' he announced and flung them to shore.

She held out her hands, but the slippery fish slid through her fingers. 'It's okay,' she shouted, scooping them from the pebbles, 'I've got water to rinse them with.' She pointed to her waterfall.

Rob started up his engine. 'Looks like rain later,' he said, his practised fisherman's eye on the distant clouds. But he didn't ask her to come home. Mairi glanced at him. Did she look disappointed? He thought so. Did she look high on something? He couldn't tell.

'Thanks, Rob,' she shouted. 'Hey, I appreciate it, really, thanks very much. For everything. The room. Your… kindness.

I'm sorry about how I've been, but I'm better now. You gave me space to sort some stuff out. I'm grateful for that. Thank you, Rob.'

'You're welcome,' he called back, but he didn't linger. He left his young lodger to feast on the fish he had provided. He moved off, leaving her gazing after him, two silver fish dangling from her hands. Watching until the *Stella* was out of sight.

Feast she did, then drifted back into the warmth of her dream, the strength of his arms, and forgot about Izzy and her final task. Izzy was dead. Mairi was alive. It was that simple.

Nothing's simple, she heard Izzy say, but no longer a maddening cry. Just a whisper, easy to ignore.

Perhaps an hour or more, into the late afternoon, she dozed, lulled by the lapping waves. Stirring, she considered returning to the cottage, but then remembered how he had turned and left. Hardly a smile from him. She felt herself fall into rejection. The unwanted place she knew too well. Now, even the rough and awkward man who had been intrigued by her, who could hardly keep his eyes off her, didn't want her anymore.

Not wot we're looking for...

The knock back after too many failed auditions.

Maybe it was reeling down into that gloom that set off the voice she thought she'd silenced; *Set me free.*

The spells, the ashes scattered over the sea. Tears welled up and spilled down her face. Whatever she did, her mother would be there with her thirst for revenge. There was no escape.

'Fuck you, Izzy Whyte,' she muttered. Mairi picked up a shell and threw it into the glinting sea. Then she picked up a stone and threw that after it, a cry wrenched from her throat. She scooped up handfuls of small stones and hurled them, one chasing the other into the sea. She was yelling now, a torrent bursting from her – 'fuck you,' each time louder, 'fuck you!' She grabbed more stones – 'It's not my fault being born. I was innocent. You hear me – fucking innocent! I didn't ruin your life. Stop ruining mine. Go wherever dead people go and leave me alone!'

Tears were streaming down her face. 'Fuck you – I'm not going to ruin his life, or the Gunns, just to give you some sick satisfaction. They're already broken. And I'm not going to push any sailor man down some fucking steps. You hear?' She punched the air like a mad King Lear. Her voice was breaking. The rain Rob had forecast came splattering down. 'Fuck the blood. Fuck the clans. Fuck revenge.'

Mairi fell to her knees and howled. She clawed at stones. 'No Judy Garland!' she shouted, throwing a stone into the sea. 'No Marilyn!' She hurled another. 'No costumes!' She hurled another and started to laugh. Soaked to the skin she stood up, as if she was about to take a bow in the best play of her life. 'No ghosts either. Just me!'

36

PET GULLS LISTENED. At least, that's what his dad used to believe. And the way this gull cocked its head and stayed by Rob's side while he lifted creels, it resembled listening. 'I know, I totally lost the plot. Don't know if you gulls get like that, but it's not good. Anyway, I'm stepping back. A man's got to have his pride, eh? Drugs or not, it's no my business. I need tae sit back, turn cool and see if she comes to me.' Rob only half believed the words coming out of his mouth, but those counsellors got some things right – it felt good to talk.

The gull seemed to nod. Rob, on a roll, carried on. 'Because this shit not knowing where you are is no way to live. okay, I've been obsessed. That's not loving; it's bloody madness. You gulls have to work hard for a mate, eh? Strut about and make a display! What about poor Albert the Albatross? Shit, I'm like him, looking for love in the wrong place!' The pet gull bent its head. Water slapped against the hull. On Rob went. 'Aye well, see with us humans, strut doesn't cut it. Humans have got to play cool, make like you don't care. Make like you're not interested, *then* she might come running! Weird, eh? See if Albert had stopped trying, one o' these gannets might actually have fancied him!'

Though he would have raced to the cave in a heartbeat, swept her into his arms and carried her home, he carried on lifting creels and tossing fish heads left over from the bait to the gull.

'You love me coz I feed you, eh?' The gull squawked. 'We've got an uncomplicated relationship, eh?' Rob laughed as he began binding the catch, coaching himself to just breathe. What's for you, he remembered his dad saying, will no go by you.

Except Rob didn't believe that. Plenty things had passed him by.

Rob steered her in on a low tide, the gull circling the boat. Other gulls wheeling above the quayside.

'Hey, how's it going, man?'

Rob glanced up, though didn't need to. He knew that voice.

'Fling me the rope, Robbie.'

Rob spat over the side of the boat then took the coil of rope and flung it up. Jake caught it and looped the end round a bollard.

'There you go, Robbie. Hey, I'm thinking,' Jake was standing on the lip of the pier, looking down at Rob who stayed in his boat, making a thing of counting his catch. Being low tide there was a good height between them. 'I'll be moving on,' Jake went on, looking down at Rob who was slowly shifting his boxes of catch. 'It's too small for me here. Too stuck back in God knows what century. Don't know how you handle it, man. If I hear one more Dolly Parton number, I'll fucking scream.'

The last thing Rob needed was to pass his paltry catch up to rock star Henderson. So he waited for him to leave, leant on the rail and rolled a cigarette. 'Drugs, eh?' Rob said, not bothering to look up, 'what the fuck do you know about owls hooting? I nearly killed myself climbing these bloody steps. What the fuck do you know about drugs in Ronester?'

'Not much, Robbie, not much these days. You know me, clean living.'

Rob lifted his head, blew out smoke and stared up at him.

'So what was the big advice, eh? What do you know about her?'

Jake looked away briefly. 'Nothing, man. I just know dealers use girls like her.'

'Like what?'

'Lost.' Jake shrugged. 'Desperate.'

'You can throw me the fucking rope back right now,' Rob said, his voice steady, with a steel edge to it.

'Not saying she's bad, Robbie.' Jake threw the rope. 'Just saying, don't get hurt. And hey, Robbie, man, I'm not saying she's desperate coz she's with you. Fuck it, man, I didn't mean it like that. But... just watch yerself.'

Rob rammed the throttle and powered the *Stella* back out, waves surging in her wake.

Only when he was out on the open water did he cut the engine and look back to the harbour through his binoculars. Jake had gone. So had the fire he had stoked in Rob. The guy was trying to say sorry. Rob could see that, but for the life of him he couldn't find it in him to forgive. He had ruined his life, simple as that.

If anybody was lost it was him, Rob Sinclair. Ten years lost and he knew it. In no mood to go back he cut the engine, dropped a line for mackerel and hunched down beside the bound lobsters.

He thought of Jake, letting a good boat rot in the water, making it in the rock world and strutting off back to Manchester where he had a wife and kid. Good riddance to him. When Rob lifted the line, already two mackerel caught, he spied Jake, the blues man, trudging up the track towards the hotel. He followed him through the binoculars, and for the first time Rob felt a stab of something like pity, seeing his old friend bent like that. He had his own weight to bear, that was clear. Doubtless not all was rolling in the rock world.

Rob watched Jake go, then turned to look up the coast to the cave.

By three o'clock that afternoon a good few mackerel lay on the deck, glinting in the afternoon sun. Rob was used to it now, but at first, when he had arrived from Aberdeen 'to help his dad out' as his dad called the mission that was saving his son, killing fish and lobsters had sickened him. He had shouted at his dad, said it was bloody cruel and his dad had looked at him. There were a good few things he could have said, about his son and cruel, but he stayed silent and that was worse. 'Shout at me for fuck's sake,' Rob had yelled. Still silent, his father bent to haul up the next creel. Rob saw the brown splotches on his father's strong arms, the blue crinkled veins on the back of his hands. 'There are worse ways of getting by,' was all he said.

Aye, right enough, well Rob knew those worse ways of getting by.

As a laddie, Robbie loved to wait at the pier for his dad. He'd go from the village school straight down to the harbour. Sometimes he'd wait there for ages. When he saw the boat, a tiny speck in the distance, he'd start to wave, then when he heard the familiar splash and pull of the oars, or putter of the engine, he'd call out his father's name, or the name of the boat – *Stella*. Which meant star, his dad had told him, for at night stars guided him. And sometimes he liked to fish at night. His dad had showed him how to find the North Star, and the constellation of Orion. 'The hunter,' he had said, 'like me.'

Back then, Robbie wanted to be a fisherman, like his father. Robbie shouted, jumping up and down, when the black bearded and blue-eyed comforting face of his father came into view. 'Hey ho, laddie,' his dad called out as he approached the pier. He'd fling the coiled rope to shore and Robbie would wynd the end of the rope round the bollard. That was his job, and he was proud of it. Loved the feel of the thick, spray-damp rope in his hands, and the way it tugged and slackened like a live thing, depending on wind, tide and the swell of the sea.

'Five silver darlings for you and your mother,' his dad said, jumping from the rocking boat to the pier. From the glittering shoal twisting in his net, he picked five fish and slipped them into the paper bag. 'Run home now, Robbie,' his dad said, after he'd ruffled his hair, giving him the briny whiff that Robbie loved. Robbie watched his dad pick up the catch, sling it over his shoulder and march on to the weigh-in shed. Already buyers were there. The hotel chef was there. The fishmongers from Wick. The van that went to Billingsgate was there. Even the van that went to Spain was there.

Robbie knew he wasn't old enough to go into the weigh-in shed. He always thought of this rickety old tin building as some magical 'way in' to somewhere. Somewhere he would be able to go when he was older. When school was over and when he was a fisherman, like his father. When he'd have a wife, like his father. The buyers were shouting out figures. Before Robbie's dad vanished inside the magical way-in shed he turned and called to him, 'tell your Mam we'll have a fine clam till go with they herring. I'll be home soon as this selling's done. Go on noo, son, off home wi' yea.'

Robbie turned and ran. His job was done. He'd caught the rope and secured the boat. He'd got their tea in a bag. And the bigger job too was done – he could tell his Ma that his Da was safe home from the sea.

Near to the cottage the young Robbie slowed his steps. No smoke curled from the chimney. No reek of peat scented the air. Robbie wanted to run back to his father, wait for him outside the way-in shed. 'Mam,' he called, but she didn't appear in the doorway like she usually did. His heart skipped a beat. 'Mam,' he called again and this time his voice caught in his throat. He walked to the door of the cottage, his steps slowing.

He lifted the door latch and slowly pushed it open. Everything was wrong. 'Mammy?' he called, his voice a halting question mark. No answer. He forced himself to step into the kitchen. The place felt cold. Nothing cooking. He ran through to the living room. Her armchair was empty. The fire had gone out. Terrified now that she had fallen and hurt herself, or fainted, for she had done that before, he ran upstairs. Everything felt changed. He ran into his parents' bedroom and cried out in relief when he saw a shape in the bed. She was asleep. She was often complaining how tired she was. He stepped closer. 'Mammy?' he whispered, reaching out to touch her, but she wasn't there. It was just the rumpled blanket.

The silver darlings turned off in their bag. The prize clams thrown till 'ee gulls.

The cottage grew chill after that. His father grew silent. Robbie was always down at the shore, looking for her. That's when the ache of loneliness took root. He was only nine years old. And they never took holidays after that, him and his dad, or had visitors. Loneliness wrapped about them both.

Rob blinked his eyes open. The reddish light off the water dazzled him. Salt tears pricked his eyes. He wanted to tell Sophia how his mother had gone to Inverness, then further south. He wanted to tell her how she had written to him, saying to look after his father, saying she was sorry, saying she needed to see something more of the world and could he find it in his heart to forgive her. Letters came from Newcastle, then Chichester. Saying she wanted him to take a bus and come to visit her. He was thirteen now. He could do that by himself. There might have been more letters for there was often paper curling in the grate. Then, five years after she had left, a letter came informing them that she had died. He wanted to tell Sophia about that.

Dusk was falling. Rob had been out for hours. There was one creel he had forgotten; one he'd dropped the day before further out than his usual grounds. Now he busied himself, hauling up this last creel, which felt heavy. Whatever was down there was no ordinary lobster. He pictured a seal stuck in the hole of the creel, gone after the bait then unable to wriggle back out. Or perhaps his creel had snagged on a rusty anchor. As Rob hauled, cursing with the weight, he pictured what he might have inadvertently caught. There were plenty wrecks down there. Once he'd hauled up an ancient outboard motor. Another time he'd lifted the rib cage of a killer whale.

He peered down. Something big had attached itself to his creel and was rising up through the water. He guessed it was a crate from a merchant ship, but as his strange catch rose, Rob, panting, saw it was a suitcase. With a final almighty yank he hauled the case, and the creel, up and into the boat. Strands of seaweed clung to the case, but that didn't disguise the pattern; leopard skin.

It was hers, he was sure of it. She had a toilet bag the same pattern. He knelt beside the bashed suitcase and shook it. Finally he would learn who she was. Her secrets were bound to be in this suitcase that she had probably tipped over the cliff edge. Clues as to who she was, and whatever it was she was running away from would surely be inside. He tried to prize the suitcase open but it was locked.

He looked about for a wrench. There was an old one under the seat. It was getting dark now and the *Stella* bobbed about, waves slapping the side of the boat. Wearing his head torch, Rob trained the beam on the lock of the case. He whacked the wrench on it, expecting the lock to spring open and Sophia's dark secrets to spill out. There might be pounds of cocaine in there. Identity papers. Letters. But the lock didn't budge.

Above him a gull cried. He pushed the suitcase to the side of the boat. There was no rush. Maybe he'd take the boat back to the cave, say, 'your suitcase, I presume?' Doctor Livingstone style. But he felt tired with this spying and guessing. Rob lifted the anchor and turned the *Stella* towards the harbour. He had caught her glove. Now, as if the stars were binding them, he had caught her suitcase.

He decided to pack the lobsters in ice, then, back in the cottage, cut bread, make a flask of tea, find a bottle of wine and candles, then deliver these chivalrous gifts to his damsel in distress. And she would look at him, as she had earlier, with a new admiration. Then, as they clinked glasses by the glow of the fire, he would casually mention something he had lifted from the sea, something animal patterned and bulky, that might interest her.

But as he made his way back to the small harbour in the gloaming of that spring evening, it was his mother he thought of, and the silver darlings. All gone.

Rob didn't go back to the cave that night. When he reached the cottage, tiredness swept over him and it was all he could do to open a beer, make toast, and crash on the sofa. He could have returned to his own bed upstairs. It was empty, but he was used to the sofa and the old sleeping bag, plus he was exhausted. Even mounting the stairs, after the mad three hundred and sixty-five steps of Whaligoe the night before, seemed too much effort. The suitcase was in the boat, under tarpaulin, and the lobsters packed in ice. They could wait.

Even next morning something stopped him rushing along the beach to the cave. He'd spent nights there himself. It was dry, warm with a fire, and of course she had the fur coat. She'd be fine. It was a good cave. If the stories were true, tinkers had lived there for months on end.

Rob laughed ruefully, turning the phrase over; *if the stories were true.*

If the stories were true then selkies did exist, and one was waiting for him on the shore. He had raised her at New Year.

Whatever she was, absence, so the saying went, made the heart grow fonder. Even forcing open the leopard-patterned suitcase no longer seemed urgent. Uncovering her secrets wasn't loving. Prying wasn't loving. This giving her space felt like something closer to love.

So, he dealt with the lobsters, giving them to the huge transporter that stopped by the harbour every week. He'd get more money delivering the catch straight to the hotel, cutting out the middle man, but sometimes the middle man was handy. After he despatched the last polystyrene box up into the fish truck he reached for his pouch of tobacco. It was empty, so Rob headed up to the shop.

37

LATER THAT AFTERNOON Rob carried the battered and stinking suitcase into the cottage. He paced around it, like a leopard himself, searching for a way in. The palms of his hands felt itchy. 'You know what that means,' he remembered his father saying, 'you'll come into money.' Aye, maybe the case was full of the stuff. Rob cracked open a can of lager and drank, eyeing the suitcase. He doubted there was money in it. Likely inside were documents, letters, traces of identity and her past. Or shells and jewels from sunken ships? Or drugs? Or stacks of photos of film stars? She had a thing about film stars.

After the second can he took an axe to it, cleaving right through the middle. The case burst apart and rotting costumes came spilling out. Rob dropped the axe and stared, at red wigs, blonde wigs, red skirts, school uniforms, aprons, old fashioned dresses, mini-skirts, jackets, high-heeled shoes, reeking of the sea and spewing out over the kitchen floor. He rummaged through the foul-smelling costumes but there was no revealing piece of paper, no handy passport. No wad of notes.

The way a red wig landed on top of a black dress reminded him of a horror film. He raked through what was still in there; clothes, tights, belts, scarves. The slimy feel of everything repulsed him. He sat back and stared, Then the penny dropped. His secretive stranger had been a prostitute. Rob laughed dryly. He was no stranger to prostitutes and their dressing-up boxes.

Though Maggie never used that word, rating herself as a friend with benefits. Strewn in front of him were slimy, kinky dress-ups. Aye, here was his mixed-up, mystery woman, taking a bus to the end of the road at the end of the year – to make a fresh start. To put this seedy stuff behind her. He felt a mix of pity, disgust and desire.

Actress! He felt a fool. Now he knew exactly what kind of actress. The way she came to him, straddling him while he lay in bed, begging him to hold her tight, moaning and rocking, whimpering and crying out, like she'd done this a thousand times. Rob cracked open a third can, toasting the stinking characters that lay jumbled before him. 'Here's tae us, wis like us... damn few and they're a' deid.'

Which was when a knock sounded at the back door. Rob kicked the clothes under the sofa. More than a bit drunk he heard the door creak open and a voice call out, 'Hey, you in, man?'

Jake.

He would see the clothes strewn over the kitchen floor. He would see the axe and the split case. Rob considered bolting out a window when Jake appeared. 'Having a party?'

'Something like that.' Rob's tone was curt. Jake Henderson was the last person he would invite to a party. Rob remained standing in the middle of the floor, a red wig slumped over the sheepskin, reeking costumes bursting out from under the sofa.

'Great.'

'What do you want?'

'Right, um...' He looked stumped for words, like the blues man of Manchester had turned up in the wrong gig. 'Hey, Robbie, got a drink?'

'You didn't come here for a drink.' Rob's woozy drunkenness had fled. 'Did you?'

'Na, right.'

Rob wasn't offering him a seat, or anything. He stood, clothes at his feet, waiting for Jake Henderson to say whatever he had come to say.

'Hey, man, look. Sorry. Big time sorry.' He pulled an envelope from his back pocket. 'Look, I know this is... I mean, can't make up for it, but... hey, I'm getting out of here, like I said. Back to Sally and the kid. They need me, and I need them. And man, it cuts me up, seeing you still suffering. Anyway, man, if you could do anything with the boat, she's yours. Sell her. Do whatever. Eh? *Wishful Thinking* I mean. I want you to have it, Robbie. Worth a couple o' thou at least.'

'You don't need to pay your guilt. It wasn't your fault.'

'Aye, but... it should have been me, Rob, and I see you having a hard time and I never forget that. You swapped shifts so I could go out on the lash. You got the fucking men on fire. I got laid.'

'Destiny,' Rob said, because one of the counsellors had said that. And because sometimes it felt like that.

'Right, well, say *Wishful Thinking* is destiny too.' Jake reached out his hand.

Rob stared at his outstretched hand, then at him. 'Getting Beth Gunn in the shit, though, that was your fault. They're still hurting, Jake, hurting like hell.'

Jake shrugged and dropped his hand. A leopard skin dress lay at his feet. 'She would have gone wild. She was off the rails. Girls like her. Come on, man. If it wasn't me and my brother she would have got gear off someone else. Anyway, Rob, mate, I didn't come to talk about her. I came to say sorry.'

Now it was Rob shrugging. 'If it's payouts you're doing, chuck a few quid Lachie's way.'

'Fuck sake, man, I don't need a lecture. Right, the boat's

yours. Let her rot if you want. You know what, Robbie, let your life rot if you want. I've said sorry. I want you to have the boat. I want things to work out for you. But man, if you're going to wallow, that's your shout.' Jake propped the envelope on the mantlepiece, next to the photo of Rob's dad on the *Stella*. 'That's the papers for the boat. She's yours, Robbie. You're made for the sea.' He nodded towards the photograph. 'Just like your old man.'

Rob stared at Jake. He had his fist curled, ready to punch, but couldn't. He wasn't that fighter anymore. Jake was still staring at the photo. 'He was a quiet one, eh? Believed in the selkies.' Jake turned to look at Rob now. 'To be honest, that's what I could do with, Robbie, a bit magic.' He frowned down at the stinking clothes on the floor, then up at Rob. 'You... okay?'

'Stuff I dragged out the bay,' he said.

'Right.'

'Threw a wee bit whisky on the sea,' Rob heard himself saying.

'Aye, I mind your dad did that.' Jake laughed now. 'Mibbe I need to give that a go.'

For a moment the two men stood, slimy clothes at their feet, looking at each other. 'You're made for the music business,' Rob said finally, managing a wry smile.

'Aye, well. But mibbe that's the problem. I need to be more there for Sally and the kid.' He sighed, stepped towards Rob and stood on a wig.

'The drug runner's outfits, in case you're wondering,' Rob said.

'Right, well... nice.' He whistled, laughed again, but nervously. 'I mean, I could have been wrong about that. I've been getting a lot of stuff wrong lately. Sally says I don't get her.'

Rob kicked a black beret aside. 'I don't get Sophia either.' He looked up then, and stared at Jake, the boy he'd gone through school with, the teenager he'd gone to Aberdeen with, the man he'd spent years wanting the worst for.

Jake reached out his hand. 'Take care, Rob.'

Rob stared at Jake's outstretched hand, breathed deeply then took his hand and shook it. 'You too, Jake.'

When Jake had left Rob bundled all the clothes back into the split suitcase and left the envelope sitting on the mantelpiece. There was a skip over by the harbour that was being uplifted the next day. Rob shoved the case and its contents into the back of the van, drove round there, dumped it in the skip, covered it with mouldy rolls of carpet, and drove back.

By the time he was back in the cottage the light was fading. She would be huddled by a fire, probably starving. Maybe the fire was out. Rob filled a small bag with cheddar cheese and oatcakes. He added a bottle of wine, two plastic cups and a few pieces of coal. Better late than never, to first foot her. He was tall, she had called him handsome and he came bearing coal. He laughed, feeling lighter in himself after Jake's visit. With the bag slung over his shoulder he went out into the dusk. He would walk along the shore to the cave, it wasn't that far.

Shame the rat took off with the chocolate biscuits. Shame the wood for her fire was damp and hissing more than burning. Shame it was growing dark. Everything turned unsettling in the shadowy dusk. Strange noises – grunting and shuffling – scared her. She could hear moaning seals in the distance, and the occasional splash. It could be waves, jumping fish, or anything. She felt jittery, mainly because the voice was back, swooping above her like a hissing bat. *One more little job to do. I'm in chains here. Set me free! You promised!*

Mairi groaned. Her stomach too; she was ravenous. The wind was up. She hugged her bent knees. The blackening sea in front, the black cave behind. In the gloom she could make out what looked like bats fluttering towards her. Mairi pressed her head between her knees, convinced ghosts were everywhere, that she was going mad, that they were heading for the cave, that they brushed her cheek. That they were out to get her. She screamed.

'It's alright,' Rob said.

She cried out in panic.

'Hey, it's me, Rob, it's okay.'

'There's things in the cave,' she managed to say, between shuddering cries. 'I don't know what. Freaked me out. God, thank God you're here.'

'Yeah, it's okay. Bats. They won't hurt you.' Rob crouched beside her. 'I brought a bit food. And a bit coal.'

She started to cry then. He put an arm around her trembling shoulder and she burrowed into him. 'Hey, it's okay, lass. I brought wine too.' He pushed a stick into the dying fire.

Rob blew what was left of the fire into life, added a few twigs then the lumps of coal. He bent towards her and kissed her. 'Wine?' he whispered.

'Yes, please,' she whispered back, 'rescuer.'

Rob uncorked the wine. The popping sound echoed round the cave.

'I was so scared,' she said, her voice a hush.

'I'm here now,' he said, holding onto that word – rescuer. That's what he wanted to do, to rescue her from whatever demon was plaguing her. And to do it right this time. To 'get' her, like Jake said. He filled a plastic cup with red wine. 'Stay with me for the rest of my life,' he said, handing her the wine and gazing at her through the orange glow. 'I don't care about the past. It's gone. Whatever it was. Whatever you've done. We can start over, lass. You and me.'

'Oh, Rob,' she cried, 'it's not that easy.' She gulped the wine, then tore open the oatcakes and ate hungrily while the voice started up, more insistent. *Push the bastard down Whaligoe Steps*. She blurted out, unsure who was speaking, herself or her mother; 'We could have a picnic at Whaligoe.'

He flinched. 'You been there?'

'Questions.'

'Yeah, lassie, questions.'

She shook her head. 'I read about it.'

'Okay, we'll go! We'll go to Whaligoe, free as birds.' He leant over and kissed her. 'And mibbe,' he whispered in her ear, 'we'll give a wee dram to the sea-spirit, ask her to make things right.' She clung to him, burrowing her face in his chest. 'And mibbe my bed will be comfier than this cave, eh?' Waves broke on the shore and a cold wind blew. 'A good bit warmer too.'

As he lifted her into his arms she was swept back into her mother's stories. How a selkie man came ashore and loved her. And how he might be the father. How her strange beginning might have been here, in this very cave. She hoped her father was a sea-spirit. Not the Polish waiter in the hotel cupboard with the tattoo. Or the Lithuanian chef, both of whom thumbed it south soon as they learnt the wild lass was 'up the spout.'

'*I am a man upon the land,*' Mairi softly sang, '*I am a selkie in the sea…*'

Feeling like some knight of old, he carried her out of the tinkler's cave, the sweep of his head torch picking out bats hanging upside down. 'I'm a man on the land, and you're my treasure,' he said, 'along with this ocean, this sky, these stars, the whole priceless lot of it.' He carried her along the beach where the wind was whipping up, then into the cottage which felt to him like his castle, and upstairs to the bed he had made of driftwood.

38

OUTSIDE A STORM raged, but indoors they sat at the kitchen table, drinking wine, listening to Gary Innes's Saturday night radio programme; intended for folks the length and breadth of Scotland to roll back the carpet and dance round the living room.

They'd been in bed, she clinging to him like she never wanted to let him go. But she didn't trust the ghost of Izzy and didn't trust herself to sleep. 'It's Saturday night,' she had said, kissing his neck then rolling out of bed. 'Wanna dance fisherman?'

Rob laughed, following her out of bed, even managed a twirl on the wooden floor. 'You're good for me,' he said, hurriedly pulling on a shirt. 'We might catch 'Take the Floor' on the radio.'

'Take the what?'

'Scotland's take-a-partner-and-dance radio show!'

There was no pretence now. Or a lot less. She was English. He was introducing her to Scottish culture. She had already wriggled into her long green dress. He took her by the hand and together they went downstairs. 'God knows the last time I danced,' he said. 'Come on, lass, let's jig.'

The resident dance band struck up, fiddles and accordions, for a 'Gay Gordons', and the radio presenter encouraging everyone to take the floor.

'Will you do me the honour,' Rob said, bowing before Mairi,

then gently leading her onto the kitchen floor. He hardly knew himself. Gone was the shy and surly man. Gone the fighter, born the lover. Here was the man glad and ready for anything.

'Well, I don't know these steps,' she said, smiling, 'but you can teach me.' She allowed herself to be guided, to turn, to step forward then back, out to the side and twirl.

Mairi birled under his upstretched arm. The music, the sea and love-making was in him. He moved like he'd been a dancer all his life. The music drowned out the noise of the rain battering on the window. It drowned out the voice in her head. 'I could learn these dances,' she said, almost shouting over the din of music and storm. 'I could learn to live here.' Live a better story, she thought.

'With me?' Rob said, twirling her round.

She nodded, 'Yes, with you.'

He laughed. The storm could rage all it liked. 'For ever?'

'Why not? For ever and ever. Free as birds.'

'Free as birds.' He took her in his arms and spun her round. 'We'll make our love nest here. It's not a bad place.'

'It's a wild and wonderful place.'

'I could fix it up.'

Outside the storm was up. Even at this distance, in the relative safety of the cottage, they heard the sea boom. It was he who winced and she held him tight.

Whether it was the crack of thunder, the closeness of her, the afterglow of making love, this new heart-warm feeling, or the fact that an old accordion tune came on, the memory broke open in Rob and now, in her arms, he was helpless to push it down. A flash of lightning lit up the room. Rob cried out.

'It's alright, Rob,' she said. Brightly, the music carried on: take your partners for an 'Eva Three Step'.

Rob grasped her arm, like he was a drowning man clutching

at the spar of a sinking boat. Another flash of lightning blazed the kitchen for a second, then plunged them into the dark. The music died. 'It's a power cut,' Mairi was saying and she fumbled for a lighter, while Rob still held to her. 'It's alright,' she said, soothingly, 'we just need a candle.'

'No!' he cried.

And he was back holding the monster hose, the man at his back shouting how he needed to lift it higher. Rob's arms were in agony. 'Up, man, up,' the man behind him yelled, over the deafening cracks and screams. 'Hold it high, man,' the one at his back roared, and Rob trained the jet on the burning rig but the fire was raging, smoke belching, the stench was terrible, the rig was a dragon devouring everything and everyone. There was a circle of rescue ships now, jets of water like white rainbows dousing the blazing monster. In front position Rob had to look up. He couldn't close his eyes or look away. He saw one man after the next ignite then jump. The fire of their bodies extinguished by the North Sea. The choice, burning or drowning? The hope, some miracle of rescue. The cries from these men like nothing Rob had heard, or knew was possible from a man. 'Hold higher, man,' the one behind him shouted, 'drench him. The one up high.' Rob saw the man up high, his hair on fire, making a halo. But the force of the jet didn't reach. 'Move her closer,' Rob yelled, but now everything was babel. Nothing made sense. Rob stared up at the flaming man. Though the distance between them was far Rob saw his face. He can't have, but thought he saw his eyes, the expression on his face, pleading for him to bear witness. See me, the burning man seemed to say. Witness this last act. This jump. Know I did exist. That I was.

Rob looked down. The force of the man's need was too great. When Rob looked back the man with the flaming halo was gone. Rob wanted to jump into the sea, find him, but he couldn't swim and he was harnessed to the man behind.

The lamp flickered in the cottage. The radio crackled then Gary Innes was back and the accordions too. 'It's alright,' Mairi was saying.

Rob was under the table, shouting, 'No! No!'

She crawled under the table and held him until his cries subsided. 'It's alright, Rob. I'm here. Whatever it was, it's over. It's alright.'

'Tak yer partners for a 'Pride of Erin Waltz',' came the cheery invitation from the radio. Accordion music filled the kitchen.

The thunder rolled, but further off now, far out at sea.

For a long time they stayed, crouched under the table, hugging each other.

39

ROB WOKE LATE and found the bed next to him empty. But he didn't feel empty. He felt light, as if some weight had been lifted from him. From the bedroom window Rob could see Betsy in her garden, pegging up her washing. Her white sheets bloated like sails. Rob went outside with his binoculars. But his lass was not wandering the shore, or swimming in the sea. All he could see was one cormorant, drying its wings on a rock. Then he spied a black-backed gull, gliding over the flapping bed sheets.

It was then Rob saw her, in Betsy's garden, and Betsy herself, stretching out her arms, as if to comfort her.

Rob set his binoculars down and ran outside, over the tufted marram grass towards Betsy's cottage. What was going on? Was it him, and the roaring that came from him. My God, no wonder she was scared.

Heart pounding, he approached Betsy's garden. The two women were behind the billowing sheets. From where he stood Rob could hear Sophia sobbing. 'It will be alright,' Betsy was saying, 'whatever is burdening you, it will lessen.'

'Oh, God, I'm sorry,' Rob blurted, pulling a sheet aside to see Betsy comforting Sophia, hugging her. 'It just got hold of me. I don't know why. I never know what's going to set it off. I'm sorry, I gave her a fright, I shouldn't have...'

'It's not about that, Rob,' Mairi cried out, wracked with sobs.

Betsy gestured for him to leave.

'She won't let me go,' Mairi was saying, choking the words out, her shoulders heaving.

The cormorant had gone.

Rob made his way back to the cottage, and to the business of organising this picnic to take to Whaligoe. Maybe it was as simple as the gender thing; maybe he really didn't understand women. His mother accused his father of that. Of not listening. Sally accused Jake. But this woman didn't want him to listen. This woman wouldn't tell him anything.

But a picnic together was a step in the right direction. That would cheer her up. Rob couldn't remember the last time he'd had a picnic, wasn't even sure what to bring. A blanket, a bottle of wine. Bread, cheese, chocolate biscuits, a flask of tea. He couldn't bring much more because everything needed carrying down three hundred and sixty-five steps.

When he heard the back door click open, he promised himself he wouldn't pry. When she came in, red-eyed and making herself a cup of coffee he casually asked her, 'red wine or white?' as he stuffed a tartan woollen blanket into his rucksack.

'Red.' She stood at the kitchen sink, gazing out the window and looking lost.

'Hey, I'm sorry about last night.' He went over to her, placing a hand on her shoulder. 'Sometimes it…'

'Whaligoe,' she said, still looking out of the window. 'The picnic.'

'You still want to go? The forecast…'

'Yes, please. Let's just go.'

Rob hoisted the bulky rucksack over one shoulder, wincing. The seaweed had worked wonders but there was still a dull ache. He watched her bend to splash cold water over her face. When she turned off the tap he tried again to reach her. 'I'm sorry about kicking off like that. Sometimes it just comes, sudden. But you were lovely. I think you're making it better. I think I can move on. The oil-rig fire, you know, I think you're helping me get over it.' He bent forward to kiss her, but she stepped away.

'That is good, Rob. It's good to move on, lets things go.' She smiled sadly and snatched in a deep breath. 'I would like to go to Whaligoe.' *I fucking loved that place...*

He glanced out of the window. 'We could wait for a better day.'

'I... I don't mind the rain. Oh, please, Rob. Let's go now.'

Rob smiled at her, aware the smile she gave back didn't reach her eyes. 'Ok, lass,' he said, 'let's go to Whaligoe!'

Driving south in the van with the rucksack slumped in the back where lobsters and crabs normally writhed, he felt his confidence return. For so long he'd been tiptoeing around her, unsure how to be, what to say. But things had changed in him. He felt lighter, younger. And she had said forever. She had said she would stay with him. And she knew him, in all his mess, and she had said she loved him. She was sullen now, but he was no stranger to dark moods.

'A penny for them,' he said, glancing round at her.

She sighed. All the pennies in the world wouldn't help. Or, she remembered a line from a failed audition; all the perfumes of Arabia.

As they drove he pointed out gulls; a black-backed and a herring gull. And the fulmars were back. Spring was surely his county's best season, everywhere primroses, dandelions, daffodils, gorse and broom. The landscape, usually so bleak, was ablaze with yellow. Rob felt proud of Caithness. Even if it had started to rain.

The sight of so much yellow bolstered him. He would get

down on his knees on Whaligoe Steps and ask her to marry him. And he'd call on the sea-spirit to help! It was the spring equinox, wasn't it? Another one of these thin times, according to his dad.

The windscreen wipers squeaked. Tyres flung water from potholes. Rob glanced round at her again, at her clenched jaw, her shut expression. 'You sure you're okay?'

'Let's just get there,' she said. *You're my blood.*

'Ok ma'am.' He picked up speed. 'Whaligoe – here we go – in the rain!'

When an old Runrig song gave way to the forecast the radio told them what they knew; infrequent but sudden downpours in the far north of Scotland. Rob laughed. 'Great weather for a picnic, eh?'

She looked baffled, hardly hearing his words for the clamouring voice. Izzy was everywhere, in the wind, in the back seat of the car, on the road. *Never too late to settle scores, eh?*

The closer they drove to Whaligoe the louder the voice grew, like feedback through speakers, like a distant London siren. *God, you'll be the death of me...* And louder... *Everything up there was wild, like me, fuck it, I was the wildest thing there, but I got packed south. Cast out.* Mairi pressed her hands to her ears. *Eye for an eye.*

'How many steps?' she blurted, to drown out the voice.

'One for every day of the year,' he said. 'Hey, lass, you sure you still want to go?'

Mairi nodded. She would sever the bond at Whaligoe. Stand up for herself once and for all. Fight with a ghost, and leave her free to love this man. Even that was in the folklore book. Stand your ground, it advised. Draw a golden light around you, command the apparition to leave. If that didn't work, she would jump. She wouldn't push him. She wasn't a puppet. Not anymore. The only blood on her hands would be her own.

They were coming out of Wick, the flat stretch of road between fields empty ahead of them. Rob indicated. 'Is this Whaligoe?' she said. A question, right enough, but what did it matter now.

'No.'

'So… what?'

Rob pulled into the lay-by and turned off the engine. He tapped his fingers on the steering wheel. 'So,' he said finally, 'I packed a picnic,' now he looked round at her, 'for you and me.'

'Great.'

'Picnics are supposed to be fun. Do you know what that means?'

She could begin by admitting that, no, she did not know what fun was. She had managed to reach twenty-five years of age with very little of it. She shrugged. She couldn't speak. Her heart raced. She couldn't even speak to Rob. How was she going to command a ghost?

He sighed and leant over the steering wheel. 'I know I'm…' he trailed off, wondering what. Awkward? Needy? Surly? Shy? 'Not a bundle of laughs,' he chose, 'but believe me, I'm trying to lighten up. I thought we were getting somewhere. But, you keep changing the goal posts, blowing hot and cold. Shit, I gave you my room, my bed. I have tried to be good with you. I know I'm not God's gift but you've got to know, I've made a real effort. I want to help you, and you won't even tell me your name. You go sobbing off to Betsy. What's going on, lass? Are you in some deep shit? Some drug thing and somebody got you framed, eh? Somebody who won't let you go? Is that why we're going to Whaligoe? Somebody going to fling you some heroin from a boat, are they?' He searched her face but couldn't fathom her shut expression. 'Or some prostitute business?'

'What?' She stared at him.

'The costumes, the wigs and stuff. I found them. Like, in the sea. But it's okay. Like I said, past is past. Whatever you've been, we can start over.'

She started to laugh, that threatened to spill into crying. 'What about Beth Gunn?'

'Her again?'

'Yes, her.'

'I don't know what Lachie's been saying but I know fuck all about Beth Gunn. Lachie was always for blaming other folk. She got away and he never got over it. End of.'

'But it's not. You... grassed on her?'

'What? Fuck, what is this? Jesus, let's go home. Whoever heard of a picnic in the rain anyway? We can come back, have fun another time, eh?' He wanted to harden himself against her but couldn't. He reached out and brushed her cheek. 'Dinna heed the old man.'

'It's not okay. It's not.'

'I'm with you, it's not okay.'

'I want to go to Whaligoe. Please, Rob.'

He turned the engine on then pulled out into the road. 'Whatever you say, mystery girl.' He sighed and the sea opened up as they turned a corner. He flicked back through the drunken index of his memory, for a time he'd ever grassed on Beth Gunn. What the fuck had Lachie been saying? Bethie had had a thing about Rob. Fancied him. Hung about outside Seaview wanting to see him, whole nights sometimes. Drove his dad mad. But as far as he could remember, he'd never grassed on her.

Push him over the edge. Then peace. Freedom. Job done.

Rob indicated left as he approached the red phone box. 'Nearly there,' he said.

As the van turned off the main road Mairi stared out through the rain-splashed window, to the cliffs and stretch of open sea. Whaligoe would be the place to finally fling Izzy off her. Though the voice was screaming louder than ever; *Go and find her, Lachie, he said, go and tame that girl. If it wasn't for the bastard Sinclair…*

Mairi saw a clump of daffodils, their heads drooping in the rain. So different from that dark Hogmanay night on that noisy old bus, heading in the opposite direction. It had been pitch-dark then and she'd seen nothing. Now it was a rainy afternoon; wide sky full of thick dark clouds and at the edge of the road clumps of yellow gorse. And daffodils.

Aye, this is the place. What took you so long? Mairi bit her lip so hard she tasted the metallic shock of blood. *Do these wee jobs for your mother then you can breathe all the fresh air you like.*

'Picnic time,' Rob said, driving along the bumpy track to the small empty carpark. The place looked different in daylight. No need to hide the van now. Welcome to the famous steps of Whaligoe, a sign said. A sodden Saltire on a wooden pole drooped above the sign. He hadn't seen that the other night.

Mairi got out quickly, fumbling with the door handle, then stood in the rain, clamping her lips. Her head was a screaming banshee; *Push him down… then the ghost of your poor mother will rest in peace.*

Rob hauled out the rucksack. 'Cheese, oatcakes, wine, chocolate biscuits, in the rain,' he said, laughing though his laugh sounded strained. Mairi, her arms wrapped characteristically around her fur coat, which was already looking like a wet dog, walked off.

The confrontation, she had decided, needed to be at the steps. She would sever this cord for once and for all. She had read the exorcist part in the folklore book, over and over. To stand firm and command the ghost to leave. To expel it. Wearing gold can help as protection, the book said. Though Mairi didn't have gold. The gold which, in a different world, would have been hers, was in a wall, its light hidden.

The voice was a shrieking banshee now; *and they banished me! They fucking banished me! Shut that window. Curtains, aye ducks, curtains!*

Rob hurried to catch her up. 'You better hold on to me, going down I mean. They're steep and, if I mind right, a few steps are crumbling.'

'You have been here before?' *I want my pound of flesh.*

Fleetingly, he considered truth but decided against it. 'Years ago. Like, when I was a kid.' Except that wasn't true either. He remembered being in this place as a teenager, how wild Beth Gunn had brought him and Jake here, and about twenty cans of lager, and how she had slipped and said Rob had pushed her. She wasn't badly hurt, just scraped her knees and got a little cut on her forehead. She was drunk, and saying how they might see a whale. Or a selkie man. She had ranted that night. Saying how Rob was a milky Sinclair and how if she fell into the sea, he wouldn't be brave enough to save her. Sinclairs weren't brave like Gunns were. Jake had told her to be quiet. She told them both to shut the fuck up, and said Whaligoe Steps had a power, and so did she.

'You know what it's like when you live in a place, you don't do the tourist stuff.' He pushed Beth and Jake from his mind.

'No other time, Rob?'

He stared at her. 'None like this, with you, and a picnic in the rain.' He stepped forward and kissed her, surprised she didn't resist, surprised she kissed him back fiercely, the rain wetting their lips. Bolstered by her sudden warmth he whispered in her ear; 'So, now we're onto questions, who is it won't let you go?'

She made to pull away, but he wrapped an arm around her waist and pulled her close. 'You can tell me.'

She shook her head. 'The picnic,' she muttered. 'The steps.'

Now it was him shaking his head. He kissed her on her wet head then led her to the tourist sign. Fuck the rain. He wanted to do this right, to show her Caithness. Although she seemed distracted, he read the sign out loud; *'Welcome to historic Whaligoe Steps where men and women involved in the herring fishing toiled in days gone by.'*

Rain splatted onto the sign, blurring the words... herring fishing. Rob wiped the sign with his sleeve and carried on, aware of her holding him tight; *'It was the work of the women to clean and cure the herring, then lift their laden creels... for export abroad... make ready for boats... walk to Wick... sell their fish.'* He paused and squeezed her shoulders. 'That's some job, eh?' He wanted to tell her it was alright, whatever her job had been. He didn't care what she had done. Prostitution, drugs, none of it mattered now.

His lips were moving. Mairi caught some of his words, like steps and fish and boats, under the other voice, driving her mad, drowning him out; *Do it. Push him down the steps... Clean the mess. You're my blood. Never too late to settle scores, eh? They made us suffer.*

Rob kissed her wet cheek. 'Well, I drive an old van to Wick to sell my fish,' he was saying, 'some things have changed, but not much.' He lifted a hand to the rain. 'Hey – you can change your mind. Come back on a better day.' He had planned getting down on one knee. He'd pictured sun, daffodils, wheeling fulmars.

She shook her head. *Then the ghost of your poor mother will let you go.*

'Ok.' This was madness, Rob knew it, but in his catalogue of crazy things a picnic in the rain at Whaligoe Steps was relatively sane.

Not for her. This gathering the courage to silence her mother for once and for all was akin to smashing the window in Tooting. Which she'd never done. Though a hundred times wanted to. She'd do it now. Smash everything. Take on a phantom, look it in the eye and for once and for all rip it from her. She stepped closer. Rob was right behind her, reaching for her hand. Another step and suddenly there they were, unravelling below, a spiral of steps going down, down, down. She turned to face him.

He looked at her with concern, with love, gripping her hand. 'Sophia?'

'My name is not Sophia.' The truth telling had begun.

His heart raced. The steps were so close behind. But Rob, clutching her hand, was wise enough to stay silent, to let her go on.

The voice was clamouring above and behind her. *Do it. Do it!* She squeezed his hand, felt the substance of him steady her.

Rob pulled her into him. 'What's wrong? Honey, please, let's move away from the edge.'

But she pulled her hand away from him. She needed to do this on her own. Izzy was coming closer, her grating voice like a razor in her brain. In terror Mairi turned and stared down the cliff steps. *Dead doesn't mean gone.* Izzy was walking up them, in black high-heel boots, hooped earrings, as if death was just another bar. *You took your time.*

Mairi gulped in air to slow her ragged breathing. She lifted her hands. 'Don't touch me, Rob.'

The commanding had begun.

Just do it, Izzy was screaming. *A quick nudge for God's sake. Not much to ask my own blood, is it?*

'I don't know what's going on here, but I'm going to take you home, put you to bed, make you a hot chocolate, put whisky in it, and whatever is wrong, lass, let me help you. Step back. Please!'

Mairi's head reeled. She turned to face him. 'Izzy... Beth... the girl... she got caught here,' she managed to push the words out. *They're all bastards...*

Rob reached a hand out. 'Come to me.'

'The Gunn girl. Was caught here.' *I was the wildest thing there, but I got banished...*

'Come home, lass.'

'She was on the steps.'

'Who?' He still had an arm extended, his hand open to her.

'The Gunn girl. Elizabeth Gunn. *You're a Gunn no more.* The girl you knew.'

'It's dangerous here. Rain doesn't help. Come on.' He kept his voice steady. 'We can come back another day, just take my hand. Please.'

'But Bethie can't. She was caught. You...' *I loved it there.*

'Mary's been telling you that. Aye, I heard about it. My dad was night fishing and found her. He never liked her, but said he sent out word because he was worried about her.'

'Your dad?'

Rob nodded. 'He didn't say much about it. Not a talker.' He grasped the sleeve of her coat. 'The Gunns and that old sorrow really got to you, eh? Doubtless you turning up reminded them of Bethie. Come on, lass. Let's go home. It's their sorrow, you don't need to take it on.'

Suddenly she tipped forward and hugged him tightly. Wrapped in his arms he manoeuvred her further from the edge. 'It wasn't you?' she cried.

'Not me what?'

She stared up at him from her sodden pelt, her face shining with rain. 'Sent word to Lachie that night?'

'Me?' He shook his head. 'Fuck, I must really look like an old man to you. It was the rig. It aged me.' There was something about the steps, the rain, the sheer openness of the place that was asking for truth. He blurted it out. 'I'm thirty-seven. Not that old. Not too old.'

But she wasn't interested in his age. The dark cloud over her face fled, and there was the sun.

'Your dad? It was your dad?' She laughed loudly. 'Robert Sinclair. Sinclair the sailor man. My God, it wasn't you!' She lifted her arms to the rain as if it was a blessing showering down on her. She could hardly speak for laughing. 'She said – do damage to Sinclair the sailor man! He was Robert too!'

Mairi held his face between her hands and kissed him. She pressed her wet cheek against his. But the blessed joy was short lived for the voice was back – howling like a banshee – *blood is blood! Father – son, it makes no difference! Push him down Whaligoe! Eye for an eye. Life for a life. Then I'll rest!*

'Christ, they really need to let her go.' He kissed her wet cheeks, kissed her neck, knowing it was easy to say. Knowing he'd been told the same. Knowing he'd regret not watching the dying man till his own dying day. He didn't hate Jake anymore. That, at least, was something. Maybe it was possible to let stuff go.

'Me too,' she cried, 'I need to let her go.' She drew back from him, her brief sun eclipsed.

'Who?' he asked, softened with her kisses, and hoisting the rucksack up his shoulder.

'Bethie,' she cried then turned and ran to the cliff edge.

'Sophia!' he yelled, but that wasn't her name. 'Lass!'

It had to be here. However this was going to end, it had to end here. As if this year of steps were somehow to blame for a life cut short. The steps zig-zagged down, cliff face on one side, grass verge on the other.

'Careful, for God's sake,' he was shouting, reaching out to her again, deafened by noise. The wind was up. The rain teeming down. Gulls screeching. 'Hey, step back. Come on! Please!' The steady voice abandoned. He was shouting now. 'Get back!'

She turned and looked at him, rain plastering her black hair to her skull, making her even more elfin, as if she had just risen from the depths.

'It's dangerous,' he shouted. The notion of a picnic in this rain was madness. He cried out, 'We're going back.'

She shook her head. She couldn't. All her life was going back. It had to be now. Fling this ghost from her – or fling herself down Whaligoe Steps. For a haunted life was no life.

'This is it, Izzy,' she called to the air above her, 'Come and show yourself!'

Rob was at her side again, pulling her arm, panic in his eyes. 'Hey, Sophia, I'm taking you home.'

'That's not my name.' Her eyes were ablaze, her face flushed and streaming wet.

'Honey, it's okay, shit happens. Let's get you home.'

'Leave me alone,' she screamed to the air above, and Rob could see her cries were not for him.

And it fell into him suddenly, how so much of her strangeness was not about him. She was in a place he couldn't reach. He held her tightly. 'It's okay.' He felt her writhing in his arms, cursing himself for going along with this.

'Go!' she was yelling, 'You had your time. It wasn't my fault.

None of this was my fault. You hear me! Izzy! I am commanding you to go.'

Rob held her tight. She was the burning man with the halo. She was begging him to bear witness. To stay. And he would this time. 'I'm here,' he called out, above her cries, the rain, the booming waves from way below. 'I am right here. I see you.'

They were wrestling now. She was strong, quick. In a flash she wriggled free, leaving Rob clutching her fur coat. 'Sophia!' he shouted.

But that wasn't her name. She swung round at the top of the cliff, wild-looking, haunted, rain sheeting down her face.

He took a step, clutching the coat, reaching out an arm. 'Please.' He took another step. 'We'll get through this. You'll get through it. I'm here.' His voice was steady again, the ground beneath him strong. But just feet away the ground was about to give. 'I love you, and whoever Izzy is, she can't hurt you.' He took another step towards her. 'Please, lass.'

The wet wind howled. Far below thundering waves crashed. 'She won't let me go,' she cried. 'It hasn't worked, Rob. I'm sorry. I'm not strong enough.'

If this was the way of letting a haunting go, so be it. Jumping would let vengeance go. Let the agony of never fitting in go. Like she'd let her mother's clothes go. The scripts. The lines. The dreams. Even this love, this tender man. He was holding her fur coat, like the first time she saw him.

'Sophia!'

At the top step she spread her arms wide.

'Sophia!' he screamed, lunging towards her.

She jumped.

Rob watched her disappear. He saw a man on fire, a halo, an angel with burning wings.

An avocet in flight.
As she fell down Whaligoe.

40

THE GULLS CIRCLED above him, screaming. Rob dropped the coat and bolted after her. At the cliff edge the steps spiralled down. He couldn't see her. 'Sophia!' he cried. 'Lass!' He lurched down the steps, two, three at a time. 'Sophia!' He slipped. His rucksack hurtled down, thudding, bouncing, disappearing from view. Rob righted himself, reaching for the cliff wall. Then he saw her, some twenty or thirty steps below, sprawled on a ledge of machair that grew at the side. In moments Rob was by her, appalled at the blood flowing from her head. 'My God, are you okay? Lass! Lass!'

Her head was at a twisted angle, wedged against the cliff. Rob felt her wrist. Unsure if it was his own racing pulse, her faint one, or both. He felt her heart. It was beating. Thank God. Her eyes were closed, her face pale and wet, streaked with blood. He drew a finger up her cheek and found the cut, at the side of her ear. Blood streamed out, mingling with rain. The step turned red. She must have hit the step, or a jut in the cliff. Rob tore off his jacket, his t-shirt, ripped it into a bandage. He remembered some First Aid from crewing supply boats in Aberdeen. Seaweed flashed into his mind, how she had tended to him. But seaweed was too far away.

Blood bloomed onto the white cotton. Rob placed his palm an inch above her mouth. Unless it was the wind, she was breathing. His First Aid training advised not to lift a patient.

That he should call for help. But he couldn't leave her. She was losing blood. She might die. Her spine wasn't broken, nor her neck, he was sure of that. He pried her gently from her twisted position and lifted her into his arms, all the time crying, lass... lass...

Rain fell on his bare torso, on her face, on her dangling twisted arm. Holding her to him, blood ran onto his chest. He carried her up the thirty or so steps she had fallen down, telling her over and over, she was going to be alright, feeling the lightness of her, the warmth. Panting hard he reached the top. 'Darling, you're going to be alright. Please, don't die.'

When he reached the van, he couldn't find the keys. Then remembered they were in the rucksack, probably at the foot of Whaligoe Steps, or in the sea. It was five miles into Wick. There was a hospital there. Rob carried her in his arms, paused at the old phone box. Emergency only, it said. Rob pressed her to him with one arm while dialling 999 with his free hand, the handle dangling down. 'I'm at the top of Whaligoe Steps,' he shouted, 'and my girlfriend fell. She's bleeding. She's unconscious. But breathing. Please, I think she's...'

'On its way,' the voice from the swinging receiver said.

He carefully adjusted her, kissing her cheek, crying himself now. He set off, walking on the side of the road heading north. She looked beautiful. And bleeding. Drops fell onto the grass verge. He couldn't stand still, waiting for an ambulance that might be hours. 'It's going to be okay,' he repeated. Tears streamed down his face and fell onto her. Everything was rain, tears, and blood. It was evening, still light but precious few vehicles passing, so Rob kept walking, never taking his eyes off the field of roses in his arms. Her eyes were shut, a strange, peaceful expression on her face. He had to keep going. He had to get her to the hospital.

She muttered something. Rob bent his head close to her mouth. 'Lass? You're okay. It's fine. You slipped on the steps, but you're going to be okay. Can you hear me?'

'Sorry,' she muttered. Then she smiled, or it looked like that. He bent to hear her. 'She's gone…' she whispered.

Her eyes were open. He didn't look away. If these were to be the last eyes she saw they would be full of love. 'I'm here,' he said. 'But lass, don't… please… don't die…'

A siren broke the spell. Rob spied the blue flashing light in the distance. Suddenly there it was, drawing up, parked, the ambulance bright. Two men jumped out. 'We'll take over from here, mate,' one said.

'But…' She was gone from him. Rob slumped onto the verge, watching a stretcher, a blanket, oxygen. How quick they moved. Rob started shaking. One of the paramedics put a blanket around his shoulder. 'Is she okay?' Rob asked, his teeth chattering. 'She… she fell down the steps. With the rain. It was mad.' But they weren't listening. Maybe they knew it wasn't true. Rob watched them carry her, on the stretcher, swiftly into the back of the ambulance.

For a moment Rob thought they might leave him there, on the verge, in the rain, and he might never see her again. 'Jump in,' one of the men said, 'sit next to your girlfriend.'

In the ambulance there was nothing for Rob to do, except shake, and stare at the contraptions and monitors. One of them made a slow bleeping noise. 'Bleeping is good,' the man said. He was busy with tubes and oxygen. They had, Rob noticed, removed his t-shirt bandage and put on a more professional looking one.

'Is she okay?' Rob said. He felt like a stuck record. It was all he could say. He wanted to hold her hand, but she was full of oxygen, tubes, a bandage, a blanket.

'She's lost a lot of blood,' the paramedic said, glancing at Rob.

'I didn't push her,' he blurted.

'I never said you did.'

'She fell.' Maybe she did fall. Or maybe, like the burning man, she had jumped. The way she had stretched her arms, maybe she really thought she would fly! 'She…' he began, but by now they were pulling into the hospital. Sophia was sped off on a hospital trolly, Rob frantically watching her go.

Then he was left in a brightly lit reception area. A woman gave him a cup of sweet tea, and another blanket. 'I heard your girlfriend took a terrible tumble down Whaligoe Steps,' she said, giving him a sympathetic look. Rob paced the room. Twice he went to find a nurse and twice he was told to rest, and did he need more tea, and they were doing everything they could. And could he please wait in the café area.

The woman there brought him yet another cup of tea. Rob slumped down on a red plastic chair. His whole body was shaking now, despite the blanket. He couldn't speak without his teeth chattering. 'How is she?'

'In good hands,' the woman said. She smiled at him and brought him another blanket.

A nurse appeared, pushing open the creaking swing-doors of the café. 'She'll pull through,' she said, nodding. 'They've staunched the bleeding and stitched her cut. She's twisted her ankle. Broken a rib, dislocated a shoulder. And there's concussion, but she'll weather it. You can stay the night here if you like. We can give you cushions. I know those sleeping pills. Your girlfriend will be out for hours.' The nurse turned to go but stopped. 'What were you doing at Whaligoe in the rain?'

'Having a picnic.'

Then the nurse was gone.

'A picnic?' the woman who was still by his side asked, raising an eyebrow.

'She jumped.' The tears came then, great sobs. Rob buried his face in the blanket. 'I mean, maybe she slipped. I… I didn't see properly.'

'But she's here now,' the woman said, 'and she's going to be alright.'

41

ROB COULDN'T FACE going home without her. Even if he had wanted to, how would he get there? His van was in the car park of Whaligoe Steps and his keys were God knows where. The woman from the café brought him an old black sweatshirt. 'It was my son's,' she said.

A faded 'Big Country' was written across the front. Rob wondered what had happened to the son. 'Um, got a clothes hanger by any chance?'

The woman bustled off to the staff changing lockers and brought him one. 'Off for some breaking and entering noo?' she asked, winking.

He tucked the hanger under his arm. 'Something like that.'

Then he walked the five miles to Whaligoe.

His rucksack was hung up on a fence post by the car park. Rob was about to unhook it from the post when he heard a voice behind him. 'A wis worried like.'

Rob swung round. A man, wearing a leather jacket, jeans and a baseball cap over long grey hair grinned at him. Rob recognised him vaguely, as the man who looked after the steps and planted a few flowers about the car park. 'Like ee band,' the man said, nodding at Rob's sweatshirt.

Rob glanced down, saw the letters upside down. 'Oh, right.' Then he reached for his rucksack, which looked remarkably intact. 'Hey, thanks, it fell off me... in the rain... last night.' He fished in the side pocket and retrieved the keys. Then he twirled the hanger. 'Won't be needing that, then.'

'A thought maybe...' the man trailed off. 'Like A said, A wis worried. Your van, is it?' He nodded to the old white van.

'Aye.' He shook the keys. 'It's these I need.'

'Glad you're okay. A was worried, like. Wait 'ere.' The man hurried back to the small cottage then was back in half a minute, carrying the fur coat. 'A thought ee worst.'

Rob took it, holding it to him as if he was holding her. Then out it came, how coming here had been her idea, even in the rain, and how she had spread her arms wide like an avocet's wings and flew. And how he carried her up the steps, and how she was in hospital. In intensive. How he doesn't even know her name. 'She's... she's...'

'Oh, man, 'at's tough. 'At's shit. A thought maybe something like 'at. A jumper. Shit.'

Rob pressed the coat to him. 'Yeah, it's shit.'

'But... she'll pull through.' The man, suddenly looking, thought Rob, like a prophet under the wide Caithness sky, added, 'she wasn't meant to go. Not her time.'

Rob drove home and slept till the next day.

42

TWO DAYS AND twenty phone calls later, Rob drove to Wick hospital, Betsy's lemon drizzle cake with him but not knowing whether Sophia would be able to eat. So much he didn't know. Even her name. She was awake, that's all he'd been told, and he was welcome to come for a brief visit. She had, the doctor added, asked for him. It wasn't only lemon drizzle cake he had with him.

Rob went through the swing doors into the long corridor. The woman from the café walked by, a bundle of magazines in her arms. 'Nice to see you again,' she chirped.

Then he was outside Ward 4. He pushed open the door. Just inside the ward a nurse spotted him. 'My,' he stuttered, 'my...' Rob glanced around. The few beds in the ward were screened with green curtains. My what? 'At Whaligoe,' he blurted, because that was one name he was sure of.

The nurse drew back a curtain. 'A visitor for you,' she called cheerily, moving a chair closer to the bed. 'Just ten minutes,' she said to Rob, then she was gone.

Mairi was propped against pillows, her head wrapped in bandages. The one eye that Rob could see was a dark slit in a mess of purple and yellow swollen cheek. Despite her appearance she grinned, showing now two gaps. 'A little dental work required,' she said. It was her voice. No acting.

'Every gap tells a story,' he said, taking her hand.

'What a story I was lost in, Rob.'

Their fingers didn't stop finding each other, entwining. This was home. He couldn't tell how long they sat, holding hands. Minutes, days, lifetimes. 'I should have brought seaweed.' He leant forward and kissed her bruised face. The one eyelid he could see was drooping, as if sleep was pulling her under. 'Hey, lemon drizzle cake from Betsy,' he said quickly, bringing the cake from his pocket with one hand and breaking off an edge. 'She says, get well soon.' He held a morsel of the sweet cake to her lips. She smiled and managed a nibble. 'Oh, and hey,' he went on, pulling a fat envelope from his pocket, 'we're rich. I came into some money. When you're out of here, how about you and me take a holiday. Eh?'

She squeezed his hand. 'I would like that,' she murmured, her chin dropping to her chest.

'Oh, and Mary Gunn came looking for you.' He wanted to keep her awake, to stretch this visit into the rest of his life.

'Grandmother,' she whispered, her eye closing.

Rob leant in closer. 'What's that?'

'My grandparents. The Gunns. My... my... family...' Then she seemed to nod off, a faint smile on her swollen face.

Rob's mind raced as the nurse beckoned for him to leave.

Back in the van, in the hospital car park, leaning over the steering wheel, Rob worked it out. At least some of it. If she was Mary and Lachie's granddaughter then she was wild Beth Gunn's daughter. He looked out at the pink cherry blossom on the trees around the car park.

He was, he had to admit, no detective. It had been staring him in the face for weeks.

When Lachie saw Rob Sinclair on the doorstep of Heatherlee farm, he looked ready to slam the door in his face. Rob raised his hands in a gesture of surrender. 'Rob!' Mary called from the hallway behind Lachie. 'How is Yulia?' Lachie was fuming, his face turning red.

'In hospital,' Rob called to her, then out it came, before the door would be shut on him forever. 'She says she's your granddaughter.'

43

WHEN LACHIE ADMITTED he wasn't up to the drive to Wick, Rob offered to take them. He cleaned out his van, cleaned himself, changed his shirt, then half an hour before visiting time returned to Heatherlee to pick them up. They were waiting for him, dressed, he guessed, in their Sunday best, and Mary holding a bunch of wildflowers. With a pang Rob wondered how long they had been standing there. Mary was wearing a blue cotton dress with a tartan shawl over her shoulders, her soft white hair pinned up, her frail hands clutching a little homemade bag, and the posy of flowers. Lachie too had made an effort. Despite the relative warmth of the spring day, he had donned a tweed suit; trousers, waistcoat, jacket and tie. 'We are ready,' he solemnly announced.

The awkward silence was eased by Caithness FM's pop music, though Rob switched it off when the news came on, not wanting announcement of a suicide attempt at Whaligoe to mar this trip. In the silence that followed, Mary leant forward from the back seat of the van and whispered, 'I had a feeling.'

'Hush, Mary,' said Lachie from the passenger seat.

'Don't hush me,' she said. 'I knew there was something.' She tapped Rob on the shoulder. 'It wasn't just my old fur coat that told me. No, it was her eyes, and strong hands, and feisty spirit.' She laughed softly.

'Your fur coat?' Rob's eyes caught hers in the rear-view mirror.

'Well, I think it's the same. It had been my mother's,' she said, almost coyly. 'I hardly ever wore it, of course. Nobody would remember it was once mine. It wasn't fitting for a farmer's wife. I kept it at the back of the wardrobe. It went the night Bethie did. Then, all these years later, it came back.' She smiled and nodded, then it was Lachie she was tapping on the shoulder; 'with our granddaughter.'

Rob let them go in to see her first. He stayed in the café, managing half a Caramel Wafer. He pictured Lachie and Mary weeping by her bed, or Mary weeping and Lachie not knowing what to do with himself. In the midst of Rob's reverie, Lachie and Mary appeared in the café led by a nurse who gave the briefest nod to Rob, sign language for – your turn now. As he had expected, Lachie looked bewildered, but not Mary. She was beaming from ear to ear like a child. 'It's our granddaughter come back to us,' he heard her say to the woman at the café counter.

'And how is she?' the woman asked, starting to make them tea.

'She's had a nasty fall and a hard time of it,' Mary said, 'but she's alright now.'

'We hope so,' Lachie added, his voice a mix of gruff and kind.

Rob heard the café door click behind him. The nurse led him to Ward 3. 'She's out of intensive,' she said.

'Thank God.'

Mary's primroses and cowslips were in a small vase by Mairi's bed. She was sitting up, bruising on her face, but the swelling down, and she was smiling. 'My grandparents came to visit,' she said, then nodded towards the flowers. 'Aren't they lovely?'

Rob pulled the seat in close to the bed, drew the curtain and took her hand.

For Rob it was enough to be holding her hand, and that she was alive, and he was alive. All his desperate need to know who she was didn't matter.

But she told him. 'Mairi,' she began. 'Izzy said it was for the sea, but I think it was for Mary, my grandmother.'

'Mairi,' Rob murmured, and gently kissed the back of her hand.

She told him how Izzy had taken the name Whyte, for them wanting to cut ties with the past, she explained. But that was the problem, she told him, she couldn't cut ties. She held them tight. And, she went on, 'maybe I couldn't either. Maybe all along I was the one not letting her go. All my talk about living in the present, but I couldn't let her go.'

He stroked her arm and felt the strength of her. 'She was the only family you had,' he said.

'I might be half a selkie,' she said, and grinned. 'I might have ancestors out there in the sea.'

'You never know,' he said, gently squeezing her hand. 'Up here anything's possible.'

Then she said how both Lachie and Mary had told her they would be proud to call her a Gunn.

'Or Sinclair?' asked Rob, leaning over and kissing her.

She smiled. 'How about Mairi Sinclair-Gunn!' she said, then kissed him.

'It's got a very good ring to it,' he said, kissing her back.

Her words swooned round his brain, his heart, his blood. And she went on, in flow now, telling him she would soon be twenty-six. How her mother had come from Ronester. Wild Bethie Gunn!

'I should have guessed.'

'Maybe I am better actress than I thought.' She laughed, then stopped. 'Sophia's gone now. So has Izzy. Yulia too. Mairi has finally arrived. God knows where I've been, lost in some strange movie probably, not knowing what was real, what wasn't. A bit crazy, I think. But I'm here now. I'm okay.'

'Very good to meet you, Mairi.'

She laughed and kissed the back of his hand. 'Very good to meet you too, Rob Sinclair.'

'You're not crazy, Mairi.' He brushed his lips across the back of her hand. 'The dead like it here. There's plenty space for them. They like the big wide skies.' He laughed softly, half embarrassed acknowledging the spectral population of Ronester. 'You get used to living with them. The trick is, not to get swayed by them. But take account of them. That way, they relax.' He laughed again. 'I've been drinking beer with my dad every night for three years.'

'You love him,' she murmured.

'Aye, but maybe he needs to move on.' He laughed softly again, part of him amazed he was saying this stuff. 'I do.'

'Something saved me, Rob,' she said. 'I felt something brush my shoulder. It was like something caught me. There was something there, cushioning my fall. Whatever it was vanished, then you were there, lifting me. And I knew I was going to be alright. That I had come back from wherever I'd been.'

He reached over and kissed her on the cheek. 'Maybe the sea-spirit saved you,' he whispered.

'The selkie?'

'Aye, the selkie.'

She told him how Mary had rummaged in her little bag and brought out a ring. How her grandmother, with a knowing smile, said an owl must have delivered it, and how Lachie agreed, it was meant for their granddaughter now. 'But... I'm not Elizabeth,' she said to Rob, showing him the heavy gold ring on her thumb. 'Izzy broke the mould.'

'She did.'

'Like, she broke free in a way.' Mairi gazed at the chunky ring. 'I'll wear it sometimes. Take her up the cliffs, or down to the shore. She loved it here.'

Neither of them heard the buzzer announcing the end of visiting time.

'You know, I never had a proper holiday,' she said, kissing him on the cheek. 'And I never saw it still light at midnight.'

'Welcome to the rest o' yer life,' he said, kissing her shoulder.

The nurse, seeing them in each other's arms, closed the curtain, and smiled.

44

LATE SUMMER AND even a few tourists browsing in Mackie's shop, perhaps because Mackie had had the good idea to prop a sign at the road-end announcing it was a sharp turn to; 'Mainland Britain's first and last shop!' To accommodate the tourists, detouring en route to Orkney, he filled some self-service shelves with Jean's Caithness tablet, Old Poultney whisky from Wick, a few green and blue pottery mugs from John O' Groats, shell necklaces, postcards of Ronester harbour, plus, wonder of wonders, crocheted tea cosies, fruit scones and fresh farm eggs brought down weekly by Lachie and Mary Gunn, and rainbow candles from Mina's granddaughter, who wanted to be an artist. 'It's looking lovely,' Gladys said as Mackie handed over her pack of twenty.

'A shop needs to keep abreast of the times,' Mackie said proudly. 'Now, how about a candle for when the nights draw in? Winter will be here before you know it.'

'Next time, maybe,' said Gladys, pocketing her cigarettes and leaning over the counter. There were tourists in, perusing the postcards, and this wasn't for broadcasting abroad. 'Mairi is not wild like her mother.'

'Ach,' said Mackie. 'Her mother wasn't that bad. She was young and that's no sin, is it? Seems to me Bethie loved the wild wind and the night sea. And things didn't work out for the poor lass. We've all done a few wild things in our time, eh?'

Gladys stared at him. 'You've changed your tune.'

'We can all change, can't we?'

'Rob has perked up,' she admitted. 'If you call that changing, he's changed. I actually got a good morning from him the other day, and that's a first. And I heard they're going to tie the knot – on the beach no less!'

Mackie smiled. 'And the harbour,' he went on, expansively, 'looks like San Tropez with his new boat in it. She's a beauty.'

Gladys Crowther thought San Tropez was stretching it a bit, but did admit, the *Stella Maris* was a real beauty.

It was.

The *Stella* springing two leaks just when Rob's bank balance was thriving, thanks to selling *Wishful Thinking*, seemed fated timing. So Rob mended the leaks, sold the *Stella* as well, and bought a beauty of a boat and named her the *Stella Maris*. The Star of the Sea. And there was still enough left over for a holiday.

It was late September when Mary smashed a bottle of champagne over the gleaming white bow of the *Stella Maris* to christen her. The golden sparkling liquid sprinkled the bow and cascaded over the sea. Lachie took the photograph while Rob and Mairi stood together at the helm, ready to take the *Stella Maris* on her maiden voyage. 'It's like the libations,' Rob said, now steering the boat slowly out of the harbour and waving to the folks gathered on the quayside.

Mairi laughed, her face turned to the soft September wind and the open sea. 'When you raised the selkie?'

'When I raised you,' he said, one hand on the wheel and the other around her shoulders. He bent to kiss her mouth, then tenderly kissed the small scar above her right eyebrow. 'We'll call that your Whaligoe.'

She kissed his scar. 'And we'll call that your Aberdeen.'

The cheers of the crowd faded behind them, where they would all be congratulating Mary and Lachie on their beautiful granddaughter, and Rob was a fine man after all, and all changing their tune, saying Bethie had been such a lively wee lass. And free as the wind now, them that knew about ghosts said. And Mary would be nodding, and softly smiling. And Lachie would be agreeing that bygones should indeed be bygones and a Sinclair was as good as a Gunn.

'Go there,' Mairi said, pointing to the open sea. If it was that free ghost in the wind guiding her, or the ring on her thumb, she didn't say, but heeding her Rob turned the boat.

'Aye, aye, captain,' he said, bringing the *Stella Maris* to the place then down with his net and three kisses later up with that same net teeming with silver darlings. They spilled onto the deck, more fish in one go than he had ever caught. Maybe more than his father had ever caught. He thought of him then, looking down on them and nodding. He'd be at peace now.

Over the glittering catch Rob gazed at this woman who had come into his life nine months earlier and changed everything. He was still trying to work out who she was. What she was. He stared at her. He would never tire of that. He stared at the fish, then out at this blue-green patch of water. 'So... you *are*...'

'What?' she asked, into the wake of his question, smiling.

Rob grinned then shook his head. It didn't matter, selkie, or not. She was here, with him. He loved her and believed her when she said she loved him. He took her in his arms. 'Yourself,' he said, laughing at the simple truth of it.

Acknowledgments

SOME BOOKS ARRIVE onto the page quickly. Others take years. *On a Northern Shore* falls into the latter camp. To further the camping metaphor, many good people have offered tent pegs and poles! It is them I would like to thank. Some read drafts, some engaged in helpful conversations, others made suggestions. All helped this book take shape.

My thanks go to my agent, Kathryn Ross. Also to my good friend and wordsmith, Jennie Renton. To my dad, Ramsay Mackay, for reading the manuscript and for his suggestions. Thanks also to my partner, Mark Norris, for his feedback and support. Also to some of my creative writing students for reading earlier versions of this story; wonderful writers all; Elaine Connelly, Sarah Naismith, Carmel Kennedy and Sabreena Malik Crook.

Thanks to all my wonderful creative writing students, past and present.

Thanks to fellow writers Susan Elsley and Louise Kelly, for listening, reading and feedback. Thanks also to the arts organisation that was Northlands Creative Glass in Lybster, Caithness, and Lyth Arts Centre, Caithness, for giving me the opportunity to live and work as a writer in the far north of Scotland. I would also like to thank Catherine Byrne, a Caithness author, for her friendship and support, and the Caithness Writers Group for their welcome.

Thanks also to the communities of the Scottish Storytelling Centre and TRACS (Traditional Arts & Culture Scotland) who help keep stories, folklore and the imagination thriving.

Luath Press Limited

committed to publishing well written books worth reading

LUATH PRESS takes its name from Robert Burns, whose little collie Luath (*Gael.*, swift or nimble) tripped up Jean Armour at a wedding and gave him the chance to speak to the woman who was to be his wife and the abiding love of his life. Burns called one of the 'Twa Dogs' Luath after Cuchullin's hunting dog in Ossian's *Fingal*. Luath Press was established in 1981 in the heart of Burns country, and is now based a few steps up the road from Burns' first lodgings on Edinburgh's Royal Mile. Luath offers you distinctive writing with a hint of unexpected pleasures.

Most bookshops in the UK, the US, Canada, Australia, New Zealand and parts of Europe, either carry our books in stock or can order them for you. To order direct from us, please send a £sterling cheque, postal order, international money order or your credit card details (number, address of cardholder and expiry date) to us at the address below. Please add post and packing as follows: UK – £1.00 per delivery address; overseas surface mail – £2.50 per delivery address; overseas airmail – £3.50 for the first book to each delivery address, plus £1.00 for each additional book by airmail to the same address. If your order is a gift, we will happily enclose your card or message at no extra charge.

Luath Press Limited
543/2 Castlehill
The Royal Mile
Edinburgh EH1 2ND
Scotland
Telephone: 0131 225 4326 (24 hours)
Email: sales@luath.co.uk
Website: www.luath.co.uk